The kiss was Theo's first surprise.

Her second was the almost volcanic eruption of emotion in the pit of her stomach. Colt's lips took, and tasted, and demanded a response. But he didn't have to demand anything.

Dizzy, dazed, breathing erratically, she opened her eyes to see him staring at her. He, too, looked dazed.

"I...I shouldn't have done that," he mumbled thickly. "Can you forget it?"

"Yes, of course..." she lied. She realized she was trembling. Trembling over a kiss. Dear God, Colt Murdoch was the most potent man she'd ever kissed, bar none.

He sent her a glance. "I don't know why I did that. I didn't plan it. Please believe me."

"Yes, of course," she said, her voice stiff and unnatural. "We don't need to talk about it. You said to forget it. I agreed. It's forgotten."

But she knew she would *never* forget it...

Dear Reader,

There's a lot in store for you this month from Silhouette Special Edition! We begin, of course, with March's THAT SPECIAL WOMAN! title, *D Is for Dani's Baby*, by Lisa Jackson. It's another heart-warming and emotional instalment in her LOVE LETTERS series. Don't miss it!

We haven't seen the last of Morgan Trayhern as Lindsay McKenna returns with a marvellous new series, MORGAN'S MERCENARIES: LOVE AND DANGER. You'll want to be there for every spine-tingling and passionately romantic tale, and it all starts with *Morgan's Wife*. And for those of you always eagerly seeking new Dallas Schulze novels, look no further, as this popular author makes her Special Edition debut with *Strong Arms of the Law*.

Also this month, it's city girl versus roguish rancher in *A Man and a Million*, by Jackie Merritt. A second chance at love—and a secret long kept—awaits in *This Child Is Mine*, by Trisha Alexander. And finally, we're pleased to welcome new author Laurie Campbell and her story *And Father Makes Three*.

Next month we're beginning our celebration of Special Edition's 1000th book with some of your favourite authors! Don't miss books from Diana Palmer, Nora Roberts and Debbie Macomber—just to name a few! We know you'll enjoy the blockbuster months ahead. We hope you enjoy each and every story to come!

All the best,

The Editors

A Man and a Million
JACKIE MERRITT

SILHOUETTE

SPECIAL EDITION

*First published in Great Britain 1996
by Silhouette Books, Eton House, 18-24 Paradise Road,
Richmond, Surrey TW9 1SR*

© Carolyn Joyner 1995

*Silhouette, Silhouette Special Edition and Colophon are
Trade Marks of Harlequin Enterprises II B.V.*

ISBN 0 373 09988 6

23-9603

Made and printed in Great Britain

JACKIE MERRITT

and her husband live just outside of Las Vegas, Nevada. An accountant for many years, Jackie has happily traded numbers for words. Next to family, books are her greatest joy. She started writing in 1987 and her efforts paid off in 1988 with the publication of her first novel. When she's not writing or enjoying a good book, Jackie dabbles in watercolour painting and likes playing the piano in her spare time.

Other Silhouette Books by Jackie Merritt

Silhouette Desire

Big Sky Country
Heartbreak Hotel
Babe in the Woods
Maggie's Man
Ramblin' Man
Maverick Heart
Sweet On Jessie
Mustang Valley
The Lady and the
    Lumberjack
Boss Lady
Shipwrecked!
Black Creek Ranch
A Man Like Michael
Tennessee Waltz
Montana Sky
Imitation Love
†Wrangler's Lady
†Mystery Lady
†Persistent Lady
Nevada Drifter

Accidental Bride
Hesitant Husband
Rebel Love

†*Saxon Brothers series*

*Silhouette Summer
    Sizzlers 1995*
"Stranded"

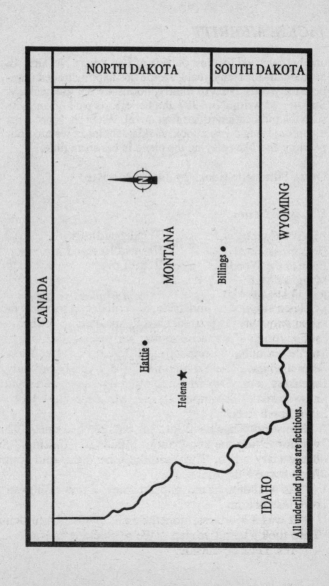

Chapter One

"Miss Hunter?"

Theo stopped in midstride. Several dozen people were on their way out of the small chapel, speaking in hushed, consoling tones. The funeral service had been simple, brief and, while undoubtedly respectful, different than any Theo had ever attended. There'd been no sign of a casket and only two speakers, a minister who had offered a prayer and an attorney, Jordan Hamilton. It was Mr. Hamilton who was standing by now.

She slipped her hand into his outstretched one. "Thank you for letting me know about Maude's...passing." Suddenly teary again, Theo withdrew her hand and found a fresh tissue in her purse.

"As Maude's friend and attorney, I only followed her own instructions."

"It was a kindness, nonetheless." Jostled from behind, Theo took a tentative step. "We're blocking traffic."

"Yes. Let's go outside."

Moving with the flow of the small crowd, they were soon beyond the doors of the chapel. The day was bright and sunny, and people lingered in the parking area to chat. Jordan Hamilton was in no hurry to leave, Theo noted while fishing a pair of dark glasses from her purse.

While he had been at the chapel's pulpit, Theo had automatically registered the young attorney's good looks. Not in a physically sensory context. Her mood had been somber and centered on her old friend, Maude Evans, who had suddenly passed away.

But Jordan Hamilton was a good speaker with a deep, resonant voice and an excellent vocabulary. And while he talked, Theo had not only listened and dabbed at her wet eyes, she had looked at the tall, slender man of thirty-odd years with sandy brown hair and mustache, wearing glasses as stylish and becoming as his impeccable brown suit. Behind the lightly tinted lenses, Theo now saw warm hazel eyes.

"Your eulogy was moving," she commented.

"Thank you. Maude meant a great deal to me."

"To me, too." She saw Jordan Hamilton's lips turn up in a rather dry smile.

"Miss Hunter, we need to set an appointment."

"An appointment? For what?" If she sounded blunt, it was due to surprise. Why on earth would she and Jordan Hamilton need to meet again? Not that there was anything wrong with the man. Quite the contrary. If they didn't live so far away from each other, there was every chance of friendship developing between them, as she liked the clean-cut type of man Jordan Hamilton represented so well.

Feeling scrutiny and a strange sort of speculation from him, Theo frowned behind her dark glasses.

Then he said slowly, thoughtfully, "You really don't know, do you?"

Theo took a quick glance at her watch. Her time in Hattie, Montana, was limited. "Know what, Mr. Hamilton? I don't want to appear rude, but I really do have a plane to catch.''

''Miss Hunter, you are the primary legatee of Maude's estate.''

There was a moment of silence. Maude's estate couldn't have any real monetary value, but how sweet of her, Theo thought sadly. ''Oh, I see,'' she murmured. ''Well, I wasn't planning on staying another night, Mr. Hamilton. And I'm sure you understand the flight situation.''

''I understand it very well. Getting in and out of Hattie by air is possible, but just barely.''

The hint of amusement in his voice at the small town's lack of convenience created a moment of communion between them. Theo's smile was friendly, but she issued a reminder. ''The commuter plane to Helena will be leaving in an hour.

Jordan looked at his own watch. ''So it will.'' His expression sobered. ''It's in your best interests to stay another night, Miss Hunter, believe me. I'm going back to my office when I leave here. We could meet there. Do you have a car?''

Theo felt a tad helpless about this. She had planned on being in Montana one night. Arriving at Helena's airport only yesterday, she had caught the five-seat commuter flight to Hattie and had stayed in a motel last night. Her tickets for the reverse trip were in her purse. Her plan was to return to the motel for her bag—it was only a few blocks from the chapel—then take a taxi to the modest little airport.

But Jordan Hamilton seemed so insistent, and, thinking about it, Theo supposed that it made more sense than not to take care of this now. Whatever Maude had left her would have immeasurable meaning to her.

''All right, I'll stay another night, Mr. Hamilton.''

He smiled. ''Would you mind if we relaxed to a first-name basis?''

''No, of course not.'' The parking area was emptying of both people and cars. Theo glanced around. ''Where is your office from here?'' Her gaze fell on a man leaning against a white vehicle. He was tall and lanky and dressed in a striking dark suit. His hair was almost black, his cowboy boots were black, and he was staring at her.

Or, at Jordan Hamilton.

Flustered and curious about the reaction, Theo tore her eyes from the man. ''I don't have a car, Mr. Ham...Jordan. Is your office within walking distance?''

''You can ride with me.'' Jordan grinned. ''Although just about everything in Hattie is within walking distance, Theodora.''

''Theo, please.''

Someone slapped Jordan on the back and drawled lazily, ''Afternoon, Hamilton.''

The attorney turned with a scowl. ''I knew you'd be here, Murdoch.''

''Why wouldn't I be? Is this Theodora Hunter?''

The craziest surge of adolescent embarrassment struck Theo. Jordan was obviously displeased at the intrusion, but the man she had seen leaning against the white car was looking at her with the sexiest grin she'd ever seen. She couldn't even remember when a member of the opposite sex had made her so instantly aware of her own appearance.

Out of deference to the somber occasion, she was wearing a simply styled black dress, dark hose and black pumps. But Theo knew she looked good in black, and this man's sassy blue eyes were saying so, as clearly as if the words were tumbling out of his outrageously attractive mouth.

Theo looked from one man to the other. Jordan Hamilton's lips were drawn into a thin, taut line. ''Theodora Hunter, Colt Murdoch.''

As if on cue, Theo murmured, ''Theo, please,'' the same thing she'd said to Jordan only a minute ago. It was a completely automatic response for her, as she had always thought ''Theodora'' to be excessively formal. Colt Murdoch's pleased expression personalized the request, though, and Theo felt another wave of embarrassment.

Colt caught the charming flush of her cheeks. He also noticed Jordan Hamilton catching the charming flush of her cheeks. Checking further, Colt saw the warning in the attorney's eyes. He himself had issued that same sort of silent warning to predatory males before, and he fully understood what it meant.

A wry grin tugged at Colt's lips. Ignoring Hamilton, he turned to Theo Hunter. "I need a few minutes of your time, Theo. Can you squeeze me in?"

"I beg your pardon?" Bewildered, Theo's gaze darted back and forth between the two men. Under ordinary circumstances she'd be thrilled to be the focus of so much masculine attention, but whatever was going on here didn't feel at all ordinary.

"Listen, Murdoch, Miss Hunter has just so much time in Hattie," Jordan all but snarled, startling Theo further.

"I don't doubt it, which is why I intruded on her privacy on such an unhappy occasion," Colt replied smoothly. He looked Jordan in the eye. "Maude was my friend, too, whether that meets with your approval or not, Counselor."

Theo didn't know where to put herself. These were both big men, and their dislike of each other was almost palpable. Or, more accurately, Jordan Hamilton's negativity was obvious. Colt Murdoch seemed more amused than anything else.

"It's about a piece of land, Theo," Colt said to her, which only confused her more.

"Damn it, she doesn't even know the terms of Maude's will!" Jordan harshly exclaimed.

Colt studied Theo Hunter. She was tall, shapely and had the most glorious head of dark red, curly hair he'd ever seen on a woman. He hadn't anticipated Maude's granddaughter looking like this, but then, it was completely obvious that neither had Jordan.

They never had gotten along, him and Jordan. Their rivalry went way back, clear to junior high school. But they viewed the old antagonism in different ways. To Colt, it had always seemed inane and humorous, while Jordan took it all so seriously.

Blatantly turning his back on Jordan, Colt smiled at Theo. "I only need about a half hour of your time. When you're through with the legal beagle here, of course."

Theo glanced at Jordan, who was glaring daggers at Colt Murdoch. She couldn't begin to guess what this was all about, but she wasn't comfortable with it. For the sake of peace, she knew she would agree to almost anything. "I'm staying at the Tip-Top Inn. I should be back there in an hour or so."

Colt nodded. "Thank you. I'll be there." He gave Jordan a brief nod, too, then strolled off.

"Insolent damned . . ." Jordan muttered.

Relieved that the two men were no longer squaring off, Theo ignored the irate comment. "Shall we go?"

"Yes. My car's right over there." While Jordan led her across the nearly vacant parking lot, Theo saw Colt Murdoch driving away. She thought he sent her another one of his dazzling smiles just before his car moved into the light traffic of the street, but she couldn't be positive.

Jordan held the passenger door of a silver gray BMW open, and Theo slid onto the seat with a murmured thank-you. A second later, Jordan was behind the wheel and starting the motor. As he drove past the chapel to the street, Theo felt a tugging of emotion again. Maybe Maude's simple funeral service shouldn't have surprised her, but it had. It still did.

"I have to ask," Theo said quietly, giving Jordan a questioning glance. "Did you plan Maude's service?"

"It wasn't what you expected?"

Theo hesitated. She wasn't trying to find fault or fix blame, but the few minutes in the chapel seemed like such an unemotional send-off to a truly wonderful woman. Jordan reached out and patted Theo's hand.

"Maude planned it herself, Theo," he said gently. "Her instructions were in writing and very explicit. You may read them, if you wish."

"Then she knew she was going to...?"

"No, of course not. But she was eighty-three. Many elderly people plan their own funeral. Maude didn't want a lot of weeping and wailing. Those are her words, 'weeping and wailing,'" Jordan said with a small smile in Theo's direction. "Doesn't that sound like her?"

A soft sigh lifted Theo's shoulders. "Yes, I guess it does."

"You knew her a long time?"

"Twenty-one years. She was a very special lady."

"Agreed." Jordan pulled the car off the street into a parking lot. Theo looked at the attractive varnished wood and native rock building and saw a bronze sign beside the front door. Jordan A. Hamilton, Attorney-at-Law.

"This is very nice."

"Thank you."

They went inside. A young woman was seated at a desk that contained a computer, a large calendar desk pad and a pretty little vase holding pens and pencils. Besides those items, the surface of the desk was bare except for a small book of message forms.

Theo looked around and saw no one else in the office, specifically no clients awaiting attention. Jordan must have kept this part of his day open for Maude's funeral and the reading of her will, Theo thought while taking in the decor.

The building's interior was decorated quite elegantly in pastel blues and grays, and tasteful background music wafted from unseen speakers. Here was another surprise in Hattie, Montana, Theo decided. Jordan must have an excellent legal practice to afford such impressive quarters and a late-model BMW car.

"Theo Hunter, this is my receptionist and secretary, Marion Roth."

The young woman stood up and shook Theo's hand. Marion Roth was about twenty-five, Theo judged, four or five years younger than herself, attractively dressed and with a lovely, warm, rather shy smile. Marion's hair and eyes were the exact same color, Theo noticed, a light golden brown, making her a striking-looking woman.

Theo smiled over the handshake. "It's nice meeting you, Marion."

"It's very nice meeting you," Marion murmured.

"Please bring us come coffee, Marion. This way," Jordan said to Theo. With a glance over her shoulder at Marion, Theo followed the attorney down a hallway, thinking that Jordan's secretary seemed inordinately shy; she really hadn't looked directly into Theo's eyes even once.

Jordan brought her to a large, beautifully appointed office. "Please sit down, Theo."

"Thank you." Theo seated herself in one of the two plush chairs at the front of the desk. Marion appeared with a tray, set it down on a corner of the desk and left.

Jordan poured coffee from a silver pot into two china cups. "Milk or sugar?"

"A little milk, please."

When he'd prepared the two cups, Jordan moved the tray to a table along the wall and settled himself in the leather chair behind the desk. He took a sip of his coffee, then opened a drawer and lifted out a file folder. Laying it on the desk, he then ignored it and looked at Theo. She gave him a tentative smile.

"Are you curious?" he asked.

Theo's smile faded. "About Maude's estate? No, why would I be? I know Maude had very little. I am pleased that she thought of me in her will. Through the years she sent me some lovely things she made. She was a genius with knitting, crocheting and tatting needles, which you must know. Her lace was—*is*—delicate and incredibly beautiful."

"Valuable?"

Theo frowned. "Monetarily? I wouldn't know about that." She met his gaze for a long moment. "I'm not sure where this conversation is heading."

"It's heading to—" Jordan leaned forward "—several million dollars."

"What?"

His expression sober, Jordan opened the file folder and took out a sheaf of papers, which he held across the desk. "This is a list of Maude's assets."

Numbly, disbelievingly, Theo took the papers. "I don't understand." Her eyes dropped to the first item on the long list. *Cash in banks... $860,000.* "This can't be right," she mumbled. "I sent Maude money because—"

Jordan sat back. "Because why, Theo?"

Dazed, bewildered, Theo stared at the list again. Words and figures representing stocks, bonds, land and buildings blurred. "Because she was living on social security."

"She lived simply."

"Yes," Theo whispered, dropping the papers onto Jordan's desk with a trembling hand. The coffee in her cup sloshed as she brought it to her lips. "I don't understand," she repeated after a sip. "All these years I believed Maude to be living just above the poverty level."

"And you sent her money."

"Not steadily, and not always the same amount. When I was in high school I would tuck a few dollars into my letters, whatever I could spare. Later, after college, it was more."

"Why do you suppose she accepted it?"

There were tears in Theo's eyes, tears of confusion and sadness. "I... don't know."

Jordan cleared his throat. "How did the two of you meet?"

"She never told you?"

"No, she didn't."

Theo sipped from her coffee cup again. Her system was absorbing the first staggering shock of this session, but unanswered questions were leaping through her mind. It was almost comforting to push them aside for a journey into the past.

"My fourth-grade teacher initiated a class project called 'Friends in Other States.' We were all given names of pen pals." She saw Jordan's left eyebrow slide upward. "Yes, I was given Maude's name," she said, somewhat defensively.

"I'm not doubting you, Theo. But you must admit... well, twenty-one years ago, Maude was already sixty-two. Why would she want to correspond with a child?"

"I never questioned it," Theo said stiffly. "A nine-year-old doesn't question such things. Maude wrote wonderful letters."

"Did your parents question it?"

"My father died when I was three, but no, my mother didn't question it, either." Theo didn't like the defensiveness she was feeling about the old friendship, but she couldn't help herself. "I sense disapproval—or something—from you," she said in an unsteady voice.

"Not disapproval, Theo. Amazement is more like it. You see, until I read this a few days ago—" Jordan held up another piece of paper from the file folder "—I thought you were Maude's granddaughter."

"What is it?"

"An explanation, a letter, if you will, written by Maude. It was in a sealed envelope, to be opened after her death. Her will, which I'll get to in a minute, clearly names you as beneficiary. There are a few minor bequests, nothing of any importance. But I think she became worried that a problem might arise during probate because the two of you were not lawfully related. This letter clarifies her position... and yours. Until I read it, I truly believed Theodora Hunter was her granddaughter."

"I see." It was a lie. Theo didn't see at all. Everyone she knew who was aware of the years-old friendship knew very well that Maude Evans was a beloved friend and no blood relation. Why would Maude lead *her* friends to believe otherwise?

"Maude did have a daughter, you know," Jordan said softly. "So a granddaughter is not out of the question. Some of Hattie's old-timers probably remember Sarah Evans."

"What happened to her? Why isn't she Maude's beneficiary?" Maude had never mentioned a daughter.

"She died, Theo. Sarah left Hattie rather suddenly. Rumor had her pregnant and ashamed. I don't know what's true or isn't about Sarah. It was years ago, and now that Maude's gone, it isn't very likely that anyone will ever know the truth. Please don't misunderstand. Maude never said to me, or to anyone else I know of, that Theodora Hunter was Sarah's daughter."

"But you assumed."

"Erroneously, apparently." Jordan began sorting through the papers in the folder. He cleared his throat again. "I will read you Maude's will."

Locating the last fresh tissue in her purse, Theo tore it to shreds while she listened. This whole thing didn't seem real. In the chapel parking area when Jordan first told her she was Maude's beneficiary, she had visualized receiving a few of Maude's personal possessions, things to remember her by. This list of assets—Theo eyed it with growing tension—made her an extremely wealthy woman.

Now she understood Colt Murdoch's reference to "a piece of land." There were at least half a dozen pieces of land on the list.

"Probate should take about six months to a year," Jordan said. He opened his middle desk drawer and reached into it. Theo looked at the key ring in his hand. "These are keys to Maude's house, which you may use. Nothing may be sold from the estate until probate is completed. If you should need money—"

"I won't!"

"If you should need money," Jordan continued evenly, "you should have no trouble arranging a loan against the estate with the local bank." His professional expression relaxed. "You own a shop, a boutique, in California, don't you?"

"In San Diego. My mother and I started out partners, although Mother's input was strictly financial and I repaid her investment with interest." Theo's green eyes glittered with tears and passion. She didn't like talking about Maude's assets, about her estate, so crassly. And she wouldn't need a loan! The shop had done well for several years now.

Her glance fell on the keys Jordan was holding. "I won't be using the house. I can't stay in Hattie." She watched Jordan get up and walk around the desk. He sat on a corner of it and toyed with the keys in his hand, jingling them. He was very close to Theo now, close enough that she caught a whiff of his after-shave.

"Theo," he said quietly. "Obviously this has been a surprise and will take some getting used to. But you should be here during probate."

"Why? I certainly know nothing of the legal process."

"I'll handle that. Don't worry about that aspect of the situation. But you should familiarize yourself with the estate. You own a great deal of land now, for one thing." Theo saw his expression suddenly take on tension. "Which reminds me. Colt Murdoch is no one for you to be dealing with."

Theo was not accustomed to having someone tell her who to deal with. Or, in this case, who *not* to deal with. Her spirit of independence just naturally rebelled at anyone issuing orders in a presumptuous tone. Worse, masculine superiority or overprotectiveness really raised her hackles. She had been in the business world for eight years now, and more than once had run into male condescension.

Jordan Hamilton was a nice guy. Theo liked his looks and his intelligence. She liked his office and his career. His questions about her relationship with Maude were perhaps understandable, and maybe there was even something about Colt Murdoch that she should know. But stating point-blank that she shouldn't deal with the man was just a bit heavy-handed.

"Why?" Theo asked bluntly and in a not-too-kindly voice. She saw Jordan blink at her.

"There are several reasons. One, he's a land developer and not to be trusted."

In spite of her grave mood, Theo nearly laughed. "You said that as if the two were synonymous."

"In Murdoch's case, they probably are."

"'Probably'? Do you know that for a fact?" She received a long stare, then Jordan got off the desk, dropped the keys into her lap and returned to his chair.

"Are you interested in my professional advice?" he asked coolly.

Theo had no problem with that. Maude had apparently trusted Jordan Hamilton, and that was influence enough for Theo to do the same. "Yes."

"Very well. If you have to return to San Diego now, make every effort to come back to Hattie as soon as possible. Maude's house and everything in it is yours. An estate of this size needs tending. Maude did that in an office in her home."

"But you said nothing could be sold until probate is completed."

"Is that what you plan to do, sell everything?"

Theo's mouth dropped open. "I don't *plan* to do anything. I haven't even digested what I've heard here today, nor do I have the slightest idea what 'tending' the estate even means!" She saw Jordan take a deep breath.

"I'm sorry. Please forgive my curtness. The past few days have been difficult." Jordan fiddled with the file folder. More than the past few days had been difficult. He had a lot on his mind, none of which he would or could explain to Theo Hunter. "Tending the estate will involve decisions, Theo. For example, there are certificates of deposit on that list. Some of them will mature within the next few months, which will require a decision on whether or not to reinvest the sum in another certificate.''

Theo wasn't convinced. ''I'm sure a decision of that nature could be discussed on the telephone.''

An impatient note had entered Jordan's voice. ''You're confounding me,'' he said sharply. Standing, he placed his palms down on the desk and leaned over it. ''Don't you *want* this estate?''

Did she want it? Frowning, Theo chewed at her bottom lip. Most people would be doing flips around this office by now, and a few years ago, she might have been as giddy with excitement about so much money as anyone else. But her life was orderly, her business doing well. She was even planning to expand. The money would make it easier, of course.

Maybe the money would make it too easy. Was that why she wasn't elated?

She wasn't, she knew. She still felt terrible about Maude, and sudden wealth because of her old friend's death was hardly something in which to rejoice.

Plucking the keys from her lap, Theo slowly got to her feet. ''I don't know how I feel about it. I do know that I have to go home tomorrow. Perhaps, in a few days, I'll see all of this differently.''

Jordan straightened. ''Shall I call you, or would you rather call me? We need to stay in contact.''

She really *had* confounded the man, Theo realized with a sudden pang of guilt. ''I'm sorry, Jordan,'' she said quietly. ''This is a shock, plain and simple. Call me whenever you need to. And I will go and take a look at Maude's house.'' It wouldn't be easy to do, Theo suspected. Her old friend's presence would be strongly felt in her home. She knew Maude's address by heart, of course, even if she had never visited her. ''Would you mind giving me directions?''

''You've never even been in Hattie before, have you?''

''No, I haven't.''

''But you and Maude saw each other. She showed me snapshots of the two of you.''

"We saw each other twice. When I was fourteen Mother and I took a bus tour to Yellowstone National Park. Maude joined us for five days. The other time was when Maude came to San Diego for two weeks."

"I see."

He didn't see at all, Theo realized with some discomfort. Jordan Hamilton had absolutely no understanding as to why Maude Evans would bequeath a several-million-dollar estate to a woman she had seen exactly twice.

Well, neither did she.

"I'll drive you to the house," Jordan offered.

"How far is it from here?"

"About a half mile."

Theo settled her purse strap over her shoulder. "Please don't think I'm ungrateful, but I really do need some air."

"If that's what you prefer, fine. I'll sketch you a map." Jordan drew a few lines and wrote street names on a small pad. "It's not hard to locate. Just follow these arrows." He tore off the top sheet from the pad and pressed it into Theo's hand. "And take this, too," he added, grabbing the list of assets. "Study it, Theo. It will all sink in eventually, and this will help."

"Thank you." Their eyes met, and Theo saw speculation, curiosity and a hint of confusion in Jordan's. She shaped a faint smile and offered her hand. "Goodbye."

On the way out, she also said goodbye to Marion Roth, but she didn't linger. Breathing deeply of the fresh air beyond the building's front door, Theo glanced at the map and started walking.

Chapter Two

Hattie was a pleasant little town, Theo decided as she followed the map. Actually, from Maude's letters she knew quite a lot about Hattie. About some of its residents, too, although Theo couldn't remember Maude mentioning Jordan Hamilton or Colt Murdoch.

Flying in from Helena, Theo had seen a vast variety of open country. There were both mountains and prairie land surrounding Hattie, at differing distances, of course. She had spotted ranches, some appearing large, some small. There were areas with stands of dense pine trees and then miles without even one tree of any kind. From the air it was beautiful country that struck her as raw and untamed, maybe a segment of America's last frontier, and she had truly enjoyed the flight from the state capital to the small town.

But admiring a part of the world she hadn't seen before was a far cry from envisioning herself living there. Her life was in California, and until today she'd never once had any reason to consider living anywhere else.

Disturbed by that idea, Theo continued following Jordan's map. She found Maude's street, then began checking house numbers. Situated about midway in the block, Maude's house was small and modest, a one-story, blue-and-white cottage. The place was enclosed by a white picket fence and the yard contained pretty shrubs, flower beds and several large shade trees.

Emotion tightened Theo's throat. Maude had invited her here, but once she'd grown up and become busy first with her education then with earning a living, there'd just never seemed to be time for a trip to Montana. Their friendship had been undoubtable, but, in retrospect, strange. Why *would* an older woman seek correspondence with a child who lived a thousand miles away from her own home? And Maude certainly hadn't been without friends. The crowd in the chapel proved that.

"Hello, there!"

Startled, Theo turned toward the voice. An elderly woman was leaning over the fence along the left side of Maude's house. "Hello," Theo said.

"Can I be of help? Are you looking for someone?"

"I'm an old friend of Maude's."

"Then you know...?"

"Yes." Theo realized that she was getting a very thorough inspection. From behind a pair of gold-rimmed spectacles, the white-haired lady's pale blue eyes were bright and curious.

"You were at the service," the woman said, as though just remembering where she'd seen Theo before.

"Yes, I was." Unlatching the gate, Theo moved into the yard. She walked over to the fence. "I'm Theo Hunter."

The woman visibly relaxed. "Of course. I should have recognized you from the pictures Maude showed me. I'm Nan Butler. Maude and I have been neighbors for years." Nan sighed. "I'm going to miss her."

Preferring not to get into an emotional discussion when she was already on the verge of tears, Theo opened her purse and took out the keys Jordan Hamilton had given her.

"I have the keys to Maude's house," she said. Nan Butler was one of Hattie's residents whom Maude *had* mentioned in her letters; her name was familiar.

Nan was silent a moment, obviously digesting the implication of Theo Hunter and the keys, and then nodded. "I see. Well, if you need anything, let me know."

"Thank you."

"Will you be moving in?"

Would she? Theo glanced at the house. If she followed Jordan's advice and returned to Hattie, it only made good sense to stay here. But there were so many loose ends floating around in her mind—her shop, her mother, her condo in San Diego.

"I really don't know," she murmured, bringing her gaze back to Nan Butler. The woman's eyes were brimming with curiosity, she saw. Maybe there was a touch of surprise behind those gold-rimmed glasses, as well.

As surprises went, though, Nan Butler's was minor, Theo thought wryly. She still couldn't assimilate everything Jordan Hamilton had told her, and owning this house was only a small part of it.

"It was nice meeting you, Nan," Theo said with some gentleness, not wanting to appear rude to Maude's old friend and neighbor. "I'm sure we'll see each other again."

"Quite likely," the elderly woman responded pertly.

Theo began backing away from the fence. "Goodbye for now." Turning, she felt Nan Butler's sharp eyes on her back all the way to the front door. It wasn't until she was inside with the door closed that Theo realized what she'd been feeling under Nan's intense scrutiny: guilt. Guilt that she should now have possession of Maude Evans's property. "The house and everything in it" was the way Jordan had put it.

It wasn't right, Theo thought with her stomach churning. Why had Maude given *her* everything?

She was in a small foyer, from which Theo could look through an open archway and see into the living room. Her first impression was of clutter. Tables and bookshelves were overflowing with books, magazines and newspapers. Feeling dazed again, Theo began walking through the house. There were two bedrooms, one bathroom, a kitchen with a dining alcove and the office Jordan had mentioned. A door off the kitchen led to one other room, a combination storage and laundry area. Every available space in the entire house was crammed with something—books, magazines, newspapers, small boxes, partially finished handiwork and various types of thread and yarn.

Theo stopped at the doorway of the little office. Two file cabinets, a desk, chair, cardboard boxes and a large cupboard crowded the room. Papers were stacked everywhere.

It was going to be a monumental task to sort through everything, Theo thought unhappily, seeing the process of going through Maude's belongings as emotionally disturbing. Was there no one else to do it?

Sighing, Theo answered her own question. As the beneficiary of Maude's estate, the job was her responsibility. She really *was* going to have to come back to Hattie, which meant considerable planning in San Diego.

She was still clutching her purse when the doorbell startled her. Hurrying through the house, she opened the front door. Colt Murdoch was standing there. "Oh! I completely forgot about you waiting at the motel."

"That's what I thought. Mind if I come in?"

He was just too good-looking to be believed, Theo thought uneasily, moving away from the threshold so he could enter. Big and confident and uncommonly handsome. He'd loosened his tie and unbuttoned the collar of his white shirt, but he still looked terrific in that dark suit.

"I figured you might be here," Colt said as he passed her in the foyer.

Theo closed the door, noting his white four-wheel-drive vehicle at the curb. "I apologize for forgetting our appointment."

"You're probably a little stunned, aren't you?"

How did he know what had taken place? He did, Theo could tell. Knowledge was in his eyes, on his face. She put the question aside, along with any sort of admission about her state of mind. "Please come into the living room."

"Thanks." Colt followed her in. When Theo sat on a chair, he took the sofa. "I wouldn't ordinarily bother anyone at a time like this, Theo. I want you to know that."

Jordan's opinion of this man surfaced again to pester Theo. Colt Murdoch didn't look untrustworthy. Actually he looked quite fantastic. His features weren't perfect, but his face was masculinely gorgeous all the same. It was because of the deep, dark blue of his eyes and the sensuous yet clipped curve of his mouth, Theo decided.

She wasn't comfortable with Colt, but suspected that could be because of Jordan's warning. "You mentioned a piece of land."

"Yes. Maude was selling me eight hundred acres."

"Nothing can be sold from the estate until probate is completed. Jordan made that very clear."

"I'm aware of that. I only want to apprise you of the situation." Colt smiled and relaxed against the sofa cushions. "Naturally, I'm hoping you'll honor Maude's commitment."

The day's events were resulting in a dull but noticeable headache for Theo. She had dropped her purse onto the floor beside her chair, so her fingers were free to press against her temples. Seeing a shade of understanding in Colt's eyes at the gesture, she folded her hands on her lap. "I can't talk about *anyone's* commitments today. You don't really expect me to, do you?"

Colt adjusted his position on the sofa, crossing an ankle over his other knee. "You have to understand my position, Theo. I approached Maude about buying that piece of land several months ago. She took her time thinking about it, but she did give me a definite yes and told me to go ahead with the paperwork.''

''Which you did?''

''I started the process, but there wasn't time to finish it. Maude gave me the go-ahead only about ten days ago.''

''You mentioned commitment. Do you have something in writing from Maude?''

''I have only her word.'' Planting both feet on the floor, Colt leaned forward. ''I'm not trying to put pressure on you about this, but that land is very important to me.''

''You're a developer.''

A faintly cynical smile altered Colt's expression. ''I see that good old Jordy's already informed you about that big bad Colt Murdoch.''

''Jordy?''

Colt sat back, his gaze on Theo, his expression amused. ''He was Jordy as a kid, but I think he's forgotten that.''

''Oh, I see. You two grew up together.''

''We both grew up in the area, yes. But we've never been what you'd call close. I hope you don't share Hamilton's low opinion of land developers.''

She was being dissected, analyzed and put back together. Only the barely perceptible movement of his eyes gave him away, but Theo knew how thoroughly Colt Murdoch was scrutinizing her. Did he like what he was seeing? It was impossible to tell, but as uncomfortable as she was with him, she couldn't help admiring the view.

His physique was great, his shoulders broad, his stomach flat, his legs long. The black boots on his feet had to be handmade. He had wonderful hair, thick and springy looking, the kind of hair that made a woman think about touching it, threading her fingers through it.

Attempting to put aside Colt Murdoch's impressive physical attributes, Theo still felt a very strong, very recognizable pull. He disturbed her, and she was too realistic to pretend to misunderstand it. Sexual attraction struck without warning. Some people's chemistries created a turbulence of sensations, and that's what she was getting from Murdoch.

She dampened her lips. "I've never met a land developer before, so I could hardly have any kind of intelligent opinion on the matter."

"That's good to hear," Colt replied softly. "Some people believe everything they read in the newspaper, and there's no question that a few unscrupulous characters have given the profession a dubious reputation."

"Are you a successful developer, Mr. Murdoch?" Theo felt well within the bounds of propriety in asking that question. If the man wanted to buy eight hundred acres of Maude's land, there would be little point to discussing it if he didn't have the means to pay for it. Not that Theo had any idea what she was going to do with the estate. Lord, she didn't even know what kind of land they were talking about!

"Moderately successful, and please call me Colt. Look, all I'm asking you to do is to honor Maude's commitment."

Theo shook her head. "No, you're asking me to believe that Maude *made* a commitment."

Colt's eyes narrowed. Theo Hunter was a strikingly beautiful woman. Without the dark glasses she'd worn earlier, he could see the startling green color of her heavily lashed eyes. He could also see a cloud of confusion and a private battle with self-control in those eyes. The day had obviously been tough on her, but he had the impression that Theo was normally well controlled. She was nobody's fool, either, and she'd grasped the gist of his dilemma very accurately. All he had was Maude's word on that land deal, and Maude was gone.

"Do you think I would come here and lie to you about it?" he asked.

If she were to believe Jordan Hamilton, Colt Murdoch would do almost anything. The attorney's body language, in Colt's presence and then later when he'd warned her about the man, had said more than his actual words, conveying dislike, mistrust and suspicion.

Whatever Jordan thought Colt capable of, though, Theo couldn't call the man a liar. She didn't judge anyone by someone else's standards, and from the few hours that she'd known of Colt Murdoch's existence, the only thing she could really accuse him of was being too attractive.

"I'm not even hinting that you'd come here and lie," she said flatly. "But I'm not prepared to discuss that particular piece of land or any other portion of Maude's estate."

Colt watched her troubled gaze slowly sweep the room. "It's overwhelming, isn't it?" he said quietly.

"Very," she answered huskily. "How...how is it that you know about Maude leaving me everything?"

"I guess I just figured it out. Maude talked about you a lot." He frowned a little. "I wish I'd listened a bit closer, to be honest. Anyway, with Jordan all bristled up and self-important today with you in tow, I put two and two together."

"Really? That's it? You simply figured it out?"

"That's it."

"Hmm. Well, there's an enormous amount to do here, and I can't stay in Hattie right now. Jordan wants me to return as quickly as possible."

"Is that what you're planning to do?"

Theo was positive she saw a speculative gleam in Colt's blue eyes, as though he were visualizing further opportunity to talk about that land. The uneasiest feeling she'd ever had began to work its way through her system. She couldn't label it, but it had something to do with money, and with power.

As undefined as the sensation was, Theo couldn't question the effects she was feeling from the unnerving events of the day, and how both Colt Murdoch and Jordan Hamilton must be thinking of her as wealthy now.

My Lord. Her, Theodora Hunter, wealthy. It was stunning, impossible to comprehend.

Theo moistened her very dry lips again, then got to her feet. "I need something to drink. Would you care to join me?"

Colt stood up. "Yes, thanks."

Theo started away. "It might only be water," she called over her shoulder as she remembered that she had no idea what she might or might not find in Maude's kitchen.

"Water's fine."

And then, standing in the middle of that small old-fashioned kitchen, Theo felt herself trembling. She couldn't force herself to open a cupboard under any circumstances. This was Maude's kitchen, Maude's house. Believing otherwise was going to take some time.

Unsteadily Theo dislodged two paper cups from the dispenser on the wall beside the sink. Filling one with tap water, she drank quickly and left the used cup on the counter. The second cup was filled and carried to the living room, where she handed it to Colt Murdoch.

"I'm going to lock up and leave," she told him. "May I impose on you for a ride to the motel?"

"Sure, no problem." Colt swallowed his water with his gaze on Theodora Hunter. Maude had talked about her "dear friend" in California many times. On those occasions, Colt had sort of let the rather vague conversations drift in one ear and out the other. Maude had been an odd duck, no two ways about it, always rambling on about one subject or another. As he'd told Theo, he wished now that he had listened a little more attentively, maybe asked a few questions. At the chapel today he'd been a little confused at first, thinking that Theodora Hunter must be Maude's granddaughter. Remembering those conversations, however, he had realized that Theo was that "dear friend" Maude had mentioned.

Then, the way that Jordan had behaved after the service had given the whole thing away. Colt really had figured it out: Theo was Maude's beneficiary. And the way Jordan had acted all protective and possessive, one would think that everyone was out to steal Theo's inheritance before she even got it. Colt wouldn't put it past Jordy to make sure *he* was the first in line. It was a damned disturbing thought.

Another thing Colt found disturbing was that Theo was a compelling woman. Jordan had to have noticed, same as him. The difference between him and Jordy was that Jordy would do something about it and he didn't think it was right.

Not that he didn't function with all of the requisite hormones of a sexually active male. There were women in his life, but no one special right at the moment, no one to bring to mind and concentrate on to displace Theo's prodigious appeal. Still, she had a lot to deal with right now, and she didn't need a man complicating her life. Jordy wouldn't be that considerate, however, Colt suspected, watching Theo through narrowed eyes.

She moved with a unique, sensual grace, first retrieving her purse from the floor beside the chair she'd used, then bearing toward the archway and foyer.

Bright, pretty and sexually stimulating, Theo Hunter was a woman he could like, Colt decided uneasily as he followed her to the door. Unfortunately, Jordan probably thought the same thing about her.

He stood by while Theo made sure the front door was locked. "You're coming back to Hattie in the near future, then?" he inquired.

"I don't think I have a choice."

They walked down the sidewalk to the front gate, where Colt unhooked the latch and let Theo precede him to the curb. He didn't speak again until they were in his car and en route to the Tip-Top Inn. "That piece of land is crucial to my plans, Theo," he said.

She glanced at him with some impatience. Her mind felt crowded with brand-new thoughts and ideas, most of them foreign and obtrusive. Her life had changed drastically today, and it wasn't her doing. The concept of wealth wasn't inconceivable. Financial security was what she and a large percent of the population worked for, after all.

But to have several million dollars dropped on her without warning was emotionally staggering. To be honest, Theo had started toying with the idea of refusing any part of Maude's estate. Could an heir do that? Just call up the attorney in charge and tell him to give the whole shootin' match to someone else?

She needed to talk to her mother. Desperately, as a matter of fact.

And she *didn't* need someone trying to pin her down about selling him a piece of Maude's land.

Theo took a deep breath to calm her nerves. She didn't want to yell at Colt Murdoch, but she felt like yelling at something or someone. She was abnormally on edge, a condition that wasn't going to fade away just because she preferred a more serene mood.

Getting out of Hattie would help. Returning to familiar surroundings would also help. But the burden of unforeseen responsibility that had suddenly been thrust upon her was influencing the very foundation of who and what she was.

"Mr. Murdoch—Colt—I need some time to absorb today's events," she said, speaking as emotionlessly as she could manage. "I'll agree to only one aspect of your request. If the land you want—*need*—is to be sold, you may have first right of refusal."

Colt nodded agreeably. "That's fair. I'm sure you'll decide to sell most of the estate's real property. It's mostly raw land, you know. The piece I'm interested in adjoins land I already own."

Theo wasn't the least bit curious about Colt's plans for the land. If she had been, this would be the opportune time for questions. But Colt Murdoch's career or profession, whatever category land development fell into, couldn't begin to compete with everything else running through her mind.

Her shop, for one major topic, was gnawing at her. She operated the boutique herself, with the assistance of two full-time and two part-time employees. Which of them had the ability to assume her position? Someone would have to do it. She couldn't just waltz off for weeks at a time, maybe even months, without a responsible person overseeing the business.

And she wasn't going to ignore the business she had worked so hard to make successful. She had invested too much time, money and emotion in the boutique to push it aside now just because she didn't need its profits.

Besides, the list of assets in her purse didn't seem real, and the boutique was *very* real.

"Here we are," Colt declared as he pulled the car into the Tip-Top Inn's parking lot. He left the engine running and turned in the seat to face Theo. "You'll be here this evening. How about having dinner together? I could come back around six or seven, whenever you say." Just to talk, he told himself. He wouldn't pressure Theo about anything, not about his buying the land and certainly not about putting the make on her.

Theo looked directly into his eyes. The man was incredible to look at, warming everything female in her system. If she wasn't so tied up in knots, she would welcome the chance to know him better.

But she had also responded to Jordan Hamilton's good looks. How odd to have met two such appealing men in the same day.

The whole day had been odd, though. And encouraging anything even remotely personal with anyone in Hattie, Montana, would be shortsighted at this point. She had to return, and until she gained a better understanding of her status in the area, it was best to keep all newly formed associations at arm's length.

"Thank you, but no. I'd like to be alone this evening."

Colt kept looking at her, saying nothing. Theo was an intelligent woman. The day had been a shock to her, and she wasn't accepting sudden wealth as a completely positive gift. Her beautiful green eyes were full of questions. Her life had been disrupted and she wasn't altogether thrilled about it.

That would change, Colt thought. Once she grasped the scope of her inheritance, she would be plenty thrilled. Who wouldn't be?

A small frown appeared between his eyes. Maybe any really thinking person would be unsettled by such a drastic alteration of his life. Wouldn't a sudden influx of unexpected resources diminish one's satisfaction with his own successes? Especially the small triumphs that meant so much on a daily basis?

He suddenly felt warmer, softer toward Theo. She wasn't just another pretty face, or the owner of the land he needed to fulfill the goals he had lined out for his future. An urge to reach her on a completely human level brought his hand up to her shoulder.

"I think I know what you're feeling," he said gently.

She laughed, a brief, brittle sound. "If you do, it's more than I know." Then her eyes widened. "I'm sorry. That was rude, and I didn't mean—"

"It's all right." Colt withdrew his hand, aware that she hadn't even noticed the contact. Not the way he had. She was an intriguing, attractive woman, and something electric had passed from her to him, whether she knew it or not. When she came back to Hattie . . . ?

No, he couldn't start thinking in that vein. Personal relationships muddied the waters. He needed that piece of land, and he intended making a clean, solid business deal with Theo to purchase it. All he could do was hope that Jordan had enough sense to maintain a strictly business relationship with her, though in truth Colt doubted it.

Theo reached for her door handle. "Thank you for the ride. No, please, don't get out," she added when Colt started to open his own door. "I'm sure we'll meet again, but . . ."

Her troubled expression bothered Colt. She knew she had to return to Hattie, but it was only one aspect of the nebulous quality of today's shock. "Fine," he said quietly. "I'll see you . . . whenever."

"Yes. Goodbye." Theo got out of the car, closed the door and walked toward the motel's main entrance. She went in without looking back.

Her image stayed with Colt while he sat there and pondered the situation. He was strangely divided, he realized, part of his mind lingering on Theo's personal draw—her pretty face, her wonderful hair and eyes, her exciting figure in that stunning black dress—and another part concentrating on the importance of maintaining a sensible business relationship.

He could really like Theo Hunter. If he let his emotions just go where they may, no telling what might happen. Assuming, of course, that she felt the same.

Colt shook his head with a rather grim tightening of his lips. Assuming anything with Theo would be a mistake. Had she seen him as anything but an irritant today? Had she picked up any of his admiration, any hint of his response to her warm and inviting femaleness?

Jordan Hamilton had recognized her magnetism, too, and good old Jordy wasn't married, either, though he definitely had a thing going with his secretary, Marion. Putting that aside, which Colt felt Jordan was perfectly capable of doing should Theo give him the time of day, the attorney was financially strapped and maybe not above wooing a woman for her bank account.

The thought sent a prickle of uneasiness up Colt's spine. If Hamilton had anything to say about it, Theo would never sell that land to Colt Murdoch. The man was a toad, he'd *always* been a toad. As a kid, his favorite pastime had been to rile the other kids, causing fights and arguments, keeping as many feuds going as he could possibly stir up.

Colt had learned long ago to avoid Jordan, and he'd always viewed his shenanigans as bizarre but funny. Nowadays Hamilton wore a little more subtle hat, but he was still a troublemaker. He was a reasonably good lawyer, most people said, but Colt didn't trust him as far as he could throw him and drove to Helena for his legal work.

That other angle, Jordan's financial situation, was a point of some gossip around Hattie. He'd built that fancy office and lived as if he had an extensive, profitable law practice, when most people knew that Hattie's legal needs couldn't possibly support Jordan's high-toned life-style. He had to be in debt up to his eyebrows.

Colt drove away frowning. Theo had been plopped down into a much bigger mess than anyone could imagine on short acquaintance. There was a weird sort of triangle in the making, Jordan, Theo and him, and he wasn't going to sit by and watch old Jordy infiltrate Maude's estate through Theo.

And he knew without pondering the subject that Jordan wasn't going to idly sit by and watch Colt Murdoch benefit in any way, either, even though his participation would be only through hard cash in exchange for that piece of land.

But there was a lot more to it—Theo, herself. A woman like her didn't deserve to end up with a snake like Hamilton, and Colt suspected that the attorney was going to be pitching everything he had at her.

Which meant, common sense to the contrary, he might have to do a little pitching of his own.

Chapter Three

Theo tried to call her mother and remembered, when there was no answer, that it was Lisa's weekly dinner and bridge night. She wouldn't be home until late.

After a bowl of soup in the motel's coffee shop, Theo returned to her room and prepared for bed. Then, with the pillows stacked against the headboard, she took the list of assets Jordan had given her from her purse and lay down. She had deliberately put this moment off, avoiding the list as if it were something poisonous.

Were her reactions to the inheritance normal? she wondered uneasily. Wouldn't most people be thrilled to tears to find themselves the recipient of so much money?

Her gaze faltered on each item on the list. She hadn't known Maude at all, she thought with a ponderous sadness. Those little sums of money she'd sent with her letters wouldn't add up to even a tiny fraction of what she was reading. Why had Maude accepted financial assistance when she so obviously hadn't needed it?

Theo tossed the list to the bed with a heavy sigh. There was so much to think about, so many whys and what-fors, so much perplexity about Maude and the estate. Leaving San Diego for an extended time was going to be difficult, and living in Hattie during that period was not a consoling prospect.

Then there were the people she'd met today, specifically Jordan Hamilton and Colt Murdoch. Two such attractive men, and so at odds with each other. Jordan's dislike of Colt wasn't at all pleasant, while Colt's attitude toward the attorney seemed almost indulgent, as if he tolerated Jordan's opinion and even found it amusing.

And she liked them both.

In the same way? Theo then asked herself. Setting up an imaginary scenario, if Colt and Jordan each asked her out at the exact same moment, which invitation would she accept?

It was an intriguing question, as both men were extremely interesting. But hadn't she felt something unusual with Colt? Something just a little out of the ordinary?

On the other hand, Jordan's crisp, almost curt personality appealed to her sense of order. He seemed so organized, so in control of his own destiny. She liked that.

Colt was an earthier man. She could place him in the great outdoors without a bit of trouble. Maybe on a horse. Or hacking down trees, wearing jeans and boots and having that marvelous hair flipping around.

Colt was sexier looking, that was it. But exteriors could be terribly deceiving. Good looks—a handsome face and an athletic body—didn't guarantee a thing, certainly not how a man treated a woman. Did either man possess the traits she really valued, like consideration and sensitivity?

Actually, a few minutes with a man, especially under today's trying circumstances, wasn't enough time to form any sort of intelligent judgment about his character. And as far as initial impressions went, both Colt and Jordan had induced a residual awareness.

She would be seeing them again, probably spending time with each of them. Certainly, when she returned to Hattie, meetings with Jordan would be necessary. As for Colt, she suspected that he wouldn't rest until he had secured the deed to those eight hundred acres.

Theo's mind wandered. The last important man in her life had turned out to be an incredible jerk. She'd never been married, and she wasn't all that positive that she'd ever been in love. Not *really* in love, not the moonbeams-and-stardust kind of love one read about in romantic novels.

For that matter, she wasn't sure if she even believed in that kind of love. Friends and her own mother told her it had happened to them, but without personal experience it was hard to imagine.

Theo made a face. She wouldn't be coming back to Hattie with an eye out for a man. Why would she even be thinking about such things when she was bogged down with so many serious concerns?

The night was far from restful. Theo slept in fitful spurts and came wide-awake so many times she lost count. When she opened her eyes and realized that the sun had finally come up, she was relieved, if yawning.

Now she had the morning to get through, she thought while showering. The commuter plane to Helena didn't leave until midafternoon, which meant some more restless hours before she was on her way home.

During breakfast in the coffee shop, it occurred to her how best to use the time: she had to go back to Maude's house. She had barely looked around yesterday, but she felt a little better about everything today and would see things differently.

And the walk would do her good. Gathering her purse, Theo took care of the check and left the restaurant.

It took a minute to get her directional bearings, then she set out. She was wearing slacks and low-heeled shoes for the flight home, and the day was bright and warm. The walk was pleasant, and she was getting a closer look at Hattie.

After a few blocks, a car horn tooted nearby and Theo glanced to the street. Jordan Hamilton's silver gray BMW had stopped at the curb. She smiled and walked over to the vehicle, bending down to see through the window that had just glided open. "Good morning."

"Good morning. I called your room, but you'd already left."

"I had breakfast in the coffee shop."

"Just out walking?"

"I thought I'd go back to the house."

"Let me give you a lift."

Theo hesitated, wishing that Jordan hadn't come along. She wanted to spend some time alone in Maude's house. The moment the idea had come to her, she'd known it was the right thing to do.

But how could she refuse Jordan's offer without appearing rude?

"A few things came to mind, Theo," Jordan said. "Nothing crucial, but we should probably go over them." He was leaning across the passenger seat from the driver's, and he opened the door in invitation.

She gave in and nodded. "Okay, thanks."

When Theo was settled and the car moving, she felt Jordan's glance. More than a glance. He was really looking her over, she realized.

"You're a beautiful woman, Theo."

The unexpected flattery struck a wrong note for Theo. "Thank you," she replied tonelessly. She'd refused dinner with Colt last night and she wasn't going to encourage Jordan today.

Not yet, at any rate. Maybe when she came back to Hattie she might consider some dating. Nothing serious, of course, but as she'd decided last night, Colt and Jordan were extraordinary men, and she hadn't met anyone else who had rated that special category in quite some time.

"You don't like compliments?" Jordan asked.

He'd spoken lightly, almost teasingly. He was flirting, Theo realized, wishing he wouldn't. He looked wonderful in his pale gray suit, clean and perfectly put together, but she wasn't in a flirty mood.

And maybe he should sense that.

"I believe you referred to something that needed discussion," she said quietly.

Jordan cleared his throat. "Yes, a couple of small matters. You should know that I have a key to the house. I neglected to mention it yesterday."

"I see no problem with that."

"I'd like some indication of when you plan to return," Jordan continued. "Only for practical purposes, of course. The house shouldn't be left in its present state indefinitely."

"Its present state?" Theo gave the attorney a questioning look.

"There's perishable food in the refrigerator, Theo, and in the cabinets."

"Oh, yes, I see what you mean. Well, it shouldn't be left to spoil, should it? Do you know of someone who might want it?"

"I could arrange to have it taken away and given to a needy family. Is that your preference?"

"I would appreciate that very much. Thank you."

"You're quite welcome. Anything I can do, anything at all, feel free to ask. Even when you're in California, if you think of something, just give me a call."

"I will, thanks."

"But I'm sure you won't delay your return for very long."

"I have obligations in California, Jordan."

"I realize that, but you also have obligations here."

Theo bit her lip. Jordan was being nice about it, but he was pressuring her all the same. She took a steadying breath, telling herself to keep cool. He was only doing what he thought best, probably as much for her sake as for the requirements of his work with the estate. "I'll come back as soon as I can. You have my word."

The car stopped in front of Maude's cottage. "Would you like me to come in with you?" Jordan asked.

"That's not necessary. I know you're a busy man and I'm really only killing time until my flight leaves. Thanks for the lift, Jordan. I'll be in touch." Theo opened her door.

"Oh, by the way, did you meet with Murdoch yesterday?"

The question struck Theo as just plain nosy, and she turned back to Jordan reluctantly. "I really don't think—"

"It *is* my business," Jordan interrupted defensively. "Did you make him any promises?"

She was not going to aggravate whatever problem existed between Jordan and Colt, Theo decided right then and there. "Let's make a deal, Jordan. I won't tell Colt what you and I discuss if you don't ask me what he and I talk about, okay?"

"You're making a mistake, Theo."

"Why do you dislike him?"

Jordan smirked. "I've *never* liked him. He's a smug, superior know-it-all, and..." He hesitated. There was a lot he could tell her about Colt, but she didn't seem to be in a listening mood. He settled for saying, "Believe me, you'll find out about Colt Murdoch the hard way if you insist on doing business with him."

"Is he dishonest? A liar? What, Jordan? Why shouldn't I do business with him?"

His hazel eyes bored into her as he again debated how far he should go with information about Colt. But Colt's sins had been committed long ago and he'd paid for them. He wouldn't appreciate Jordan or anyone else digging up old dirt and passing it on to Theo. Not that Jordan was afraid of Colt or anything he might do if Colt should happen to hear that he'd been the person to enlighten Theo Hunter.

But for the present, Jordan decided, he would focus *on* the present. "You did promise him something, didn't you?"

he said to Theo. "I hope you're not sorry later on. The value of what you've inherited, especially the land, is increasing daily. I hope you didn't talk about price."

"Neither of us so much as mentioned money."

"Well, that's something. Just go slow and easy with him, Theo, that's all I'm suggesting."

He had suggested a lot more than that, going so far as to accuse Colt without defining a crime. But Theo didn't want to get in the middle of it, whatever "it" was. It was possible for two people who'd grown up in the same small town to dislike each other without a definitive reason. Maybe some incident from the past still goaded their tempers.

Whatever the reason, it was between Colt and Jordan. She liked both men, and how they felt toward each other had nothing to do with her.

Theo offered her hand. "Goodbye, Jordan. I'll call from San Diego."

He accepted the handshake with a smile. "Please do. I look forward to your return."

"Thank you." Their gazes met and held for a moment, then Theo moved away and got out of the car. She knew Jordan hadn't immediately driven away, and she sent him a little wave from the front stoop of the house.

She inserted the key in the lock and opened the door, and as she crossed Maude's threshold, the BMW slowly left the curb.

Theo sighed and closed the door, her thoughts instantly shifting from Jordan to her old friend, Maude. The house was warm from the sun beaming through its east windows, and dust motes danced in the bright rays. Theo stood in the living room doorway and felt a pleasant serenity, a sensation she hadn't experienced during yesterday's visit.

For some reason Maude had wanted her to have her earthly possessions; it was up to her to figure out why.

Theo arrived in Los Angeles at seven that evening. Her car awaited her in general parking, and she drove concentrating on the heavy traffic, which seemed worse than usual, probably because of Hattie's quiet streets.

Instead of going directly home, Theo drove to her mother's house. Lisa let her in with a sympathetic smile. "How did it go?"

"It was unbelievable." With a sigh, Theo plopped down onto the sofa. "I don't know where to begin."

"Are you talking about Maude's funeral service?"

"No. I'm talking about Maude's will."

"Her will?"

"She named me as beneficiary."

Lisa drew a quiet breath. "What a lovely gesture. She thought the world of you, Theo. Her letters were always so pleasant, weren't they?"

"Yes, they were." Theo's gaze remained on her mother. "Your first reaction to that news was the same as mine, so I know what you're thinking, Mom, that Maude left me a few mementos."

"Yes, of course. Why? Is there something else?"

Opening her purse, Theo extracted the list of assets and rose slightly to pass it to her mother. "This is what Maude left me."

Lisa took the list and began reading it. Her eyes got bigger and bigger. "My Lord," she whispered. "This is impossible. There must be some mistake."

"Maude's attorney gave me that. There's no mistake."

Lisa lowered the papers to her lap and looked at her daughter. "You're right. It *is* unbelievable. Why did she name you as her beneficiary?"

"I have no idea."

"What are you going to do?"

Theo sighed. "I have no idea." After a pause, she added, "That's not completely true. I have to go back to Montana to help with the estate. To *tend* it, Jordan Hamilton said. He's the attorney. What I don't know is what I'm going to do with so much money."

Lisa's expression was serious, yet she gave a small laugh. "Is that really a problem?"

"It shouldn't be, should it?" Theo got up to pace. "Why don't I feel better about it? This is like winning the lottery. I should be thrilled. I will never have to work another day of my life if I don't want to. I can travel, buy things, a new house, a new car, anything I want."

"That's true."

Theo faced her mother. "Then why do I feel like the rug has just been pulled out from under my feet?"

Lisa slowly shook her head. "I don't know. Maybe it will just take some getting used to."

Prowling again, Theo verbalized her unease. "I've worked so hard with the boutique, and it's suddenly unimportant. Maybe that's what's bothering me. This is going to change everything."

"Possibly. If you allow it."

"How can I prevent it?" She placed her hand on her chest. "I already feel different, Mother. I don't want to, but I do."

"How *do* you feel, honey?" Lisa questioned gently.

Theo thought a moment. "Unsettled. Restless. Like I've suddenly become a huge loose end flapping in the breeze. Does that make any sense?"

Lisa smiled. "I think I know what you mean." She stood up. "Have you had dinner?"

"They served a snack on the plane," Theo said absently, retrieving the list from her mother's hand and returning it to her purse. "I'm going to go home, Mom. I only stopped by to tell you what happened."

They walked to the door. "When are you going back to Montana, Theo?"

"As soon as I can get things ironed out at the shop. Someone's going to have to be in charge while I'm gone, and I've been debating on who to appoint."

"Well, short of actually working at the boutique, Theo, you know I'll do what I can to help."

Theo leaned forward and kissed her mother's cheek. "I know, Mom. Thanks. I'll call you tomorrow."

Driving home, Theo wrestled with the question of which employee to put in charge. Lisa would gladly do it if her health permitted, but her medical problems greatly limited her activities. Bringing in someone new didn't seem wise to Theo, so her decision really rested with her two full-time employees. Her first step should probably be a chat with each, she decided while parking the car in her garage.

Inside her condo, Theo carried her suitcase to her aqua-and-cream bedroom. She had always enjoyed the condo, though small, but now she could afford to buy a house. Was that how she wanted to use Maude's estate, in luxuries for herself?

The thought was surprisingly discomfiting. There had to be a better use for so much money.

A week later the commuter plane landed at Hattie's modest airport. Theo deplaned. Jordan Hamilton was waiting with a welcoming smile and a warm handshake.

"I'm glad you followed my advice and came right back," he told her.

"It seemed best," Theo murmured, strangely annoyed at the comment. She wanted advice, she *needed* advice, and yet she wasn't accustomed to dealing with it.

After gathering her luggage, they walked to Jordan's car. When they were settled within the BMW, he looked at her. "You're staying at the house, of course, rather than at a motel."

"Yes."

"Good girl."

It was another annoying remark. Subtly patronizing. Theo told herself to stop being so damned sensitive. Jordan Hamilton intended to assist her through this and she should be grateful. Maybe he saw her as helpless at the moment, but he would learn otherwise in the course of their association.

He pulled the car smoothly away from the small terminal building. "Are you better used to the idea of sudden wealth, Theo?"

Her smile appeared, albeit weakly. "I'm still digesting it. Jordan, when Maude gave you instructions for her will, did she say anything about why she left everything to me?"

"No, but as I told you before, I thought you were her granddaughter. Which, of course, is the reason I didn't ask questions." Jordan sent her a glance. "Don't look a gift horse in the mouth, Theo. Does it matter why she did it? You're a wealthy woman now. My advice is to relax and enjoy it."

"That's a little easier said than done. Wouldn't you be questioning Maude's motivation if she had named you her heir?"

Jordan's laugh fell a little flat, Theo noticed, though he conceded her point with a dryly stated, "Guess you're right." The BMW pulled to a stop in front of Maude's house. "I'll carry in your luggage."

"Thanks." Theo got out. She wasn't traveling light this trip. Her luggage consisted of three pieces, each of them crammed full and heavy. Jordan took two suitcases, and she carried the third along with her purse. She unlocked the front door and pushed it open.

Stepping inside, Theo stopped dead in her tracks. The house looked different. Instead of the previous clutter she'd seen, everything was tidy. "What happened here?" she asked, instantly shaken.

Jordan came in wearing a big smile. "I had it cleaned as a surprise."

It was a surprise, all right, but it wasn't one that Theo appreciated. The furniture looked barren, the stacks and stacks of magazines and newspapers were gone, and who knew what else? Not that she was worried about anything of value being missing. But the idea of going through Maude's things had been growing in appeal, and why else had she put her life in California on hold to come here?

Theo set her suitcase near the sofa and dropped her purse onto a cushion. "I wish you hadn't done that, Jordan."

"I thought you'd appreciate a clean house. You said to give the food away." Jordan lowered the suitcases he was carrying to the floor.

"The food, yes, but not anything else. Not until I—" Shocked at the proprietary tone coming out of her mouth, Theo stopped herself. Obviously Jordan Hamilton was turning himself inside out to help her. How could she be so ungrateful as to start finding fault with his generosity?

"Thank you, Jordan," she said firmly.

"You're welcome. Anything I can do, Theo, anything at all, just name it."

Theo glanced around—the absence of the clutter she'd expected still bothered her—then smiled at Jordan. "I'll keep that in mind." Subtly she began easing toward the door. Jordan followed, as she'd hoped.

"I intend to personally show you each and every piece of real property you inherited, Theo," he said as they reached the door. "Maybe we could start tomorrow."

"Uh, I'm not sure. May I call you?"

"I'll call you in the morning, how's that? There's one piece, an eight-hundred-acre tract, that's the most beautiful piece of land I've ever seen. I'm sure you'll enjoy seeing it."

An eight-hundred-acre tract? Wasn't that the same number of acres Colt Murdoch had mentioned?

"I'm sure I will," Theo agreed quietly, though internally disturbed that the dissension between Jordan and Colt was already presenting itself.

Jordan finally left. Theo closed the door with a feeling of relief. Strolling through the house wasn't comforting. Even Maude's office had been invaded. Possibly nothing had been discarded, but it certainly had been rearranged. Whoever Jordan had hired to "clean" the house had been thorough.

The phone rang within fifteen minutes, just after Theo had carried her suitcases into the smaller of the two bedrooms, assuming the larger to be Maude's room and thinking it would still contain her things. Theo slipped into the office to take the call. It was Jordan on the line.

"Theo, you're going to need a car. I meant to mention it right away, but it slipped my mind. I have a loaner for you."

"That's thoughtful, Jordan. Thank you. If it's putting anyone out, though, I can easily rent one."

"Nonsense. I'll have it delivered within the hour."

Forgetting her suitcases for the moment, Theo wandered into the kitchen and idly opened the refrigerator, anticipating empty shelves. To her surprise there was an array of fresh items, dairy products, meat, condiments and vegetables. Everything was new and unopened, the catsup, the mustard, the cellophane packages.

Frowning reflectively, Theo closed the fridge. It was Jordan's doing, of course. Who else would think to replace the old food? He was a very considerate man. Attractive, too. Obviously he went far beyond the norm one expected from a business associate. Was that the underlying reason for his success, which was so apparent in his office, car and clothing?

The restiveness that Theo had told her mother about hadn't abated a whole lot. Her boutique was being managed by Helen Sorenson, the older of her two full-time employees. Age hadn't influenced Theo's decision. Rather, Helen had displayed a sincere interest in the added responsibility, while the other woman had started talking about family obligations.

Returning to the office telephone, Theo dialed the boutique's number. "Hi, Helen, it's me. Everything all right?"

"Just fine, Theo."

They chatted for a few minutes and Theo hung up feeling a little better. Leaving her shop in someone else's hands was no trivial matter, but she was at least beginning to believe in Helen's desire to do a good job.

Before Theo could get to her unpacking, the car was delivered by a young man who, though pleasant, seemed reluctant to linger. After he'd gone, Theo inspected the vehicle, which was a late-model red sedan in excellent condition. Who owned it? she wondered, uneasy again about imposing on someone's good nature. Renting a car would be a simple matter. Assuming Hattie had a car rental agency, of course. Whether it did or didn't, perhaps Jordan was being a little *too* generous, and few people functioned completely unselfishly. Colt Murdoch might be nice to her because he wanted that piece of land, but what was Jordan's motive?

A few minutes later the glaringly empty closet in the bedroom startled Theo. Suspicious suddenly, she hurried to the larger bedroom and threw open the closet door. It, too, was empty.

Stunned, Theo checked the room's two bureaus. All of Maude's clothing was gone, every stitch. Anger welled, and indignation. Jordan had been too damned thorough! How dare he remove Maude's personal possessions from the house? She had a strong, boiling urge to call him and tell him how she felt about such gall.

She didn't do it. Instead, fuming, she emptied her suitcases and put away her clothes. By the time she carried the luggage to the storage room off the kitchen, her feathers weren't quite so ruffled. Jordan was merely a little too zealous, she told herself. A straightforward conversation with the young lawyer probably wouldn't hurt. How could he understand her preferences if she didn't explain herself?

A knock at the front door drew Theo's attention. She opened the door to Nan Butler, her elderly neighbor. Theo smiled. "Hello, Nan."

The tiny woman held out a cardboard box. "I brought you some supper. Didn't figure you'd feel like cooking your first day here."

Theo took the box and peered in it to see a casserole and a pie. "Oh, this looks wonderful. You shouldn't have gone to so much bother, but thank you."

"I won't keep you." Nan began leaving the front porch. "Maybe after you're settled in you'll drop by for coffee. Or a cup of tea. I enjoy both."

"I'd love to. Thanks, Nan. I'll return the dishes...."

"There's no hurry." With a wave over her shoulder, the sprightly little woman walked down the sidewalk to the gate.

Smiling, Theo brought her supper inside and to the kitchen. How thoughtful of Nan. Apparently Jordan wasn't the only considerate person in Hattie.

The phone rang. Again Theo heard Jordan's voice. "I would be very pleased to escort you to dinner in one of Hattie's restaurants, Theo."

No longer indignant or angry about Maude's clothes, Theo was able to speak without rancor. "Some other time, Jordan. One of the neighbors brought over a delicious-looking casserole, and I really do prefer staying in this evening."

"Think you'll be in the mood to inspect your property in the morning?"

Theo sighed to herself. Jordan wasn't going to let her procrastinate on that inspection tour, and she might as well do it and get it over with.

"All right, fine," she conceded. "Around nine?"

"Nine it is. See you then."

Chapter Four

It was nearly five when Theo thought of Colt Murdoch, and that maybe he should be told of her arrival. Debating it for a moment, she went to the office, checked Hattie's phone book for Colt Murdoch and saw a number for a Murdoch Ranch and another for a business, Murdoch Land and Cattle Company.

"Hmm," she murmured in perplexity. If Colt owned and lived on a ranch, she knew nothing about it. There could be other Murdochs in the area, she decided, though it was strange that Colt didn't have a listed home number. At any rate, she dialed the business number. A woman answered with the company name.

"This is Theo Hunter. I'm not sure I have the right number, but have I reached Colt Murdoch's company?"

"Yes, you have, ma'am."

"Is Colt there?"

"Colt's out at the ranch today, Ms. Hunter."

Okay, so he did own a ranch, Theo thought. "I see," she murmured.

"You could probably reach him there, although sometimes everyone's outside and they don't hear the phone ring. He calls in for his messages, however, and I could give him your number. Whichever you prefer."

"I merely wanted to let him know that I'm back in Montana. Just pass on my message, if you will. Tell him I'm staying at Maude Evans's house."

"I'll see that he gets the message. Goodbye, Ms. Hunter."

"Goodbye." Theo put down the phone. Jordan wouldn't approve of this call, but notifying Colt of her arrival satisfied her own sense of duty.

Theo stood at the office doorway that evening and weighed the task awaiting her. Regardless of Jordan's cleaning person stacking everything into tidy piles, going through Maude's myriad papers, desk drawers and filing cabinets was going to be a major undertaking.

Not tonight, Theo decided, opting for a bath and an early bedtime. Tomorrow she would be occupied with Jordan's tour of her inherited properties. Perhaps the following day would be a good time to start on the office.

After a leisurely bath, Theo put on a nightgown, robe and slippers. Her face was shiny, devoid of makeup. With her hairbrush in hand, she switched on the TV set in the living room and curled up on the room's recliner chair. Using the remote control, she ran through the available channels and stopped at one broadcasting an old movie. Absently she brushed her hair; just as absently, she stared at the TV.

Realizing that darkness was encroaching, she reached out to the lamp on the table next to the chair and turned it on. The movie flicked by; Theo was barely aware of it. Instead, the quiet of the house, Maude's house, and the strange twists of her own life played in her mind. What she was going to do with Maude's money was a recurrent question. It was going to change her life; it had *already* changed her life.

But she couldn't see herself as living without purpose, which would be an easy pattern to fall into. Seeing Europe would be fantastic; journeying to China, to Japan, to Australia, would be incredible. Shopping without a wary eye on price tags was everyone's favorite dream. But a lifetime based on leisure? No, that wasn't for her.

She could, of course, use some of the money to expand her business. A second boutique had been her goal for the past year now; her inheritance made not only a second shop possible, but a third and a fourth, as well.

Oddly, Theo's conscience shied away from that idea. Realizing it, she sighed. Maude's money should be used for something besides multiplying itself. Theo had never thought of herself as a philanthropist—she'd never been able to afford that generous attitude—but behind the lure of expensive trips and shopping excursions in her mind's eye was a seedling of something much larger, something important. What it could be escaped her, but perhaps in time...?

Lost in thought, Theo jumped when someone knocked on the front door. Laying the hairbrush on the table, she got up and went to the foyer. "Who is it?"

"Colt Murdoch."

Theo's eyes widened. She was wearing nightclothes and no makeup. Her hair was flattened from the thorough brushing she'd just given it. Quickly, a little nervously, she began fluffing it with her fingers. "Uh, I'm not prepared for company, Colt," she called through the door.

"Oh. Sorry. I should have called, but it's still early and I thought it would be okay to stop by. I'll go somewhere and find a phone."

How silly. He was standing at her door, and he was right, the hour wasn't late.

Theo unlocked and opened the door. "Come in."

Before he did so, Colt took a moment to absorb Theodora Hunter in a robe and no makeup. Without high heels she seemed smaller. Without cosmetics she seemed younger.

He had admired Theo before; this Theo hit him hard and precisely where it counted for a man. His instantaneous response was unusually strong, and startling.

Theo might have appeared quite calm, but Colt's worn jeans and shirt were outrageously becoming to his lean torso, wide shoulders and long legs. She liked his cowboy boots, which looked aged and comfortable, contoured to his feet.

But it was his eyes, deep and dark in the dimly diffused light behind her, and his shock of black hair that reached the female core of her. He was big, towering over her, seeming taller than she remembered and much too handsome for any woman's comfort.

Clearing his throat, Colt passed by her and entered the house. Theo's heart skipped a beat as she inhaled his scent, which shook her. This guy was dynamite, and if there was anything she didn't need right now with all that was going on, it was a man who positively exuded sexuality.

Her expression became cooler, which Colt didn't miss. "I really should have called," he said.

Determining to be polite but distant, Theo closed the door. "It's all right. Come into the living room." Walking in, Theo switched off the TV.

They sat down. "I got the message that you called my office."

Theo made sure her robe was securely closed. It wasn't a suggestive robe, but neither was it completely utilitarian, being made of a shiny blue-green fabric that certainly clung more than a garment of terry or chenille would have.

"I thought you should know I was here," she replied.

"I appreciate it. When did you arrive?"

"Only today."

Colt leaned forward. "Then you haven't seen the eight hundred acres."

"No, nor anything else."

"Will you let me show it to you? I'd like you to see it through my eyes. It's a fantastic piece of land, Theo."

She was beginning to believe it. Jordan had said virtually the same thing about the property. Still, it seemed unusual for a prospective buyer to tout the positive aspects of something he wished to purchase, possibly driving up the price with his own praise.

Theo lifted her chin slightly. "Did you and Maude discuss price?"

"Only a little. I expect you'll have your own ideas on price, Theo. I won't try to kid you. It's valuable land."

A smile toyed with Theo's lips. "You're an unusual man."

Colt grinned. "Glad you think so."

Her smile flickered slightly. There was suddenly something personal in the air, and it made her want to flirt with this sexy guy. He *was* unusual. Different from anyone else she knew. His difference went beyond good looks, perhaps clear to the heart of him. A whole barrage of questions hit Theo, most of them centered on Colt's private life. She felt, sitting there in the quiet with him, simultaneously shivery and too warm.

Colt felt it, too, a throbbing electricity that he knew, if nourished, would evolve into a meltdown of ethics and standards.

He got up, deliberately breaking the spell. "I have some free time tomorrow and could show you that land."

Theo rose. "I'm sorry, but Jordan already asked me to go with him on a tour tomorrow. He wants me to see all of Maude's land."

"Oh. Well . . ." Frowning, Colt looked away. After a moment he brought his gaze back to Theo. "I'd still like to show it to you myself. Will you go with me the day after tomorrow?"

"To see the same land again?" The idea startled Theo.

"I want you to see it as I do. Jordy understands land about as well as I comprehend the law."

Colt's persistence was disturbing. Yet she didn't want to be unfair. At the same time, she didn't want to get involved in Jordan's and Colt's animosity, and there could be some of that going on right now.

"Colt...I just don't know," she murmured uneasily. "There's an enormous amount to do here, and—"

"It would take only about half a day. We could do it in the morning. You'd be back here by early afternoon."

An adamant refusal seemed so pointless. For one thing, what was she going to do with raw land in Montana? Selling it would probably be her ultimate goal, and Colt was a built-in buyer. Her business experience was thus far limited to retail sales, but anyone with a lick of sense knew that one didn't heedlessly discourage a prospective buyer's interest.

"All right," she conceded, just as she had with Jordan earlier today. She was in their territory, after all. Obviously each man had his own ax to grind. Jordan's concern focused on settling Maude's estate as quickly as possible; Colt's was in furthering his business. Neither could be faulted for pressing her for cooperation.

Colt's broad smile sent a thrill up Theo's spine. His perfect teeth flashed white against his darkly tanned skin. "Thanks, Theo. I appreciate it." He started for the doorway between living room and foyer.

Almost lamely Theo followed. Colt Murdoch unsettled her, and she wasn't accustomed to inner turmoil because of a man.

At the front door Colt turned. "Do you prefer getting started early on Wednesday?"

Theo nodded. "I think so, yes."

"Then I'll pick you up around seven in the morning."

"Seven will be fine. I'll be ready."

He hesitated, his gaze on Theo. Their eyes met. Hers darted away, nervously, Colt saw, and he realized that she, too, was aware of the magnetism between them. He thought of Jordy, who was probably planning an extensive campaign to win Theo's attention. Along with her physical appeal, she possessed a fortune, and if Jordy Hamilton was nothing else, he was a man who rarely overlooked opportunity.

An urge to warn Theo was on the tip of Colt's tongue. He could almost hear himself doing it. *Theo, watch your step around Jordy Hamilton. His nice-guy facade covers a multitude of sins.*

But it seemed a petty sort of thing for a man to do, and how would he explain the instinct behind such a warning?

Colt turned the knob and opened the door. "See you on Wednesday."

"Yes . . . good night."

Something hadn't been said, Theo thought while locking the door behind Colt. He had stumbled over an idea or topic and decided against mentioning it. For some reason she suspected it was personal, maybe a suggestion that they see each other socially.

On the other hand, her ego could be getting in the way of common sense here. Even if Colt had thought her attractive during her first trip to Hattie, he couldn't possibly have seen anything interesting in her appearance this evening.

Sighing, she turned off the lamp and went to bed.

Theo wore jeans, a loose-fitting blue T-shirt and athletic shoes for the tour. Jordan arrived wearing tan slacks, a beautiful cream-colored shirt and brown loafers. He looked great, but Theo immediately realized that he didn't intend to do any hiking. She had envisioned them getting out of the car and tramping over portions of the land he was taking her to see. Apparently not.

"Good morning," Jordan said cheerfully when Theo opened the front door.

"Hi," Theo responded. "I made some sandwiches and lemonade to take with us. They're in the kitchen. Let me get them and—"

"Theo," Jordan interrupted with an indulgent smile. "I've planned our day to include lunch at the Blue Moose

Lodge. You'll like the place. Good food and a marvelous view.''

"Oh. Well . . . sure. In that case I'll put the food in the fridge and be right with you.''

In the kitchen, Theo placed the sack of sandwiches in the refrigerator. The lemonade was in a thermos jug, so she left it on the counter. Wondering if her clothing was a little too casual for the lodge, she hurried back to Jordan.

"Should I change? I mean, am I dressed all right for lunch at the Blue Moose Lodge?''

His expression was admiring. "You look wonderful. Anything goes up there, Theo. It's a nice place, but casual dress is completely acceptable.''

She already liked the lodge better and she had no idea what it was, other than a "nice place.'' But in her estimation today was not the day for dressing up and "doing'' lunch. Maybe Jordan thought *he* was dressed casually, she thought with a bit of inner amusement.

After locking the front door behind them, Theo preceded Jordan down the sidewalk to the gate and eventually his car. They were soon heading out of town. As this was still new country to Theo, she looked at everything they passed with genuine interest.

She felt Jordan's glance and returned it. "So,'' he said, "did you find the house comfortable last night?''

"Oh, yes. It's a pleasant little house.'' She paused. "Jordan, what happened to Maude's clothes and things?''

"I had them boxed up and stored. I thought it was a little too much to expect you to take care of that, along with the necessity of getting acquainted with the estate.''

"Stored where?''

"In my garage.''

"In your garage?'' No, she told herself. She was not going to get upset about this, even if it did strike her as nervy and overbearing. Jordan was doing everything possible to make things easier for her, and she should appreciate his efforts.

"Well . . . thank you," she murmured.

"Anytime you wish to go through those cartons, just let me know."

"Thank you, I will." Maybe she didn't want to "go through" Maude's clothing, anyway, although certainly someone was going to have to decide where it should eventually end up. Just giving it to a charity sight unseen didn't feel right, however. Maude had entrusted her with her things, *all* of her things. Theo felt a strong obligation to do her best with each and every possession her old friend Maude had passed on to her.

Which meant, of course, that she would one day have to look through those cartons. Actually, it was darned presumptuous of Jordan to have removed *anything* from the house.

Theo took a deep breath to drive away that particular resentment. Again she told herself that he was only hoping to ease the many tasks that had been dropped on her, and that she shouldn't be feeling resentful for a kindness.

Jordan had made several turns on country roads. Hattie was only a few miles back when he stopped the car. "On the right are eighty acres of your property, Theo."

She looked at the huge stretch of vacant land on the right side of the road and tried to visualize eighty acres out of it. There were a few trees and about a hundred head of wandering cattle, but the land itself consisted mostly of sagebrush and bunchgrass. Frankly, she couldn't imagine it having much value.

Jordan got the car moving again. "Those beeves belong to a man named Tom McCray. I advised Maude to charge him for the grazing rights to her eighty acres, but she shrugged it off. Said something about what grass there was just going to waste if McCray's cattle didn't eat it. I strongly recommend your contacting McCray and changing the status quo. Unless you sell it, of course. McCray might even be interested in buying it."

Each piece of land that Jordan showed her was accompanied by comments about what *he* thought she should do with it. None of his remarks struck Theo as bad advice, but she wished he weren't quite so free with his opinions. She needed time to think about it all. Didn't he realize that?

The Blue Moose Lodge was a pleasant surprise. Set in the mountains on a rugged rock ledge with a view that stretched so far that the most distant point appeared hazy to her eyes, Theo found herself feeling a personal kinship with this vast, beautiful country. Their table was next to a wall of windows, and she could barely tear her gaze from the view long enough to order lunch.

"This is incredible," she said.

Jordan looked pleased. "I thought you'd like it." Reaching across the table, he laid his hand on hers. "Theo, you belong in this country."

She turned her head to smile at him. "I do?" His hand on hers felt only friendly, so she didn't shy away from his touch. "On what do you base that observation?" she asked, truly wanting to know. After all, she'd been thinking something similar to Jordan's remark only a moment ago, and found it rather amazing that he would sense her feelings, particularly since they were so new to her.

Jordan's eyes narrowed slightly, as though he himself needed to figure out what had been behind his observation.

"It's difficult to put into words," he said slowly. "It's just that you seem to fit in so well. Look at you, lovely in the most casual apparel."

There were others in the dining room dressed as she was. In fact, Jordan's fine clothes were much more noticeable than her jeans and sneakers. To be honest, she realized while looking around the room, Jordan was the most attractive man there. Suddenly proud to be with him, she smiled at the waitress as the woman placed their food in front of them.

Theo had ordered iced tea, and she took a thirsty swallow. "Hmm, good." She picked up her fork to spear a piece of lettuce from her salad. "Jordan, maybe this is none of my business, but have you ever been married?"

"No, I haven't, Theo. Have you?"

She shook her head. They smiled at each other. "What do you think?" she asked. "Are we a pair of old maids, or what?"

Jordan laughed, exposing his very nice teeth. "In my case, I think the 'or what' is more appropriate." His smile faded. "But no one should ever have the nerve to label you an old maid. I'd be willing to bet anything that you have to constantly fight off interested men."

It was Theo's turn to laugh. "Not guilty, Counselor. Actually, I've been so busy with my business since its inception, I've hardly even dated." She shook her head with good humor. "No, I can't say I've had to do any fighting off of the opposite sex."

"I find that really hard to believe. A woman like you? Beautiful, intelligent, savvy? You know, we really don't know each other, but I could still go on and on singing praises in your behalf."

Theo chuckled again. "Very nice words, Jordan." She arched her left eyebrow. "But enough about me. I'm sure there must be an important woman in your life."

The change in his expression startled Theo. From relaxed and friendly, he became stiff and . . . good Lord, was he angry? "I'll bet Murdoch told you that, didn't he?" Jordan all but snarled.

Theo blinked in surprise. "He did nothing of the kind. I was merely making conversation. Why are you angry?"

Jordan pushed back his chair and laid his napkin on the table. Rising, he said, "Would you excuse me for few moments?"

"Yes, of course." Perplexed, Theo watched him cross the room and enter a hall bearing a sign that read Rest Rooms. Why on earth would he think that Colt had told her he had a lady friend? And what difference would it make if Colt, or anyone else, for that matter, had done so? If Jordan had a girlfriend, someone important to him, more power to him. Why the anger over the introduction of a perfectly normal topic?

Theo toyed with various possibilities while she sipped her tea and waited to finish eating until Jordan returned. Maybe Colt was in the habit of spreading untruths about Jordan, and maybe Jordan was fed up with it. Certainly there was something very wrong between the two men.

And yet, it was difficult to picture Colt gossiping about anyone, especially if the gossip was groundless.

Sighing, Theo turned her face to the bank of windows and immediately felt a renewed sense of awe over the scenery. How lovely it was up here, looking down on the valley below. Was that Hattie she could see in the distance?

"Sorry about that," Jordan said, resuming his seat. He smiled, which Theo saw as a little weak, though she couldn't doubt the sincerity in his eyes. He truly regretted losing his temper, and she certainly wasn't a person who held a grudge over something so petty.

"Forget it," she told him, conveying her own sincerity with a big smile. "Tell me what's left that I should see," she added, picking up her fork to finish eating her salad.

"Just a few more pieces of land," he said, picking up his own fork.

She wanted to ask about the eight hundred acres, but no way was she going to initiate a topic that might bring Colt back into the conversation.

"There are three buildings in Hattie you should take a look at, also," Jordan said.

"Fine," she agreed, recalling the buildings from the list of Maude's assets.

After they finished lunch, Jordan paid the check—though Theo had rather adamantly offered to do so—and they left the lodge and returned to the car.

They were only a few miles down the road when Jordan sent her a glance. "Tell me about your life in California."

"Well..." Theo laughed a little. "I was born and grew up. End of story." She laughed again, this time at her silly answer. "Sorry. I was just kidding. What do you want to know, Jordan?"

"Well, let's see. You said you haven't been dating anyone, so how about telling me about your business?"

Theo chuckled within. If she'd told him she *was* dating someone in California, would he have wanted to hear about that?

"My shop is about fifteen hundred square feet in size, and I carry a little of just about everything. Slanted toward women, of course. My inventory consists of a lot of unusual things. Like feather boas and especially filmy lingerie, the sort of items you don't find in every department store you enter. I have a small shoe department, but there again, I lean toward the unusual."

Jordan sent her a smile. "Apparently you don't dress out of your shop."

Theo had to laugh. "Only occasionally. My own personal taste is mostly traditional, but there are many women out there who love looking different."

Jordan's smile faded. "You're different, Theo, you're *very* different, and you don't need unusual clothing to accomplish it. You're the most beautiful woman I've ever known."

A mixture of pleasure and embarrassment colored Theo's cheeks. Jordan had said something like that before, but this time there was raw emotion in his voice.

"Thank you," she said in a near whisper.

"Please don't be embarrassed because I think you're beautiful," Jordan exclaimed. "Theo, you're the kind of woman I've been waiting for all my life."

"Oh, really, Jordan. You shouldn't—"

"Yes, I think I should." He suddenly pulled the car to the side of the road. "To your right is another piece of your land."

Theo kept looking into his eyes. He liked her. He *really* liked her. It was thrilling to be so openly admired, and by such a successful, attractive man.

But he was moving a little too fast. "Jordan, whatever happens between us, *if* anything does, it must mature slowly," she said quietly.

He gave a quirky smile. "In other words, slow down, Hamilton."

She nodded while returning his smile. "Something like that, yes."

He reached out and touched her hair, ever so gently. "It won't be easy to do with you. You knocked me for a loop the first moment I set eyes on you." His hand dropped. "But I'll respect your wishes."

"Thank you." Theo turned her head to look at her land. "It's very nice, isn't it?" This piece had lots of trees and a meandering creek.

"It's very valuable," Jordan answered. "Because of the creek."

"Valuable" was an important word to Jordan, Theo realized. He used it often. Strange that when she looked at the land she saw its beauty, and when Jordan did he saw dollar signs. They might be getting along quite well, but there was a world of difference in some of their attitudes.

Oh, well, she thought. No two people felt the same way about everything, and besides, they were just starting to get acquainted. Obviously Jordan hoped for a personal relationship, while she felt that only time would tell on that score. There was one thing she knew about herself that Jordan would learn, perhaps the hard way: she didn't rush headlong into anything, not decisions and especially not relationships.

It wasn't until late afternoon that Jordan took several turns on gravel roads and finally stopped the car near a grove of trees. "This is your largest piece of land—eight hundred acres," he said, turning off the ignition.

Theo's heart skipped a beat. This was the land that Colt wanted. She knew it, Jordan knew it. It was the most isolated of her inherited real property, lovely land with trees and what appeared to be a small lake some distance from the road. Its background was rolling hills and beyond the hills, to the west, heavily treed mountains.

"May we get out?" Theo said. Without waiting for a reply, she opened her door and stepped out. There was a small ditch that she crossed, and she heard Jordan's door open and close, and his footsteps as he caught up with her.

"Do you know the boundary lines?" she asked, her gaze on the distant horizons. As there were no fences, she saw nothing to indicate where her eight hundred acres began or ended.

Jordan pointed to the left. "Do you see that outcropping of white rock?"

Theo finally spotted it. "Yes, I see it."

"That's approximately your southwest boundary. Now, mentally draw a straight line to that road way over to the right."

Theo did it, and her eyes widened. "My word, it goes that far?"

"Eight hundred acres is a lot of land, Theo."

"Indeed it is. And this road is another boundary line?"

"That's right. Almost everything you can see from this point is yours."

Theo was silent a moment. "It's remarkably beautiful land, isn't it?"

"I think so."

She wanted to bring up Colt's offer of purchase, to discuss it, but Jordan had gotten so angry in the Blue Moose Lodge because of Colt that she hesitated to do so.

She cleared her throat. "Well, what do you suggest I do with this parcel?"

"Sell it." Jordan's voice became low and tense. "But not to Murdoch. Do you know what he'll do with it? He'll cut it up in small chunks and sell it to people who'll bring in those awful little trailers or throw up a shack to call home. The land will be ruined, destroyed, Theo. All of this beauty will be gone."

"Oh," she said in a thin little voice. Was that what Colt did as a developer? Sell to just anyone without building restrictions in the sales agreement, thus permitting them to destroy a beautiful piece of land like this?

"There are other buyers out there besides Murdoch, believe it," Jordan said emphatically. "Come on, let's get going. I want to drive you by your buildings in town before dark."

Theo was mostly silent during the drive back to Hattie. She had a lot to think about.

Chapter Five

It was dark when Jordan pulled the car to a stop at the curb in front of Theo's house.

"Let's have dinner, Theo," he said. "I'll go home and change, and you can get ready while I'm gone. I could be back here in an hour."

She drew a breath. "Jordan, thank you, but I'm really very tired. It's been a long day," she added, smiling to soften the refusal. "Incidentally, thank you so much for today. I know you must be very busy with your legal practice, and your spending the entire day with me was extremely generous."

"It was my pleasure, Theo. You have to know that."

She put her hand on the door handle. "It was my pleasure, as well. Please, don't get out. I can see myself in just fine. Good night, Jordan."

"I'll call tomorrow."

"If you wish."

Then he surprised her. Sliding across the seat, he tipped her chin and pressed his mouth to hers. It was...pleasant. Not exciting, not arousing, but pleasant. His lips were warm, smooth and gentle, and Theo realized that in the back of her mind she had wondered what a kiss from Jordan would be like. The brush of his mustache on her skin was also a pleasant sensation. He smelled good, and, since she felt nothing repellent in either the kiss or in the man administering it, she permitted it to last quite a long time.

When he lifted his head, he smiled at her. She smiled back.

"Good night," she said again, and opened the door. Striding up the front walk, she sighed a little, because she had just been kissed by a man she found attractive and nothing much had happened to her. How disappointing.

Jordan drove away frowning. Scowling, actually. Was Theo an iceberg? She looked sexy as hell, but it must all be on the outside because he sure hadn't felt any passion from her. Sad to admit, he hadn't felt much passion himself. Damn!

Instead of going to his own home, a large, striking house on an acre lot in Hattie's one good subdivision, he headed for a little house on the other side of town. He pulled into the driveway, then drove around the side of the garage to park in the shadows. Getting out, he went to the house's back door and knocked.

It was opened almost immediately. "Jordan!"

He stepped inside and took Marion in his arms. "Baby," he whispered before claiming her lips in a feverish kiss. She was wearing a silky nightgown and robe, and his hands glided over her body in utter possession.

Moaning, she curled into him. Between kisses she whispered raggedly, "You said you weren't coming by anymore."

"I know what I said." Bending, he scooped her off the floor and into his arms. He knew the way to her bedroom as well as he knew the layout of his own home, and he carried her down the hall to the pretty room, laid her on the bed and followed her down.

His hands and mouth were all over her. Tears were streaming from Marion's eyes, tears of happiness. "You've changed your mind about Theo Hunter. Oh, Jordan, I'm so glad."

Jordan raised his head and looked at her. "Do you love me?"

"You know I do. I fell in love with you the day you hired me to be your secretary."

Jordan pushed the robe from her shoulders, then the slender straps of her gown, exposing her breasts. "I fell for you, too, baby," he whispered, taking a nipple into his mouth. He needed to talk to her, to convince her of the wisdom of his plan, but first things first.

Getting to his knees, he shed his shirt. Wriggling out of his pants, he kicked away his loafers, then got rid of his socks and undershorts. Hurriedly then, he peeled away Marion's robe and nightgown.

Kissing her ardently, he thrust into her. Her response was what he'd needed so badly. She writhed beneath him, moaning his name, caressing every part of his body. She wasn't sexy on the outside and cold inside. To the contrary, it was almost the other way around. She was pretty, with soft brown curls around her face and a nice figure. But she didn't look flamboyant and blatantly sensual as Theo did. What a disappointment kissing Theo had been. No fireworks, no excitement, nothing. Still, he had to make his plan work.

Making love to Marion was so good, he made it last as long as he could. Then, finally, the blinding explosion came, and it was gratifying to know she was experiencing the same mindless pleasure.

They collapsed then, lying in a tangle of arms and legs, their skin wet with perspiration and both of them utterly replete.

After a period of utter immobility, Marion released a long, extremely contented sigh. "That was wonderful. It always is, isn't it?"

Jordan rolled to the bed. "Always."

Marion got up and disappeared into the bathroom. Jordan wiped himself with a handful of tissues from the box on the bedstand, and then lay back on the pillow with his eyes narrowed in thought. First of all, he'd gotten so carried away that he hadn't used a condom. That had been stupid and would never be repeated. He had to be especially careful now.

He'd broken off his personal relationship with Marion to be free to pursue Theo, and now he'd discovered that he couldn't put Marion aside that easily. But he was smart enough to handle both women, wasn't he? All he had to do was convince Marion of the soundness of his plan.

A sudden pang of conscience hit Jordan, unexpected and startling. A deep frown furrowed his brow as he thought about what he was doing—or planning to do. Alone in that room he struggled with necessity and basic decency. But his back was against a very frightening wall, and did he have the luxury of choice? Could he face failure in his own town, see it on every face he looked at?

He took a deep breath and shoved guilt and conscience into the far recesses of his mind. With any luck, neither would plague him again.

Marion returned smiling. Lying beside him, she snuggled into his arms. "I've been so miserably unhappy without you. Today was especially horrible, knowing you were with her."

"It wasn't great for me, either."

"What happened, darling? Something must have happened to change your mind."

Jordan was staring at the ceiling. "I haven't changed my mind. I'm still going to marry Theo."

Marion bolted upright. "Then what in hell are you doing here?"

His voice became soft and caressing. "Making love to the woman I love."

Confusion entered Marion's eyes. "I don't understand."

"I know you don't." He drew her back down into his arms. "Let me explain it to you," he said while running his hands over her warm, smooth skin.

"Jordan, you can't have us both," Marion whispered tearily.

"Honey, you know my financial situation as well as I do. I'm broke and in debt. I've got to get my hands on some money, some big money, and Theo Hunter's the route to a carefree future for you and me."

Deeply hurt, Marion moved away from the man she all but worshiped, left the bed, found her robe and put it on.

"I see what you're thinking, Jordan, that you can marry Theo and have me on the side. Do you know what that will make me? Your whore!"

"No, baby, no!" Jordan jumped up and went to her. "I'll only have to stay married for a short time, a year at the most. I'll be handling the estate, Marion. I can legally charge exorbitant fees, and—"

"And illegally siphon off some of her funds, as well? Jordan, I don't like this. I don't like it at all."

"Honey, I have to do it, with or without you. I'd much rather you were on my team. I'd much rather know you were with me, loving me and looking forward to the day when I can get a divorce and marry you."

"Oh, God," Marion groaned. "I can't believe this is happening. You'll be sleeping with her. Am I supposed to overlook that?"

"Believe me, sleeping with Theo won't be any big thrill. I kissed her tonight and there wasn't a drop of emotion in either her system or mine."

Marion winced, then crossed her arms over her midriff. "If that's the case, what makes you think she'll marry you?"

"Because I'm going to *feign* passion. I'm sure I can get her worked up. She's just a little cautious right now. After all, we hardly know each other." His features tautened. "Marion, work with me on this. Baby, we'll be rich. Don't you get it? We'll have the world by the tail, and it won't take that long. I promise you."

Marion still looked only wounded. Sighing inwardly, Jordan returned to the bed and sat on it with his head down. Covering his face with his right hand, he worked up a few tears and a sob.

The mournful sound knifed through Marion's soft heart, and she went to kneel in front of him. "Jordan? Are you crying?"

"I thought breaking off with you was the right thing to do, but I can't do it. I'm facing bankruptcy, but I can't give you up." His shoulders heaved with another sob.

"Oh, my poor darling." Rising to sit beside him, she put her arms around him. After a minute of holding him, she saw that he was becoming aroused. Tenderly her hand slid downward until she was encircling his manhood.

"You're the most exciting woman in the world," he whispered hoarsely. "She's nothing, baby, nothing. Our marriage would have no meaning, except what I'd lead her to believe. Trust me in this, Marion. Please trust me."

A great sorrow was gripping Marion, but this was the only man she had ever loved, the only man she *would* ever love.

"I trust you," she whispered sadly. "Do whatever you think best."

Theo showered and put on her nightclothes, warmed the rest of the delicious casserole Nan Butler had brought over yesterday and sat down to her supper. After eating, she tidied the kitchen and went into the living room to curl up on the recliner chair. Putting her head back, she closed her eyes and thought about the day.

A smile touched her lips. Jordan's kiss had been sweet. He really was an exceptionally nice guy, and even though there had been no sizzling emotions involved in that kiss, it was a pleasant memory. There was a good chance of their relationship evolving into something important, she thought with a contented sigh. She liked what Jordan represented, stability in his career and life, and certainly a kindly, generous nature. The whole day had been . . . well, nice. Except for that one moment during lunch when he had become angry over Colt. But he even handled anger well, having left the table to calm himself. Yes, she liked Jordan Hamilton, quite a lot to be factual.

Now . . . what would tomorrow bring? A small frown appeared between her eyes. Colt unnerved her in a way Jordan did not. Was it because she didn't trust him the way she did Jordan? Whatever the cause, she felt a turmoil in Colt's presence that she certainly didn't feel with Jordan. Looking at the same piece of land two days in a row seemed inane. She should probably call Colt and cancel tomorrow's outing.

Rising, Theo went to the phone in the kitchen. Sitting at the table, she decided to call her mother before Colt. Lisa was really her best friend, the one person she had always been able to talk to without reservation. She knew women who didn't get along with their mothers, and Theo felt sympathy for them.

Besides, she lived with a constant if private worry for Lisa, who was a diabetic needing daily shots of insulin and who also suffered from several less serious ailments. Lisa had a good attitude about her failing health. "I'm like an old car, honey, wearing out part by part."

Theo laughed at her mother's jokes, but she worried about her all the same. In California, she talked to Lisa at least once a day and went to see her often. There was no reason not to continue the frequent telephone calls, certainly none related to cost. She dialed the long-distance number.

Lisa answered on the third ring. "Hello?"

"Hi, Mom. It's me. How're you doing?"

"Theo! Oh, it's good to hear your voice. I'm fine, honey, just fine. How are you?"

"Well . . . busy, I guess. Today Jordan Hamilton took me on a tour of the real property I inherited, so I saw a lot of the country around Hattie. Some of it is really beautiful, Mom. You'd like it, I'm sure. When you're feeling up to it, maybe you could come and see it for yourself."

"You won't be there that long, will you?"

"I really don't know. I've just begun to scratch the surface of all that has to be done. According to Jordan, anyway. One major job is going through the things in Maude's office, which I haven't even started."

"I'm sure you can handle it, Theo."

Theo had to laugh. Lisa's belief that her daughter was the smartest, brightest, most intelligent woman walking around on the face of the earth never wavered.

"I'm going to give it my best shot, Mom. Anyway, are you sure you're all right?"

"Absolutely. You're not to waste your time in Montana worrying about me. You know how my neighbors are, always clucking around and checking on me. If something should go wrong, they would see that I was well cared for. And I have any number of friends that I could call in an emergency."

It was true. Lisa had dozens of good friends, unlike Theo, who had many acquaintances but not too many people she felt were friends. In that respect, she and her mother were quite different. Lisa was one of those people that everyone liked, being so open and friendly herself. Theo's personality was more reserved. Even in high school and college she hadn't made many friends. Then, once she'd started her business, she had worked such long hours, there just hadn't been time for personal pursuits.

Maybe that was one reason she had enjoyed today with Jordan, she thought. There'd been no pressure on her to hurry back to the boutique. Her thoughts went to tomorrow's plans, and that it just might possibly be another pleasurable day. She shouldn't be judging Colt by Jordan's standards or anger, anyway. When had she started doing that?

"Enough about me," Lisa said. "Are you planning to tackle Maude's office tomorrow?"

"No. Colt Murdoch asked me to go out to that eight hundred acres he wants to buy from the estate. I told him I'd go."

"But . . . Theo, I'm confused. Didn't you see that land today along with the rest?"

"Yes, Mom, I did. But Colt said . . ." Theo frowned slightly. Was this going to sound silly? "He said he wanted me to see it through his eyes."

"Oh. Well, I thought land was land. I mean, wouldn't it look the same no matter who was showing it to you?"

"He said that Jordan knows land like he knows the law."

"In other words, there are aspects of the property Mr. Murdoch expects Mr. Hamilton to have missed showing you."

"I think that's it. What's peculiar about Murdoch's attitude, Mom, is that he praised that land very highly to me. Wouldn't you think a prospective buyer would do just the opposite?"

"That's the way it's done in California," Lisa said dryly.

Theo chuckled. "Yeah, it sure is. Well, guess I'll sign off now. You have my number, so call anytime. Call collect, Mom. I can afford it."

They laughed together and said goodbye.

Theo hung up feeling good. Talking to her mother had definitely elevated her spirits, which hadn't really been low before the call. But now she felt pumped up and not at all tired. Maybe she'd start on Maude's office.

Entering the little room, Theo stopped just across the threshold. Where should she begin? The file cabinets? The desk drawers? The stacks of files and papers on the desk? There were also some boxes stacked in a corner. They were probably full of papers, too.

Her heart sank. This wasn't a job to begin at this time of night. No, she would wait until she could approach the job bright eyed and rested, maybe the day after tomorrow.

Returning to the living room, Theo switched on the TV, located a movie on one of the channels and sat down to watch. She woke up two hours later, groggily turned off the set and went to bed.

Theo awakened to the ringing of the doorbell. Who on earth . . . ? she wondered, then glanced at the clock. It read 7:10 a.m., and Colt had told her he'd pick her up at seven.

"Good Lord," she muttered, bounding out of bed. Grabbing a robe, she yanked it on while hurrying to the front door. After unlocking it, she pulled it open. "As you can see, I overslept," she said rather grouchily.

Colt grinned. Apparently Theo Hunter was not a morning person. "No problem. I'll wait in the Bronco."

"Do you know how to make coffee?"

"Sure. Want me to make some while you get dressed?"

Theo stepped back, holding the door open for him. "Come in." Leaving Colt on his own, she returned to the bedroom. Five minutes later, while she was still trying to wake up and figure out what to put on for the day, she wondered if she hadn't lost her mind. Colt probably thought she was a moron, dragging him in to make coffee for her.

And he'd seen her at her positively worst—hair flying, sleep-filled eyes, old bathrobe. Honestly, she should be horsewhipped.

Well, maybe she didn't deserve that much punishment, but why in heaven's name had she forgotten to set the alarm last night? Oh, yes, she'd fallen asleep in the living room and trekked to bed still half-asleep.

Drawing on jeans and a T-shirt, the same kind of clothing she'd worn yesterday, she at least knew she was dressing right today. Colt was wearing jeans, a blue shirt, his cowboy boots and a big hat.

The smell of brewing coffee assailed her senses. Hurrying to the bathroom, she brushed her teeth, washed her face, moisturized it and put on some makeup. Then she brushed her hair and anchored it at the back of her neck with a bone clasp. There, she thought, assessing her appearance in the mirror. It wasn't great, but it would have to do.

The second she walked into the kitchen, Colt handed her a mug of coffee. "Careful," he cautioned, "it's hot."

She took a sip. "It's perfect. Thanks." She took another sip. "I've got to eat something. Did you have breakfast?"

"About two hours ago."

"Oh, an early riser. Well, would you mind if I made some toast? I'll hurry."

"Take your time." Colt pulled out a chair at the table and sat down with his own mug of coffee. Watching Theo move around the kitchen was a pleasure. Damn, she was pretty. And sexy. *Very* sexy. The way her behind filled those jeans was a sight for any man's eyes. And, as he'd noticed before, she had an especially graceful way of moving.

Theo was finally becoming alert, and she felt Colt's eyes on her as solidly as if he were touching her. Dropping the bread into the toaster, she turned to face him.

"Getting your eyes full?"

Colt grinned. "Yeah, guess I am." He let his gaze slide down to her jeans, which Theo didn't miss.

"Is there something wrong with my jeans?"

"Not that I can see."

"Then you must like them." She was speaking sarcastically.

"They're just jeans, as far as I can tell. It's what's in 'em that's so interesting."

Theo's left eyebrow rose. "Oh, really."

"Yes, really." Colt couldn't keep the amused grin off his face.

"It must be nice to be entertained so easily," she said. "A pair of jeans on a woman? You probably walk around with that perpetual grin, because here I've noticed that nearly every woman lives in jeans.''

Colt laughed out loud. ''You're sure not a morning person, are you?''

The toast popped up, and Theo quickly transferred it to a small plate. ''I don't like being visually undressed at any time of day, Mr. Murdoch.''

''Ouch,'' he said with a small chuckle. ''I wasn't undressing you, honey. I was admiring the shape of your, uh, your shape.''

She gave him an openmouthed glare. ''Well, honestly!''

''That's what I am, an honest man.''

''Not according to Jordan Hamilton,'' Theo retorted while getting a jar of jelly from the refrigerator.

''Oh, him. Well, Jordy doesn't like me. He's apt to say anything.''

Theo sat at the table with her plate of toast. ''Would you like some?'' she asked, holding up the plate.

''Thanks, but no. By the way, I've got a sack lunch in the Bronc, just in case we get hungry before we get back.''

''You said we'd be back early.''

''We should be, but sometimes when I'm walking a piece of land, I lose track of time.''

''Well, you've seen this land before—we *both* have—so I'm sure we won't have any trouble with time.'' Theo took a bite of her toast. Colt Murdoch was not Jordan Hamilton, and obviously today wasn't going to resemble yesterday in the slightest. There was a bit of dismay mixed in with the knowledge that yesterday she had liked being with Jordan, and today she was enjoying Colt's brass and sass. A woman couldn't fall for two men at the same time, could she?

No, of course not. What a ridiculous idea.

At least she could mention Jordan's name without Colt coming unglued. Jordan had gotten genuinely angry yesterday over the very same sin, and come to think of it, she hadn't brought Colt's name into the conversation—*he* had. Hmm.

"So, how was your day with good old Jordy?" Colt asked.

"Interesting," she said.

"He showed you all of your land?"

"Yes, including the acreage you want to buy. You know, looking at it two days in a row really doesn't make a whole lot of sense." Finishing her last bite of toast, Theo got up and brought the plate to the sink.

"Did you get out of Jordy's fancy car even once?"

Theo turned and saw the amusement in Colt's eyes. "Yes," she said with a perfectly straight face. "We had lunch at the Blue Moose Lodge."

Colt laughed with genuine relish. "Figured as much. Jordy wouldn't want to get his pretty shoes dirty. Might step in a cow-pie."

Theo couldn't help laughing herself. "You're terrible."

"But I'm cute." Colt got to his feet. "Ready to go?"

"In a minute. I need to get my purse." She was still chuckling under her breath on the way to her bedroom. But then she remembered how nice Jordan had been yesterday, and she felt guilty over laughing at Colt's remarks about him.

As for his conceited *but I'm cute* remark, truer words had never been spoken. Not only was he the best-looking guy she'd ever seen, he made her laugh.

Damn, maybe it *was* possible to fall for two men at once.

Chapter Six

"**Y**ou have to see this," Colt said, leading Theo in yet another direction on the eight hundred acres. They had been tramping around for hours, and Theo was tired.

"Colt, please, what else is there to see? I've looked at creeks, trees, views, grass and even plain old dirt. I don't mean to be uncooperative, but my feet hurt, my legs ache and—"

This was her first complaint. Willingly she'd trudged with him over hill and dale. He grinned and interrupted. "Okay, I get the picture." He put his hands on his hips and let his gaze wander. "But isn't this an incredible piece of land?"

"Yes," she said without equivocation. "It's everything you said, and more. But you know, you're acting like you plan to live here rather than break it up into little chunks to sell to other people."

Colt frowned. "Did I tell you that's what I was going to do with it?"

"Uh, someone said that." Theo frowned, trying to recall who had said what about this piece of land.

"Ah, good old Jordy," Colt said, nodding knowingly. "Well, it's like this, Theo. I'm going to have to sell some of it. How much depends on ... well, you're not interested in my financial situation. But I plan to keep as much of this land as I can manage." He grinned. "If you sell it to me, that is. Will you?"

"You're first in line. I told you that, Colt."

"But you haven't made up your mind about selling anything yet, right?"

"That's about it, yes." Bending over, Theo broke off a long stalk of grass and stuck the stem in her mouth. "Sweet," she said.

"Sweet grass, sweet water, sweet soil," Colt murmured. "See that bank of hills?" He pointed.

Theo found the hills. "What about them?"

"My ranch is on the other side. That's where I grew up."

She looked at him. "I thought you grew up in town."

"No, ma'am. I was born and raised right on that little ranch. Would you like to see it?"

"Hmm ... not today, if you don't mind." Colt had put her through the paces. They must have walked ten miles, back and forth across this eight hundred acres, and she really didn't want to look at one more piece of Montana today.

"Whatever you say. This land connects almost dead center of those hilltops with the Murdoch Ranch. I've always loved this piece, and I've always wanted it. It was my biggest fear that Maude would take the notion to sell it before I gained the credit and financial responsibility to make her an offer on it."

He stopped admiring the land and looked at Theo, who was visibly wilting. "Hey, you really are done in, aren't you? I didn't mean to wear you out." He took her by the arm. "Come on, we'll head back to the Bronc."

The "Bronc," as Colt called his Bronco, was a good half mile away, parked on a rutted little road Jordan had omitted from yesterday's tour.

After only a few steps, Colt stopped. "I've got an idea. Wait here. Sit down and rest. I'll be only a few minutes."

She was too tired to even ask what he intended doing. Actually, she didn't care what he intended doing. Gratefully she sank to the ground, and after a few seconds of watching him striding toward the Bronco, she stretched out full-length with a satisfied sigh. At first she closed her eyes, but then she opened them to look at the big puffy clouds changing shape in the vivid blue sky.

For yesterday's tour with Jordan she could have worn high heels and never been uncomfortable. Today with Colt, she realized that she wasn't in nearly as good a shape as she'd thought. She exercised on a pretty regular basis, but jumping around in her living room in time with an aerobic exercise tape definitely hadn't prepared her for a morning of looking at land with Colt Murdoch. The man was tireless. Why, he hadn't even breathed hard when he'd led her up that steep incline so she could get a bird's-eye look at the entire eight hundred acres.

"Hmm," she murmured, contentedly stretching her legs and arms to their fullest. Easily she could fall asleep on this patch of sweet grass. A nap out here in the warm sun would be unique and quite wonderful.

The sound of a motor getting louder made her sit up. The Bronco was in motion, bouncing across the uneven ground, heading her way. Shaking her head, she smiled. Had she looked so fatigued to Colt that he thought she couldn't have walked another half mile?

Whatever the reason, it was thoughtful of him to bring the vehicle to her instead of her having to walk to it.

He pulled up next to her. "Get in." He reached across the seat and pushed the passenger door open.

Dragging herself to her feet, she climbed in. "Now, this is what I call service," she quipped.

"Service with a smile," he returned, smiling at her to prove it.

Lord, he was handsome. Theo had been aware of his looks all morning, though she had taken refuge in pretending that he was just an ordinary Joe. He wasn't. Colt Murdoch could be in the movies, if he were so inclined.

But when he really smiled at her, as he was doing now, flashing those gorgeous white teeth, with his eyes crinkling at the corners, pretense was a joke.

She realized she was staring when he said sassily, "Getting your eyes full?"

An embarrassed flush reddened her face. She'd said the same thing to him this morning in her kitchen when she caught him staring, only his saying it didn't seem nearly as funny as when she had.

Even in her embarrassment, the truth came tumbling out of her mouth. "You're a good-looking man."

He chuckled and got the Bronco moving. "What I am is a hungry man. How about a picnic before we head back?"

Oh, yes, he'd said something about a sack lunch, Theo recalled. "Sure, sounds good."

"Hang on. This ground is bumpy."

He drove slowly, but the bumps made her bounce around. She buckled her seat belt and hung on. "Where are we going?" Since they weren't pointed at any road she knew of, the question was reasonable.

"To a special place."

"On my land?"

"On your land."

"Don't tell me you missed showing it to me," she drawled.

"I was saving the best for last." The grin he sent her had a devilish quality, making Theo smile.

"And everything else I've seen will pale by comparison," she said teasingly.

"Well, I don't know if I'd go quite that far, but I think you'll like it."

"It just occurred to me that since you're obviously not afraid of damaging your Bronco by driving in open fields, we could have seen almost everything you showed me this morning through its windows."

"Yeah, we could have. But be honest. Didn't you enjoy the hike?" Another devilish grin flashed.

Theo laughed in spite of her aching legs and feet. "I guess so." Up ahead was a thick stand of trees. "Is that where we're going?"

"Yeah, it is. Getting hungry?"

"Starved."

"Good. Watch it. We've got a dip coming up."

Colt had enjoyed the morning with Theo so much he felt that he'd do almost anything to prolong their time together. He liked that she laughed when he said something corny, and that she wasn't above doing a little teasing herself.

Still, he had no passes or any such nonsense in mind. He'd wanted this land for so long that risking the friendship he felt was developing between him and Theo seemed too foolhardy to consider, even if she was one luscious lady and kept him constantly reminded of his own masculinity.

"There," he said, nodding toward the windshield. "You can see it through the trees."

What Theo saw through the trees was water, but she could only see bits and pieces of it. "What is it?"

"A pond . . . spring fed." He sent her a grin. "Great spot for a picnic." He stopped at the edge of the trees and turned off the ignition. "Let's go."

It was the water she'd thought was a lake yesterday, Theo realized. She got out on her side while Colt exited through the driver's door. They met at the back of the Bronco, where Colt opened the two doors, one up and one down, and reached inside.

Spotting a wicker basket, Theo laughed. "A sack lunch, huh? That looks to me like an honest-to-gosh picnic basket."

"So it is." Giving her one of his bone-melting smiles, he lifted the basket by its handles. With his other hand he pulled out a bright red blanket.

He'd thought of everything, even a blanket to sit on. Theo experienced a burst of affection for this man who actually knew how to throw a decent picnic.

"Let me carry the blanket," she offered.

"Sure, thanks." Colt held it out.

He led the way into the trees. Theo followed behind him, admiring the width of his shoulders and the sexy fit of his jeans. He'd all but said right out that he'd been staring at the shape of her butt, and she had to chuckle inwardly because she was doing the same with him.

She suddenly wasn't at all tired. The day was fabulous, with sunshine and cooling breezes, and certainly she'd never been in a prettier spot. Her companion was . . . well, he was a special person, fun to be with and handsome beyond description. How could she think he was anything but a nice guy, despite Jordan's opinion?

"Oh, it's pretty," Theo exclaimed when they had cleared the trees and were standing on the bank of the pond. "Since it's fed by springs, though, it's probably really cold."

"Feel it," Colt told her, setting the basket down in the shade of a huge old cottonwood.

Dropping the blanket, Theo knelt and swished her hand through the crystal-clear water. Her expression became surprised. "It's warm!"

"Thermal energy," Colt said. Picking up the blanket, he spread it on the grass in the cottonwood's shadow.

Theo straightened and looked around. What a beautiful spot for a homesite, she thought. Incredible scenery, trees, grass and a built-in swimming pool. Who could ask for more?

But what would she do with a house here, for pity's sake? she thought next. After only a few days in Montana, was she forgetting that her home, business and family were in California?

"Chow time," Colt announced, pushing the handles of the basket aside to remove its lid.

Theo walked over to the blanket and sat down. "What do you have in there?"

"Sandwiches, fruit and iced tea. Sound okay?"

"Sounds great."

He also had large paper napkins, plastic plates and glasses, and little plastic containers of celery, carrot sticks and dill pickles.

Colt set out the array on the blanket. "Help yourself."

"Thanks." Theo took a sandwich, unwrapped it and bit into it. It was breast of chicken, lettuce, a mild white cheese and what tasted to her like honey mustard. "Very good," she told him.

"Glad you like it."

The sandwiches she'd made yesterday morning and ultimately left home in the refrigerator would probably end up in the garbage, Theo thought. Jordan preferred the Blue Moose Lodge over a picnic lunch. Colt actually planning a picnic was evidence of a vast difference in personalities between the two men.

What a peculiar situation to suddenly find herself in, she thought. Two exceptional men had popped into her life, when she'd gone on for years without *any* interesting male companionship.

Enjoying the sandwich and a piece of celery, Theo glanced back to the hills Colt had pointed out. "So your ranch is on the other side of those hills. Do you raise cattle?"

"About two hundred head."

"And horses?"

"We have about twenty horses right now."

"'We'? Meaning your parents?"

Colt shook his head. "My mother died when I was seven, and my father went when I was eighteen."

Theo noticed that his mouth had taken on a rather grim aspect. Talking about his parents must be painful for him. "Sorry," she said quietly. "I shouldn't be prying."

"Hamilton didn't talk about my, uh, family?"

There was that antagonism again, though Colt sounded curious, not angry. And maybe a little defensive, Theo realized after a second. Also, he had hesitated, as if he'd been going to use a word other than *family* and then changed his mind.

"No," she said, putting a finality in her voice that ended the topic. "In that case, should I assume you made this excellent lunch yourself?"

Colt's good humor returned with a twitch of his lips. "Ruth put it together for me."

Ruth? Theo felt a strange crunch in her midsection. Who was Ruth? Well, of course he would have women friends. A man who looked like him? He probably had *droves* of female friends.

"I see," she murmured, looking off into the distance.

It was obvious what Theo was thinking, that Ruth was a personal friend. Well, she was, of course, but not in the way Theo was visualizing her.

Colt said nothing to alter Theo's impression. It was stimulating and a little exciting to think she might be unnerved by the idea of an important woman in his life. She must be feeling that same tug of attraction he'd been noticing with her. Colt's thoughts went further. If she would once commit to selling him this land and their business dealings were out of the way, a friends-only attitude would no longer be necessary. *Prudent* was a better word, he decided. It really wasn't necessary that he put business first, it just seemed sensible.

"You know," he said, after a swallow of tea, "Maude talked about you quite often. As I said before, I wish I had listened more closely. Until the day of the funeral, I was under the impression that you were her granddaughter."

"Jordan believed the same thing," Theo replied, putting aside her peculiar jealousy over Ruth making this lunch. "Colt, do you remember Maude actually saying that?"

He thought for a moment. "No." His eyes narrowed slightly. "Surprises me that Jordy didn't know the truth from the get-go, though. With him being Maude's attorney, you'd think he would have been privy to most phases of her life."

"Which makes me wonder if she didn't deliberately mislead people on the true nature of our relationship. She left a letter with Jordan, to be opened after her death, explaining who I really am, in case of any legal problems over my inheriting her estate."

Colt's narrowed gaze swung to her. "And who are you, Theo?"

"A friend. A pen pal."

"A pen pal! You're kidding."

Theo related the same story she'd told Jordan about how she and Maude had become acquainted. "We corresponded for over twenty years. She wrote lovely letters. I kept every one of them."

"I bet she kept yours, too."

"Do you really think so?" Maybe they were somewhere in Maude's little office. Wouldn't it be fun to find them and read what she had written as a child?

Colt chuckled. "If what I've seen of Maude's house is any measure, she never threw anything out." He blinked then. "Hey, it just occurred to me. You must have gone through the house like a white tornado. It isn't cluttered now."

"No, it isn't. But I didn't do it." Theo looked off into the distance again. Jordan's benevolence in this case was still a sore point. "Jordan had someone clean the place while I was in California."

Colt was studying her. "Do I detect a touch of resentment over that?"

Theo suddenly felt the strongest urge to take sides in Colt and Jordan's feud—Colt's side. She actually had to clamp her lips shut to stop herself from not only admitting resentment over Jordan overstepping what she considered a lawyer's duties with a client, but to keep herself from asking

Colt if Jordan was as honest and trustworthy as he appeared.

The moment startled her. Deliberately getting in the middle of their animosity would be a terrible mistake. It was just that she liked Colt so much.

But damn it, she also liked Jordan! What was wrong with her?

"No resentment," she answered a trifle coolly. "Jordan's been nothing but kind."

I'll bet he has, Colt thought wryly, wondering if he'd mentioned his relationship with Marion Roth to Theo and knowing damned well that he hadn't. Jordan might be a pain in the haunches, but he wasn't stupid. Colt had expected Jordan to be kind to Theo. More than that, really. Maybe he hadn't advanced to the courtship stage yet, but Colt felt positive that he would. What Jordy was going to do with Marion was a mystery. Come to think of it, he hadn't seen Jordan and Marion out together since...since Maude's funeral!

Ah, he thought, the plot thickens. Marion Roth was a real nice gal, but a woman in love was apt to do anything for her man. Still, would Marion go so far as to stay in the background while Jordan wooed Theo for her inheritance? That scenario really didn't compute, not with Marion the third leg of such a manipulative triangle. Colt frowned. If he jumped into the melee brewing, did that make the situation a rectangle? His frown turned into a chuckle he couldn't hold back.

Theo sent him a look. "Is something funny?"

"It might be," Colt said with an amused twinkle in his eyes. "It just might be."

After the picnic basket had been emptied of everything but used plastic implements, Colt got to his feet.

"How about a swim?"

Looking up at him, Theo laughed. "Yeah, right. Did you bring a suit? I sure didn't."

"We could swim in our underwear."

A flash of heat bolted through Theo. "Uh, I don't think so."

Shrugging, Colt sank back down to the blanket. But there was a teasing expression on his face. "Someday we'll take a swim together in that little pond."

"Not in our underwear, we won't."

"How about in nothing?" Even though he knew he shouldn't have said that, he liked the pretty pink hue that appeared in Theo's cheeks. "Sorry," he said, lying back with his hands locked behind his head. "I shouldn't be teasing you like that." He closed his eyes.

Teasing, huh? Theo eyed him suspiciously. If she had agreed to swimming in her underwear, he probably would have done his level best to get her to swim in nothing. His apology was as phony as a three-dollar bill.

Regardless, the image of them naked and in the pond was disturbingly exciting. Theo had had only one sexually memorable affair in her entire life. It was just after college and had lasted for three months. They had talked about marriage, children and growing old together, and then, out of the blue for her, he had changed his mind. Said they were too young, and that he wasn't ready for commitment. Oddly, she'd gotten over him very quickly, which later on had made her question the validity of her feelings for him. Out of bed, that is. In bed they'd been great.

Looking at Colt Murdoch stretched out on the blanket brought back the memory of good sex much too clearly, and with the memory, some startling inner pressures.

She got up abruptly. "Colt, if we're through out here, I really need to get back to town. I have a million things to do, and I can't stay in Montana indefinitely."

He opened his eyes. "A million?"

She shook her head in mild disgust. "Let's not nitpick, okay? I have a *lot* of things to see to, and I can't do them out here." He must have things to do, too, she thought. How could he waste time like this when he had both a ranch and a business to run?

"All right," he said agreeably, rising slowly to his feet. "We'll head back."

Theo stepped off the blanket so he could pick it up. He gave it a shake, then folded it into a neat square. He carried the basket and she the blanket for the walk through the trees to the Bronco. When everything was put away, Colt opened the passenger door for her to get in.

"Thank you," she said, then stopped when he took her arm. Her gaze went from his hand to his face. "What?"

"Just this." Dipping his head, he pressed his lips to hers.

That was Theo's first surprise. Her second was the almost volcanic eruption of emotion in the pit of her stomach. Like Jordan's, Colt's lips were warm and smooth. Unlike Jordan's, Colt's took and tasted and demanded a response from her.

He didn't have to demand anything; her pulse had gone completely wild. If she wanted a sexual affair in Montana, this was the guy for it. Easily she could melt into his arms, although she was vaguely aware that she wasn't *in* his arms. Other than his hand on her arm, their only connection was the kiss. Then he lifted his head and broke that bond.

Dizzy, dazed and breathing erratically, she opened her eyes to see him staring at her. He, too, looked dazed, she realized.

"I . . . I shouldn't have done that," he mumbled thickly. Damn, where had that impulse come from? "Can you forget it?"

She swallowed and lied. "Of course."

"It won't happen again, Theo. I swear it."

Confusion and disappointment hit her. He *had* to be involved with someone to be so upset by a kiss.

"Fine," she said in a wispy little voice. Turning, she sat on the seat and swung her legs around. Colt closed the door.

She realized that she was trembling. Trembling over a kiss. Dear God, Colt was the most potent guy she'd ever kissed, bar none.

She registered the grim line of his lips as he climbed in behind the wheel and started the engine. Buckling her seat belt for the rocky ride to the road, Theo put on what she hoped was an unaffected expression.

When they were on the road, he sent her a glance. "I don't know why I did that. I didn't plan it. Please believe me."

"Yes, of course," she said, and judged her own voice as stiff and unnatural. "You said to forget it and I agreed. It's forgotten. We don't need to talk about it." She would never forget it, never!

"Good. Thanks." She'd kissed him back, Colt was thinking. Kissed him in a way that women did when they wanted more. His jaw clenched. Maybe a personal relationship wouldn't damage their business transaction. Or was he still feeling that kiss so strongly that he was grasping at straws?

Theo didn't want to talk at all. "You wouldn't mind if I caught a little nap on the ride back, would you?"

"No, of course not."

Laying her head back against the seat, Theo shut her eyes.

But she didn't sleep one wink during the drive to Hattie. All she could think of was that kiss and the racking desire it had caused in her body.

Theo was home for about an hour when the phone rang. As frustrating as it was, she hadn't been able to settle her emotions down enough to accomplish anything, and she'd been sitting at Maude's desk shuffling papers without grasping their content.

She picked up the phone. "Hello?"

"Theo, I've been calling all day and getting very worried. Thank goodness, you're all right."

"Hello, Jordan." It was an effort to adjust her thinking from Colt to Jordan. It was as though she had to erase Colt from her mind and insert Jordan, a peculiar sensation. "You shouldn't worry just because I don't answer the phone."

"Yes, but I drove by the house and your car was there. I've been going in a circle ever since."

She sighed quietly, knowing that Jordan wasn't going to like her explanation. But she wasn't going to lie to either him or Colt.

"I was with Colt Murdoch, looking at that piece of land he wants to buy from the estate."

"Damn it, I showed it to you yesterday!"

This time his temper angered Theo. "Yes, and if I decide to look at it again tomorrow, I'll do it," she snapped. "Jordan—" She was all set to let him know how ridiculous his attitude was, when he cut in.

"Wait, Theo, please. I'm sorry. I have no right to fly off the handle with you over that jerk Murdoch. Please forgive me."

Theo was silent a moment. Was this getting out of hand, or what?

"Jordan, how you and Colt feel toward each other has nothing to do with me. I'll tell you right now that I like you both."

"Murdoch and I are so different from each other, that almost seems impossible."

"Well, it isn't impossible, although I do agree that you are very different men."

"Theo, as your legal adviser, I strongly urge you to have nothing to do with Murdoch, either in business or..." Jordan cleared his throat. "I'm sure you're much too smart a woman to get involved with him personally." His heart was beating a mile a minute and he was sweating. He didn't like Colt and there were a few missteps in Colt's past that might alter Theo's good opinion of the man. But it was also possible that she was the sort of person who rooted for the underdog, and besides, he'd heard rumors about Colt's prowess with the ladies.

"Jordan, you are my legal adviser. I like and respect you, but no one, *no one,* tells me who I can or cannot see. In *any* capacity. Do you understand?"

Jordan's heart sank clear to his toes. At the same time a murderous rage built in his system. To think that Colt Murdoch was his rival for Theo's affection was almost too much to bear.

"Of course I understand," he said, nearly choking but striving to sound normal with every cell in his body. "I didn't mean to step on your toes, Theo. Please accept my apology."

Theo took a calming breath. "Apology accepted. Now, was there a reason you've been calling me all day?"

"I have some papers that need your signature. Also, I was hoping you'd have dinner with me tonight."

Theo felt suddenly weak. Even if she hadn't said anything to him that wasn't her right to say, she'd been hard on him.

"All right, Jordan. I can be ready around seven, if that suits your schedule. You could bring the papers with you."

He drew a relieved breath. "Thank you, Theo. I'll see you at seven."

Putting down the phone, he got up from his desk and paced his office, cursing under his breath. He had to get to Theo before Colt did.

That was the one thing he hadn't factored into his plan, another man, especially Colt Murdoch, being interested in Theo.

Damn Murdoch! Damn him to hell!

Chapter Seven

"May I bring you the dessert menu?" the waitress asked.

"Yes, please do," Jordan replied.

Dinner had been so pleasant, with the food delicious and Jordan utterly charming, that Theo was feeling wonderfully mellow and relaxed.

"Jordan, I have an idea. Instead of ordering dessert here, let's go back to my house and finish the apple pie Nan Butler brought over my first night in town." Theo was smiling.

Jordan's heart skipped a beat. Things had gone incredibly well this evening. As he'd hoped, Theo had signed the stack of papers he'd provided with only a cursory examination of their content. Not that there was anything amiss in tonight's supply of legal documents. The papers were necessary but mundane notifications for the court of the probate process. But Theo barely glancing at them before signing was extremely encouraging. It had been a test, really. If she had insisted on reading every word, he would have had to proceed with his plans very cautiously. As it was, he felt that things would move along quite smoothly.

He smiled warmly. "Homemade apple pie? I like your idea. Very much." He laid his napkin on the table.

The waitress appeared with the dessert menus. "We've decided against dessert, Joanne. Please bring the check."

In short order they were in Jordan's car, on their way to Theo's house. She still thought of it as Maude's house, and wondered if that ever would change for her. There were moments, right now, for instance, when she felt caught up in some sort of fantasy. Nothing that had occurred in Montana thus far had given her a sense of reality. Maybe it would come in time, she reasoned, but she felt as though she were a million miles from California. It wasn't an unpleasant sensation, just different.

Take tonight, for example. Jordan had arrived at the house in his beautiful car, impeccably dressed, and had proven to be a remarkably entertaining dinner companion. He had regaled her with stories of growing up in Hattie and of his college and law school days, and not once had he referred in any way to Colt or the fact that she had spent most of the day with him. Nor had he conveyed any irritation over her speaking her mind on the phone. All in all, it had been a lovely evening, and bringing Jordan home for dessert and coffee seemed perfectly natural.

When they arrived at the house and went in, Theo stopped in the living room. "Please sit down, Jordan. I'll put on a pot of coffee and be right back."

"Thank you." Smiling nicely, he sank down onto the sofa and watched Theo sail from the room. The skirt of her emerald green dress danced around her thighs as she moved, creating a sensual picture. Sighing, Jordan sat back with one arm strung along the top of the sofa. If there were no Marion, he might fall in love with Theo. That would be the perfect scenario, of course, if he and Theo could actually fall in love with each other. Too bad it wasn't feasible.

Thank God Marion had finally grasped the sensibility of his intentions. Oh, it still bothered her, make no mistake. Right now she was probably morose and miserable because he was spending the evening with Theo. Spending the night if he could manage to get her in the mood, to be factual. He'd wondered during dinner about the most propitious way to get himself invited in when he brought Theo home, and then she'd gone and solved the problem without even a subtle hint from him.

Yes, things were working out. To hell with Colt Murdoch. Was he in Theo's living room tonight? No way. It was Jordan Hamilton that Theo was drawn to, not that yahoo Murdoch.

Theo returned and sat in a chair facing the sofa. "The coffee will be ready in about five minutes. Nan's pie is exceptionally good. I'm sure you'll enjoy it."

"I'm sure I will." Jordan kept his gaze on Theo. "Did I tell you how beautiful you look tonight? That dress is perfect for your coloring. You have the most incredible hair, Theo, and your eyes..." Jordan frowned, as though unhappy with himself. "Guess I'm giving myself away, aren't I? I've told myself a hundred times not to rush you. It's just that... well, what can I say? Something very special happened to me the moment I laid eyes on you, and it's very difficult to laugh and talk and act as though I think of you as just a friend."

Theo hadn't moved a muscle throughout Jordan's little speech. Certainly she hadn't expected it, and she wasn't sure how she felt about him being so candid.

"Jordan, we're just beginning to know each other," she said gently.

"You're right, but why do I feel that I've known you forever? Theo, do you believe that everyone has a soul mate?"

"I'd like to believe it. It's a lovely concept, but given the divorce statistics..."

Jordan leaned forward. "That's because most people don't marry their soul mates. I believe that only a fortunate few even recognize their soul mates. Theo—"

She held up her hand, stopping him. "Jordan, please don't tell me that you feel I'm your soul mate. I'm not saying it's impossible, but I am saying it's too soon to know."

"That's where you're wrong, Theo. It happens instantaneously. I knew the minute I met you."

She shook her head. "If that were the case, I would have known, too." She paused. "Wouldn't I?"

He spoke softly. "I think you did, but there was so much going on that day it got lost in the shuffle. Tell me you didn't like me right away."

She gave a short laugh. "I can't do that. I did like you right away." She still liked him, but this conversation was making her nervous. "I think the coffee's done." Quickly she got to her feet and hurried to the kitchen.

The coffeepot was still gurgling. Frowning and uneasy, she took the pie from the refrigerator and got plates, cups, forks and napkins from the cupboards. Jordan was getting very serious very fast, while she . . . ?

Colt's handsome face was suddenly in her mind. Groaning, she laid her forehead against a cupboard door. A woman couldn't be soul mates with two men, for God's sake. And if for some unimaginable reason she had to make a choice right now—Jordan or Colt—who would she choose?

My Lord, this was becoming ridiculous. They had each kissed her, signifying interest, granted, but she couldn't say that she really knew either man.

Noticing that the coffeepot was finally silent, she prepared a tray and carried it to the living room. Jordon got to his feet. "Here, let me take that. It looks heavy."

Rather than debate the weight of the tray, she let him have it. "Just put it on that table," she said, pointing out the little oval table at the end of the sofa.

They each helped themselves to a cup of coffee and a plate of pie, took a fork and napkin and resumed their seats.

"This room could do with some rearranging," Jordan said, while balancing his coffee and pie and finally setting his cup on the floor next to his feet. "It's not much of a place, is it?"

"Apparently Maude liked it."

"She could have lived in a mansion," Jordan said with obvious distaste. "I can't figure out why a woman with her assets lived so frugally."

"She never spoke to you about it?"

Jordan gave his head a shake. "No, she didn't. I never asked, of course, though I was aware of her net worth. She was . . . well, a rather strange person."

Theo bristled slightly. "She was a wonderful person!"

Jordan saw his mistake. "Yes, of course she was. Don't misunderstand, please. But you have her money now. Do you intend living as she did for the rest of your life?"

"Certainly not, but then this isn't my home. I'll be returning to California as soon as possible." Theo took a sip of her coffee. "I really won't have to be here for the entire probate process, will I?"

Jordan's stomach muscles clenched, but he spoke calmly. "At this point I can't give you an intelligent answer to that question. Maybe in a few weeks I'll be better prepared to recite an approximate departure date."

With a heavy, sorrowful expression he got up and brought his plate and cup to the tray. Turning, he looked at Theo. "But you have to know that I don't want you to leave. Not ever, Theo." He lifted his hand and held the back of it against his forehead in a forlorn gesture. "If I could only say what's in my heart. Theo—"

"No, Jordan." Rising, she brought her own cup and plate to the tray, brushing against Jordan to reach it.

Instantly he put his arms around her. "Theo..." His eyes were brimming with emotion. "Please let me speak freely."

She tried to disengage his arms. "The evening has been so pleasant, Jordan. Please don't spoil it."

"A kiss would spoil it? Theo, don't you realize that I've fallen in love with you? I want you so desperately."

"Oh, my God," she whispered, wresting herself out of his embrace and quickly putting space between them. "Jordan, listen to me. I like you very much. You're intelligent, kind, successful and nice looking. To be honest, you're the type of man that draws a woman's attention. But you're moving too fast. What you're calling love could only be some sort of...of infatuation."

"Infatuation?" he said sadly. "Oh, Theo, you're so mistaken. Please give me a chance."

"Have I said I wouldn't? Jordan, I enjoy your company. All I'm asking is that you go slower. You couldn't possibly know that you're in love with me when we've spent so little time together."

Cold, he was thinking. She was as cold as he'd thought the night he'd kissed her. She looked like sex and sin on two beautiful legs, and she was as frigid inside as an iceberg. Getting her warmed up wasn't going to be easy. Who ever heard of a kiss "spoiling" a pleasant evening? *Bitch,* he thought angrily. Rich as Croesus and a bitch. Maybe he *couldn't* go through with this.

In the next heartbeat he'd decided that he could do anything, even warm up an iceberg, to get his hands on so much money.

There was pathos in his smile. "Maybe we'd better call it a night."

An enormous relief hit Theo. "Yes, I think we should."

She walked him to the door. "Good night, Jordan. It was a very nice evening. Thank you."

His gaze roamed her face. "You're so beautiful, you take my breath." Leaning forward, he kissed her cheek. "Sometime, very soon, we're going to make love," he whispered. "I live for it. Good night."

Stunned, Theo watched him saunter down the sidewalk toward his car. With her heart hammering she closed the door and leaned against it. She didn't like what Jordan had just said, not one little bit. Maybe, given his attitude now, she didn't like *him* as much as she had, either. What was wrong with the man? Was he really so sure of himself that he felt she was going to sleep with him just because *he* wanted her to?

It didn't work that way. Not with her, it didn't.

Colt spent the morning in his office at the Murdoch Land and Cattle Company. His development company was a small operation in a small building on the outskirts of Hattie, and he had only one employee, Terry Driscoll. Terry answered the phone, typed up sales—when he sold a piece of ground—and handled the books for both the land sales company and the ranch. Around forty-five years of age, Terry was experienced in all phases of clerical work, and in Colt's estimation, a find. She was quick, efficient and good-natured. Whenever he brought potential buyers into the office, Terry instantly put them at ease with her friendly, outgoing personality.

Around one-thirty, Colt told Terry he was going to the ranch and left the building. All morning, while trying to concentrate on paperwork, his thoughts had repeatedly been interrupted by images of Theo Hunter. He'd told himself it was because of her eight hundred acres he wanted so badly, but deep down he knew differently. It was Theo getting under his skin, not her land. That kiss, which he shouldn't have taken, had sizzled. Recalling it made the fine hairs stand up on the back of his neck.

He got into the Bronco with a brooding expression. What he'd like to do was to see Theo. He felt a pulling from her, though they were miles apart, a tugging that was answered by his own system, as though they were each sending silent messages through the air to the other.

Shaking his head at such an inane thought, he got the Bronco moving and almost immediately had to brake for a stop sign at the highway. Turning left would head him for the ranch; a right turn would bring him into Hattie. He'd dropped in on Theo once before without calling; he shouldn't do it again.

But maybe she was out in the yard. If he drove by her house and she was outside, it would be rude not to stop and say hello.

"Hell, Murdoch, you're losing it," he muttered. She'd see through that ploy quick as a wink.

But maybe she wouldn't care. Maybe she'd be glad to see him. The sizzle in that kiss hadn't all come from him, had it? No, it sure as hell hadn't. Theo had kissed him back. In fact, he'd been the one to back off, not her.

Colt turned right onto the highway. He'd drive by Theo's house. Maybe he'd stop and maybe he wouldn't. But that crap about not mixing business with pleasure didn't fit anymore. Theo had told him he was first in line on that property, hadn't she? Well, that sure sounded like commitment to him. She would sell the land, he was sure of it. What else would she do with it? And he'd be there to buy it.

Fine. That was settled.

What wasn't settled was how he felt about Theo, and how she might be feeling about him. Something sure had happened during that kiss yesterday, something he couldn't and didn't even want to ignore. Oh, sure, he'd thought of it as a mistake, but that was yesterday. After a night of waking up countless times to remember it, he'd changed his mind on that score. It hadn't been a mistake at all, not when Theo's lips had responded to his as though she couldn't get enough of them.

Granted, she'd been awfully quiet afterward, but so had he. Obviously neither of them had expected such fireworks from a simple kiss.

That was the problem, Colt thought grimly. It hadn't been a simple kiss. Probably no kiss between him and Theo could ever be labeled "simple." It was like that between some people. Chemistry and lots of it. Hadn't he felt it the day Hamilton had introduced them in the chapel's parking lot? Damned right he had, and if he was lucky, so had Theo.

Of course, he, like a horse's patoot, had been so hot after that eight hundred acres, he'd thought cozying up to Theo would muddy the waters. That error in judgment had given good old Jordy the time to *make* time with Theo.

But if she was smitten with Jordy, would she have kissed *him* the way she had?

Scowling, Colt drove into Theo's neighborhood.

Theo had opened the two windows in Maude's little office, hoping to catch any cross-breeze that happened by. The day was hot. Accustomed to air-conditioning and a cool, even temperature inside any building on even the hottest days, Theo was noticing the heat. She had started the day in slacks and a knit top as the morning had been cool, but by eleven the house had become stifling and she had changed to shorts and a cotton flowered blouse that tied just below her breasts, leaving her midriff bare.

She had decided that the place to start in the office was the stacks of papers and file folders on top of the desk. It made sense to her that those items were on the desk because they had been Maude's most current projects.

It was slow going. Theo would read a letter, such as:

Dear Mrs. Evans,
The term of your Certificate of Deposit No. B55532T in the sum of $10,000 expires on May 23. Please inform us if you wish to renew at the existing interest rate, which is 5.25%.

Theo would then search for some indication of Maude's decision, a copy of a reply and the file folder of the institution that held the CD, for example. Finally she got out the list of assets Jordan had given her during their initial discussion on her inheritance and looked for the CD. If it was on the list, she would continue searching for a file folder for that institution until she found it.

Maude's filing system left something to be desired, she discovered very early in the day. Apparently it had made sense to Maude, but it was pure Greek to Theo. Slowly, very slowly, she was making a very small dent in the many items on top of the desk. The problem was that Theo didn't know what was or wasn't important. Some letters obviously were, but there were many that touched on topics completely foreign to Thco's knowledge of the estate. Those she placed in a stack of her own.

By noon she knew without a doubt that this task was going to take a great deal of time. She felt that once she'd gone through everything, the file cabinets, the desk drawers, the cupboard and the boxes, she would know what to do with her growing stack of "unknowns." But there was no way to hurry the process. She had to read every piece of paper to grasp its content, some of which were merely hand-scrawled notes that Maude had apparently written to remind herself of something. Occasionally Theo would immediately locate a folder in one of the file cabinets related to a letter or note, which would momentarily elevate her spirit. But until every scrap of loose paper was connected to some file and/or previous correspondence, she felt that she really couldn't begin to do what was ultimately necessary: go through all of the files in the cabinets and tie them to the items on her list of assets.

Around noon she stopped for a sandwich and a glass of lemonade, but immediately after returned to the office and her overwhelming chore of reading, puzzling and deciding.

Through the open windows sounds drifted in: three young boys riding by on bicycles, a lawn mower somewhere in the neighborhood, a car passing by. Theo would sometimes glance up from her reading to look out the window just above the desk. She was forcing herself to do this job, and it gave her precious little pleasure, especially when it was so hot inside and so nice outside.

She was staring out the window when a white four-wheel drive, moving at a snail's pace, came into view. Colt! she immediately thought with a crazy sort of joy rocketing through her system. He would know she was home. Her red loaner car was parked in the driveway, impossible to miss.

Jumping up, she ran through the house to open the door, only to see the Bronco disappear down the street.

"Hmm," she murmured. She must have been mistaken about it being Colt's vehicle.

Standing in the open doorway, she bit down on her bottom lip, realizing that she wasn't eager to go back to work. Then she spotted Nan Butler puttering in one of her flower beds, and she dashed to the kitchen and then back to the door.

Going outside, she called, "Nan? I have your dishes." Theo approached the fence. "I've been meaning to return them."

Nan took off her garden gloves and laid them on the ground. Smiling, she got to her feet and walked to the fence. "I told you there was no hurry."

Theo passed the dishes across the fence. "The casserole and pie were wonderful. Thank you so much."

"You're quite welcome, young woman. Glad you enjoyed them. I've always liked cooking and baking, but I don't have much opportunity anymore. My children are scattered from one coast to the other. Oh, they come to see me every so often and then I have a merry old time cooking their favorite dishes, but most of the time it's just me."

Nan's bright eyes checked out Theo. "You're looking mighty pretty today."

Theo laughed. She had anchored her hair back from her face with a piece of yarn, and her old shorts and midriff blouse were very plain fare.

But maybe plain was what Nan thought of as pretty.

"Thank you," she said. "Hot today, isn't it?"

"Oh, my yes. But I do so enjoy the sunshine. Our winters are so long and unpleasant. For people my age, anyway. Maude and I used to talk about selling out and moving to Arizona or Florida." Nan looked nostalgic for a moment, then sighed. "It was just talk. Neither of us ever really wanted to leave Montana."

"Because it's home," Theo said quietly.

Nan smiled. "Yes, because it's home. Theo, it's all over town that Maude left what she had to you. Will you be living here now?"

"Only until probate is completed, Nan."

"I hope you don't think I've been spying on you, but I just can't help noticing your comings and goings. My kitchen window faces this way, and even without doing a lot of cooking, it's always been my favorite room." A teasing little smile appeared on her face. "Two such handsome beaux. You're quite the fortunate young woman, I must say."

Theo laughed. "You're referring to Jordan Hamilton and Colt Murdoch. They're not beaux, Nan. Jordan is settling Maude's estate and Colt wants to buy a piece of her land."

"She had land? Where, honey?"

"This particular piece is about twenty miles south of town. You didn't know?"

Nan was looking perplexed. "How odd that she never mentioned it. I thought we told each other everything."

Theo caught on immediately: Maude hadn't spoken of her wealth to her friend. Nan thought the only thing Maude had left her was her house. In fact, given Nan's remark about it being all over town that Maude had left her "what she had," it was quite likely that most of Hattie's residents believed that Maude had had very little.

Indeed, Maude had been an unusual person. A true eccentric, Theo decided, thinking of her many peculiarities.

Nan's gaze suddenly darted to the street. "Looks like you have company, Theo."

Theo turned around to see Colt's vehicle stopping at the curb. Again she felt that ricocheting elation.

"It's Colt Murdoch," she murmured a trifle breathlessly, then looked at Nan. "Do you know him?"

"I know of him. Jordan Hamilton, too."

It occurred to Theo that this tiny woman could tell her all there was to know about each man, and she doubted that Nan would be at all averse to doing so. That *could* be a very interesting conversation.

"Nan, may I drop by later? Maybe this evening?" Theo asked.

Nan nodded with a perceptive smile. "Come anytime, honey." She glanced at Colt getting out of his rig. "If you can't make it tonight, do it another time. We'll have a cup of tea and a nice long chat."

"Thanks, I'll come over at the first opportunity. Talk to you later."

Leaving the fence, Theo walked out to greet Colt.

Chapter Eight

Colt nearly choked when he saw what Theo was wearing. Not that her shorts were too short or her top too skimpy, but Lord above, the way she filled out common old clothes was positively sinful.

"Hi," he said while walking through her gate.

"Hello."

Her smile caused a spasm in his chest; she was glad to see him.

"I was in the neighborhood and thought I'd stop for a minute."

"I'm glad you did." Her smile turned rather wry. "I've been working in Maude's office all morning, and any interruption is more than welcome."

His spasm went away. She would have been just as glad to see the trash collector.

"Come in," she invited. "I'll get us something cold to drink."

"Thanks," he muttered.

His dark tone of voice garnered a curious look from Theo. "Anything wrong?"

"Everything's just perfect," he said with drawling sarcasm.

Something *was* wrong, she thought with a frown as they entered the house. Maybe it had to do with their arrangement on the eight hundred acres. That was something she couldn't change, however, and if he was impatient he'd just have to get over it.

In the living room, she gestured cordially. "Sit down. What would you like? I have lemonade already made, or I could fix some iced tea if you'd prefer."

Colt remained standing. "Got anything stronger?" He never drank hard liquor during the day, and only rarely did it after dark. What in hell was going on with him?

"No," she said with a surprised expression.

Colt cocked an eyebrow. "Are you sure? Maude used to take a little nip of brandy now and then."

"Oh, really?" Theo had her doubts about that, but why would Colt say such a thing if it weren't true? "Just how well did you know Maude?" she asked.

"Better than you, apparently."

This was the first time she'd seen Colt in his present mood. So, she thought, he wasn't *always* sweetness and light. Jordan had hinted at Colt having a dark side, and maybe this was it.

Theo squared her shoulders. "If Maude kept brandy in the house, it was probably taken away along with the food. I told you Jordan had someone clean the house after my first trip to Hattie. Well, the food was given to a needy family." At least that was what she thought had happened to it.

"Good of him," Colt said dryly. "Look in that cabinet over there." He nodded at a small cabinet in the corner of the living room. "That's where she kept it."

"Oh." Theo walked to the cabinet and knelt to open its two doors. It was crammed full of books and, oh God, not more papers! She groaned silently, wondering if she'd live long enough to go through all of Maude's papers. Shoving them aside, she blinked in surprise. There were two un-opened bottles of blackberry brandy on the shelf.

Colt could see that she had located Maude's stash. "Forget it," he said gruffly. "I don't even like brandy. I didn't come here for a drink."

Slowly Theo got to her feet. "Tell me what's wrong."

Now he had her worried. Damn! A muscle in his jaw clenched and unclenched. She was so beautiful it hurt to look at her, and yet he couldn't stop looking.

"Nothing's wrong, except for..."

They stood there staring at each other. Theo's heart started beating faster. "Colt..." His name came out as a husky whisper.

"You know why I'm here, don't you?"

"Uh, no. No, I don't. Should I?"

His eyes narrowed as he took a step toward her. "Am I confusing you, Theo?" he asked softly. When she didn't answer he took another step. "I haven't stopped thinking of that kiss since it happened."

So *that* was it. Her nerves began jumping around. She'd thought of that kiss, too, much too often for comfort. But did she want a repeat performance? There'd been so much passion between them, too much when they barely knew each other. Yet that was what she saw in his eyes, another kiss. Maybe more. Definitely she wasn't ready for more, and with Colt she just didn't know if she could speak so boldly about going slowly, as she'd done with Jordan. Nor did she know for certain that Colt would listen and back off, as Jordan had done.

She'd been thinking of the two men as so different from each other, and they were, of course, but now she realized that the biggest difference was in herself. She reacted differently to each of them. Control was sane, sensible and easily attained with Jordan. With Colt she felt awkward, slightly tongue-tied and certainly not in control.

But she had to say something. After clearing her throat, she found her voice. "Yes, you're confusing me," she said in what she hoped was a normal tone.

"That's because you're feeling what I am."

She ducked around him just as he took the final step that would have put him right in her face. From the other end of the room, she spoke firmly.

"Don't presume to tell me what I'm feeling, Colt. Not about anything. Look, if you came here to chase me around the house, I'm going to have to ask you to leave. If there's something else, then sit down and let's talk about it." Aha! Maybe she *could* keep Mr. Murdoch at a nice safe distance. Feeling rather proud of herself, Theo folded her arms across her midriff, only to feel her own bare skin. Oh no, she thought, visibly wincing. Why was she half-naked at a time like this?

Okay, enough was enough. She wasn't a child and no man was going to talk her into something she didn't want. She dropped her arms. "I'm going to have a glass of lemonade with lots of ice cubes. Would you care to join me? It appears to me that you could use a little cooling off."

Shaking his head at her brass, Colt couldn't help chuckling. "Yeah, I'll join you. Thanks."

He plopped down on the sofa to wait.

In the kitchen, Theo sank onto a chair and sucked in a big breath. When she released it, she blew it upward, rearranging tendrils of damp hair on her forehead. God, it was hot! At least a hundred degrees hotter than before Colt had arrived. Wild-eyed, she looked around the kitchen, as though there were an answer somewhere in this little old-fashioned room to . . . to . . .

What in hell is the question?

Confused? Theo Hunter, you'd better believe it!

Okay, get yourself moving. You can't sit here all day and pretend Colt isn't in the next room.

After another deep breath, Theo got up and went to the refrigerator. Taking out ice cubes and the pitcher of lemonade, she filled the tallest glasses she could find in Maude's cupboards with ice and added lemonade. Carrying the two glasses, she returned to the living room and gave one to Colt, managing to do so without looking into his eyes. Then she retreated to the chair farthest from his spot on the sofa.

Instead of taking a drink, he held the cold glass to his forehead. "Hot out today," was his explanation.

Sipping her own drink, Theo saw his manhandling of that glass as utterly sexy. "Very," was her reply, said rather primly. She crossed her legs, making sure her shorts didn't hike up in the process.

Colt's gaze slid down from her face to her legs. Even from that distance Theo felt the heat of his look. She took another swallow from her glass.

"Um . . . is there some sort of problem you needed to see me about? Something about the land?" she inquired, realizing at the same time that she was in a state of denial. He'd told her why he was here, hadn't he?

Why did he have to be so blasted handsome? His clothes—a blue shirt with the sleeves rolled up, jeans and boots—were commonplace and practically a uniform in Montana. His head was bare, probably because it was too hot for a hat. But going hatless left his marvelous shock of hair in full view. And his eyes. How could anyone have eyes that blue?

Colt rolled the glass against his forehead for another moment, then lowered it for a drink that nearly emptied it of everything but the cubes of ice.

"I do have a problem, yes," he said. "Maybe you can help me figure it out."

She made a small throat-clearing sound, hoping her nervous discomfort didn't show. "I suppose I could try."

Colt smiled. "Thank you. Well, it's like this. When we met I thought you were the most terrific-looking woman I'd ever seen. But since I anticipated doing business with you, I decided to keep my distance. Yesterday things changed." He paused briefly. "Theo, you're the one."

She stared blankly. "The one what?"

"You're the woman I want in my life." He set his glass on the floor and leaned forward. "I've heard it happens this way. A man sees a woman, maybe clear across a room, or walking down the street, or as happened with us, at a funeral, and he knows that she's the one."

Good Lord, Theo thought frantically. First Jordan, now Colt. They had each put it differently, but the gist of their verbal idiocy was the same. What was this, some kind of moronic contest to see which one of them could get into her panties first?

The breath she took conveyed exasperation. "That's a ridiculous theory," she said, also with exasperation.

"Is it?"

The bedroom quality of his voice raised goose bumps on her skin. "Yes, it most certainly is," she said with a sharp edge on her own voice, denying the effect he had on her.

"You're not ready to hear how I feel, are you?"

"Well, you must admit that you're declaring something pretty darned important a little early in our relationship. In any relationship, for Pete's sake. What's with the men in Montana? Do you all go around finding soul mates at the drop of a hat?"

"Finding what?"

Her lips pursed. "Never mind."

"Who's been talking to you about soul mates? Don't bother to answer, I already know. Jordy isn't wasting any time, is he?"

"Are you anyone to talk?" She saw him getting up from the sofa. "Don't, Colt," she warned. "Stay where you are."

He walked over to her, bent down and put his hands on the arms of her chair. His face was no more than an inch from hers.

"Tell me you didn't like that kiss yesterday," he said huskily.

"A kiss is not a lifelong commitment. At least it's not in California."

"Yeah, but then there are all kinds of kisses. Ours was special." He inched his mouth closer to hers. "If I kiss you again, are you going to renege on our business deal?"

"Don't kiss me again," she whispered, darting glances into his eyes, which, she noticed, contained not only a serious light but a very suspect twinkle. Was this just fun and games to him, or should she believe what he'd said about her being the "one"?

"Give one good reason why not."

"Because...because..." She couldn't think of a reason, good, bad or indifferent. Except she knew they shouldn't be fooling around like this. How she knew that wasn't clear in her mind, but the knowledge felt real and something to which she should pay attention. "Colt, please don't..."

The rest of her plea was trapped in her throat. His lips were on hers, moving seductively with just enough pressure to push her head back against the chair. She felt the glass being removed from her hand, so Colt must have dislodged his hand from the arm of the chair, she thought within the stormy sensations suddenly bombarding every inch of her anatomy.

This was why they shouldn't be fooling around, she thought with a touch of panic. Kissing Colt was like taking a nibble of forbidden fruit and suddenly wanting it all. One could overdose on his brand of kisses.

The low moan in her own throat startled her, but her arms went up around his neck all the same.

Colt sank to his knees and wedged his hips in between her knees. This was much better, he thought, gulping a breath of air and then kissing her again. Or maybe she had kissed him again. It was hard to tell who had started kissing whom when they were both so heavily involved. Her fingers caressing the back of his neck were driving him crazy, but then so was the taste of her mouth.

He put his hands on the waistband of her shorts, then found a much more thrilling attraction just above: her bare midriff. His breathing became more erratic as his fingers drifted over her smooth, warm skin. His desire for this woman was starting to run wild, but he didn't seem able to put on the brakes.

"Theo, baby," he whispered raggedly, his lips against hers, a second before he thrust his tongue into her mouth. Her responsive groan and the way she tried to snuggle closer to his body were like touching a match to bone-dry tinder; an explosion of inner heat had him sweating.

He kissed a path from her lips to the opening of her summery top and then buried his face in the very center of her bosom. Each of his cheeks could feel a breast, soft, full and lush, and he knew that if he should happen to die this very minute, he'd go to the great beyond a happy man.

Theo was holding his head. Her eyes were closed. Her breathing was rough and uneven. Her heart was pounding so hard she could hear it. Inside her head was an attempt to rationalize her own wild behavior. Was there anything wrong with making love with Colt? Was it sinful or criminal? They were both free agents, weren't they?

But hadn't he mentioned a woman named Ruth? Yes, Ruth had prepared their lunch yesterday.

Before Theo could completely analyze that event, Colt raised his head to mate their mouths again and her mind went spinning away to never-never land. Only dimly was she aware of him unbuttoning her top. As it contained its own built-in bra, she wasn't wearing anything under it.

Colt's hands on her bare breasts made her gasp. His mouth and tongue on her nipples made her moan. Her body was in flames and she wanted him naked, too. Almost greedily she tore open the buttons of his shirt. Her hands roamed his chest, lingering on his tiny, hard nipples and in the patch of hair between them, then moved lower. His belly was rock hard. She went lower still, down to his belt buckle.

"Do it," he whispered thickly when she hesitated. "Don't stop."

But she had stopped. Breathing hard enough to wake the dead, she threw her head back, eluding his persuasive mouth, which was again seeking hers. "Colt . . . wait."

"No, baby, no," he groaned.

"We . . . can't do this," she panted.

"Yes, we can." He nuzzled her breasts again, taking a nipple into his mouth and sucking gently.

Oh, no! She was sinking again, and something urgent inside of herself was telling her they were going much too far. She pushed on his shoulders. "Colt . . . stop."

His spine went limp from frustration, and he all but collapsed on her. "Why? Tell me why?"

"It's just not . . . right."

"That's funny, it's the most right thing that's ever happened to me." It took all the strength he had, but he managed to lift his head and look directly into her eyes. "Theo, you're not just any woman. I told you what you mean to me."

Yes, he had. But so had Jordan. More misery than any decent person deserved descended upon Theo. Had she unknowingly encouraged both Jordan and Colt to think she was easy prey? And, God help her, what if they were both sincere in their declarations of deep and meaningful feelings for her?

No, she couldn't do this. She had to sort out her own feelings for these two men before she permitted theirs to influence her.

She spoke hoarsely. "I'm sorry if I somehow gave you the idea that I would welcome a pass of this nature, but please believe that I never meant to do it."

Colt gaped at her. "You never meant to kiss me back? Or to unbutton my shirt and make me crazy with your hands all over me? It all happened accidentally? Without your knowledge or consent?"

"Now you sound angry." She pushed on his shoulders again, and this time he moved away from her. Quickly she buttoned her top.

Colt was sitting on the floor, staring up at her. "I'm not angry," he finally said. "Just confused."

"That's two of us," she mumbled. Actually, Jordan was probably as confused as her and Colt, so that made three people in Hattie who didn't know which way was up. This was getting out of hand. Who ever heard of two men falling in love with the same woman at the same time? Especially when she was positive that she'd done nothing to encourage such serious feelings. Other than being friendly, that is. And they were both pretty weird if they considered ordinary friendliness a bid for the most serious relationship a man and woman could have.

She should tell them both to go to hell, she thought with sudden asperity.

But just looking at Colt made her mouth dry and her palms wet. She didn't *want* to tell him to go to hell; she liked him.

And, Lord help her, she also liked Jordan.

Sighing, she got up, dodged Colt's long legs spread all over the carpet and went to sit on the sofa. He got up, too, uncoiling his six-foot-plus height until he was the tallest thing in the room. Looking steadily at her, he buttoned his shirt and tucked it more smoothly into his jeans.

"Do you want an apology?" he asked, his mouth set in a grim, thin line.

"Do you feel that an apology is in order?"

"No."

"Then, by all means, don't compromise your principles." She looked away from him.

"What about your principles? Did I compromise them?" When she didn't answer, he asked, "Theo, what's the real problem here? Do you dislike honesty in a man?"

Her head snapped around. "Of course I don't dislike honesty. I can't abide *dishonesty,* for your information."

"Then be honest with me. Didn't you kiss me back? Weren't you thinking of making love a few minutes ago?"

Flames flickered in the pit of her stomach again. She cleared her throat. "All right, yes. I . . . I was thinking . . . probably the same thing you were. But it's too soon, Colt. You and Jordan are both pushing me too hard."

Colt rocked back on his heels. His eyes narrowed dangerously. "Be careful with Jordan, Theo."

She smirked. "Funny you should say that. He said the same about you."

"Did he tell you about Marion?"

Her forehead creased in puzzlement. "Marion? Do you mean Marion Roth, his secretary?"

Colt wished he hadn't mentioned Marion. But Jordan "pushing" Theo made him see red. Apparently he was actually courting Theo, talking about soul mates and, damn it, pushing her when he had no right. And no sincerity, either, not when he and Marion were so close.

Or they had been. Colt frowned. Maybe Jordy and Marion had broken up. He'd better say no more on that subject until he found out the score. But then, by God, if he learned that Jordan and Marion were still a hot item, he was going to tell Theo. She didn't deserve the big come-on from a man who was already tied to another woman. And if he was still tight with Marion, he was only wooing Theo for her inheritance.

A light bulb went on in Colt's head. Jordan Hamilton was the reason Theo was so damned confused about *him!* Two men declaring themselves? Hell, yes, that would confuse any woman.

He closed his expression. "I really don't know anything about Jordan's love life, and I shouldn't have mentioned Marion. She's a nice woman, that's really all I know about her."

Like hell it was all he knew. Theo's body tensed. There was a Ruth in Colt's life and Marion was in Jordan's. So why were they both so hot on *her* trail?

And then it came to her: Maude's estate. Her heart sank clear to her toes. She had almost made love with Colt. She'd come so close it was frightening. And Jordan's little kindnesses were completely phony. Both of these men wanted her money a hell of a lot more than they wanted her!

She stood and spoke bluntly, coldly. "I have work to do. Please call before dropping in again. I expect to be very busy for the next few weeks. I don't have time for unannounced visitors."

"Are you going to tell Jordan the same thing?"

"What I tell Jordan is none of your business."

Colt saw what was happening, and he was suddenly sick to his stomach. "Theo, you don't understand."

"I understand plenty, a whole lot more than you think I do. Please leave." She walked to the door and realized that she had left it open. Anyone could have come to the house and seen what was going on inside. And stupid her, she'd been so lost in Colt's arms, she wouldn't even have known it.

He followed her to the door, then took one last stab at clearing up her misconceptions. "Theo, I meant every word I said to you. Will you give me that?"

Her expression was completely emotionless. "You and I have a business agreement. If I sell that eight hundred acres, you have first right of refusal. That's the extent of our relationship. Please try to remember that from now on."

"Theo..." He sounded helpless, which was only a true reflection of how he felt. He'd screwed things up royally, and he wasn't even sure how it had happened.

"Goodbye, Colt."

He had no recourse; she was giving him none. "Bye," he mumbled, and stepped across the threshold to her front stoop.

The door closed before he took two steps.

"Nan? This is Theo Hunter, from next door." Theo had located Nan Butler's number in the Hattie phone book. "I mentioned my dropping in later, but something's come up and I really can't come today."

"Oh, think nothing of it, honey. Like I told you, come whenever you can. You're welcome anytime."

"Thank you, Nan. Bye."

Theo put the phone down, picked up a pencil from the desk and threw it violently across the room so that it bounced off of the office wall and fell to the floor. Her jaw was clenched in the most abiding fury of her life. How could she have been such a fool? Jordan and Colt were nothing but . . . but gigolos!

Her anger failed her then, and she put her head down on her arms and wept. Her own ego was astounding, believing that two such attractive men had fallen in love with her in such a short period of time. Where had her normal good sense been hiding? Why hadn't she figured the fortune she had inherited might have had something to do with their interest?

Raising her head, she blew her nose and wiped her eyes. Was this to be her life from now on, with every man she met overlooking her in favor of her wealth? How would she ever know if he wanted her or her money?

She had to get out of Montana and away from Colt and Jordan. They had taught her a harsh lesson, one she wouldn't easily forget. At any rate, she couldn't leave without finishing the job she'd started that morning: sorting through Maude's papers and file folders.

Fine. She would do nothing else until that was accomplished. Then she would go home, back to California where she belonged. At least there, no one would know about her inheritance unless she told them, which was the last thing she would ever do. She would ask her mother to keep mum, as well. If the next attractive man she met liked her, it was going to be for herself, not because she had an impressive net worth.

Theo stayed up until midnight, sorting and filing the papers on the desk. Bleary-eyed but thrilled that she had cleared the top of the desk, she went to bed and fell asleep instantly.

Chapter Nine

"Good morning, Theo. And how are you on this beautiful day?"

Jordan's cheery voice on the telephone made Theo's spine go stiff. "I'm fine," she said tonelessly. She was seated at the desk again, having started working in Maude's office immediately after breakfast. The sooner she got this job done, the sooner she could go home. Her course seemed clear this morning. Once probate was completed, the real property she had inherited, other than the eight hundred acres she had promised to sell Colt, would be put in the hands of a Realtor. Everything else, the cash, stocks, bonds, etc, would be transferred to her bank in California. She was going to wash her hands of Hattie, Montana, Colt Murdoch and Jordan Hamilton, but those very hands were tied until she saw through to the end of what she'd come to sincerely believe was her responsibility. For some reason Maude had left her a great deal of money; along with a sense of duty, her respect for Maude's memory precluded leaving prematurely just because she'd been duped by two of Hattie's residents.

Jordan, in his own office, frowned at the coolness he heard in Theo's voice. Immediately he smelled trouble. Not the small, trivial kind of trouble he could eliminate with a few well-chosen words, but big-time trouble. His voice even quavered a bit as he inquired, "Is everything all right, Theo?"

"Why would you think it isn't?" Each syllable had its own icicle.

Deadly suspicions cramped Jordan's stomach. "Uh, no reason. Listen, there are some more documents needing your signature. I could bring them over right now, if that's convenient for you." The documents were genuine and definitely required her signature. But seeing her was suddenly far more important.

Thinking about how she wanted to handle this—having to meet with Jordan was undoubtedly going to happen again and again—she hesitated a moment before speaking. "Tell you what, Jordan. I'll come to your office. What time would be convenient for you?"

"But..." He stopped. He didn't like Theo's attitude this morning. She wasn't her usual friendly self, and in fact sounded a little belligerent. It worried him to near nausea, but he couldn't begin to guess what the problem was until he saw her face-to-face.

Getting hold of himself, he managed to speak as though nothing were amiss. "Come anytime, Theo. My morning is relatively free." His entire day was free, as far too many were, and he had intended delivering the papers to Theo and then inviting her to lunch. With any luck at all, they would have spent the day together. His mouth thinned irately as he tapped the eraser end of a pencil on the desk top.

"Then I'll see you in about an hour," Theo said.

"Wonderful. See you then."

They both hung up, Jordan with a sour expression, Theo with an angry one. But she was going to keep her anger under control, she had decided even before Jordan's call. She felt used and deceived, but neither Jordan nor Colt was going to hear it from her lips. However, her friendliness had come to an abrupt end, which they would both soon discover. From now on it was strictly business with each man, and it wouldn't even be that if she weren't trapped in this unnerving situation.

Leaving the office, Theo went to her bedroom to change clothes. As another hot day was obviously in the making, she had donned shorts and a sleeveless T-shirt after her shower. Shedding those garments, she slipped into a rust-and-cream sundress and sandals without stockings. After putting on makeup and fixing her hair, she took her purse, locked the house and went outside to the car Jordan had loaned her.

Sitting behind the wheel, she wondered again whose car it was. For some reason it suddenly seemed crucial to find out. Leaning to the right, she opened the glove compartment and looked for the registration. She found it in a little plastic case, which also contained a proof-of-insurance card.

The name on both documents leaped out at her: Marion Roth.

Theo was stunned. Jordan had actually loaned her his girlfriend's car! What unmitigated gall! And just how did Marion view his generosity with her vehicle? She had to know about it, which ostensibly made her an accomplice to Jordan's deceit. What was this, some sort of conspiracy where everyone knew what was going on except her? *My God, did they think her a complete fool?*

Tears were suddenly very close, stinging Theo's eyes and nose. She was *not* a fool, and she had put her trust in these people. In Jordan, especially. He knew the extent of Maude's estate, down to the penny, while Colt could only guess at it. Unless Maude herself had confided in him, which Theo doubted, considering that she hadn't even discussed her financial affairs with her good friend, Nan Butler. Maybe Colt had declared his feelings so brazenly thinking she might sell him that land for a pittance if they were personally involved.

Lord help her, she had come so very close to making love with Colt yesterday. A chill went up Theo's spine. What kind of men were these? Jordan had said right out that they would be making love very soon, after coming up with that hogwash about the two of them being soul mates, and Colt had done his level best to get her in bed after spouting lies about her being the one.

Disgusted and more upset than she'd ever been in her life, Theo inserted Marion Roth's key into the ignition and started the engine. With her jaw set at an angry angle, Theo drove to Jordan's office building. His car, she noticed, was the only one in the parking lot. She pulled up next to the BMW and turned off the motor.

Realizing that she was much angrier than she'd been before discovering who owned the car that Jordan had insisted on loaning her, she sat there for a few minutes to calm herself. She would not go into that office and prove she was a fool by making a scene, but there were a few things that had to be said.

Her uneasy gaze took in Jordan's striking building, then his costly car. She thought of the expensive clothes he wore, and a frown furrowed her forehead. Jordan's affluence was everywhere she looked, and she would bet anything that his home wasn't a common little house, like Maude's for instance. Why would he shame himself, and her, by wooing her for her inheritance? He had to have a lucrative law practice to afford such costly accoutrements. Something didn't add up.

Then there was Colt, who owned not only a business but a ranch. If he had the wherewithal to purchase those eight hundred acres, he certainly wasn't living at the poverty level.

But the smell of money brought out the worst in some people. Apparently neither man gave a damn that she might get hurt from their phony pursuits. Their lies were abominable. *Oh, Theo, you're the most beautiful woman I've ever known.* Hadn't they each said virtually the same thing? And she'd been flattered. Flattered! Maybe she *was* a fool.

With a disgusted grimace Theo pulled the keys from the ignition, opened the door of the car and got out. Carrying her purse in one hand and the keys in the other, she walked to the large and imposing front door of Jordan's building and dragged it open.

Entering, Theo immediately saw Marion, who appeared to be concentrating intently on the computer screen on her desk. Also on her desk was a scattering of file folders, loose papers, pens, pencils and several red-bound books, one of which lay open. She looked like a very busy secretary, Theo thought, which was what she probably was. Along with being Jordan's girlfriend, of course. But it seemed a little peculiar to Theo that when she'd come here the first time, Marion's desk had been almost completely bare. Yes, she remembered that very well. The computer had not been turned on and Marion's desk had been bare except for a small pad of message forms and a pen.

Marion looked up. "Hello, Miss Hunter. Mr. Hamilton said to expect you." She stood. "I'll show you to his office."

Theo noticed that Marion's eyes never met hers, not even close. "That's not necessary. I know the way to his office. Marion, I have something for you." Theo moved closer to the desk. "Hold out your hand, please."

Warily Marion lifted her hand. Theo dropped the car keys into it. "Thank you for the use of your car, but I really don't need it. Incidentally, while it was parked in my driveway, not being used until today, how were you getting around town?"

Marion's face looked blotched from the combination of paleness and pink spots that covered it. "I...managed," she said weakly.

The shy young woman didn't know where to put herself, Theo realized. Marion was utterly and completely embarrassed, bearing an I-wish-I-could-sink-into-the-floor demeanor.

It was proof enough for Theo. Colt had alerted her to the truth: Jordan and Marion were indeed an item.

Colt's "item" was probably a woman named Ruth. A pain of enormous dimensions suddenly squeezed Theo's heart. Not a physical pain, an emotional one. It was at that shuddering moment she realized that Colt had wormed his way into her system. It was not a good time for such a disastrous revelation, and she could barely contain the urge to run, to dash from this building and seek sanctuary in Maude's little house.

But, of course, she had to see Jordan and sign some papers. Squaring her shoulders, she gave Marion a feeble smile. "I'll go to Jordan's office now."

Marion had been standing as though frozen in place. She suddenly came to life. "Miss Hunter, please. Jor...Mr. Hamilton is going to be very upset about your returning my car. He...he wanted you to have it."

"Oh, really? Well, you know something, Marion. I really don't care if Jor...Mr. Hamilton gets upset about it. If I need a car, I'll rent one, and if there isn't a car rental agency in Hattie, I'll walk."

"There's one," Marion said timidly. "Sort of. Bob Turlow has a used car dealership, and he sometimes rents his cars. He's in the phone book under the name of Turlow's Used Cars."

"Thank you for the information." Theo started away.

"Please...at least permit me to announce your arrival," Marion said in an unsteady voice.

"If you don't mind, I'd rather just surprise Jordan," Theo replied coolly. See him in his natural habitat. Catch him unawares, she was thinking. Although that idea was probably silly when he was undoubtedly hearing every word spoken between herself and his secretary-paramour!

Marion sighed soulfully. "All right."

Theo left Marion standing behind her cluttered desk and walked down the hall leading to Jordan's office. This time she noticed details. The carpet, for one. She had shopped for and purchased carpet several different times, and what she was walking on was a high-grade wool carpet, which she knew ran at least fifty dollars a square yard. What she had bought in each instance had cost under twenty dollars a square yard.

Then there were the closed doors she passed to reach Jordan's office, four of them. What was behind them? Empty offices? Conference rooms? Why did Jordan have such a large building? Maybe other lawyers worked here and she just hadn't met them or heard about their association, Theo thought, trying to come up with a feasible explanation.

Jordan's door was wide open. As busy as Marion had looked when Theo arrived, Jordan looked ten times more involved. His suit jacket was draped over the back of a chair. His shirtsleeves were rolled up, his collar unbuttoned and his tie loosened. His desk was twice the size of Marion's, and it was completely covered in file folders, some open, some merely stacked one on another, and loose papers, dozens and dozens of loose papers. There were also several red-bound books on the desk, and a glance at the bookshelves on the wall opposite to the door told Theo what they were: law books. Apparently both Marion and Jordan used them.

Jordan's head was down, a pencil in his hand, and he was writing on a legal-size yellow pad. Theo rapped on the doorframe. "Jordan?"

He looked up and blinked, as though bringing himself out of an extremely serious thought process. Then he jumped to his feet. "Theo! Why didn't Marion announce you?"

"You didn't hear the two of us talking?" It was possible that he hadn't heard, but highly unlikely, given the silence within the building. Even the muted music she had noticed during her first visit was absent today.

Jordan cleared his throat. "No, I didn't." He glanced at the mass of paperwork on his desk and smiled boyishly. "When I'm really working on something, the only thing that sinks in is the ringing of the telephone. One-track mind, I guess.

"Please," he said, walking around the desk to get his jacket. "Come in and sit down." Quickly he rolled down his shirtsleeves, put on the jacket, buttoned his collar and straightened his tie.

Theo walked to the same chair she'd used during her first visit to this office and sat. Jordan returned to his chair behind the desk. His smile was as broad as his face. "Well, you're looking very pretty today."

His flattery raised Theo's ire, and it was all she could do not to let him have it.

"You said there were papers to sign?" she said coldly.

"Uh, yes." My God, he thought frantically, what had happened to change her attitude so drastically. "Let me clear some of these things away, and we'll get right to them." Hurriedly he began stacking files and papers.

"How many clients do you have, Jordan?" Theo asked.

"Pardon?" Her question took him by such surprise he couldn't prevent the heated flush creeping into his neck and face. Clearing his throat, he regrouped his defenses. "Actually, I've never made a head count. Why do you ask?"

Theo lifted one shoulder in a shrug. "Just curious."

Someone's been feeding her information, Jordan thought with rising panic. He strove for nonchalance. "You posed an interesting question. One of these days, when we're not quite so busy around here, maybe I'll have Marion draw up a client list." He smiled weakly. "Then we'll all know."

Theo couldn't believe he didn't already have a client list. Even in her boutique she kept track of her steady customers. Not that a retail sales establishment and an attorney's practice were all that similar. But it only made sense to her that Jordan would know the number of clients he serviced. At least an approximation, a figure he could have recited without looking it up somewhere. Or, to be truthful, she would have respected him a whole lot more if he'd told her in no uncertain terms that that information was really none of her business. Instead, he sat there with a simpering smile that lowered her opinion of him, which had already dropped to a lethally low level.

He was sucking up to her, she thought with a surprising sadness. Hoping for what? With Marion in the picture and obviously aware of Colt's every move, what possible gain would he derive from acting as though he just couldn't help falling in love with her? Her inheritance, of course, but what about Marion?

Well, the complexities of such a peculiar relationship were way over her head, Theo admitted with a rather weary-sounding sigh. "Please," she said dully. "Let's get this over with. What papers need my signature?"

Jordan had cleared the center of his desk. Reaching into a drawer of the desk, he pulled out a very thick file. Opening it, he put on a studious expression and thumbed through the papers in the file. Though he appeared relatively calm, his mind was racing. Who had turned Theo against him?

His lip curled. Who but Colt Murdoch? Colt wanted Theo for himself, the sneaky bastard, and he'd probably not only told her everything he knew about Jordan Hamilton, he had probably embellished the truth and exaggerated gossip.

Well, Murdoch wasn't the only one who could tell tales. For damned sure Colt wasn't lily-white.

But maybe he'd better think about this a bit. Let Colt look like a jerk with his stories. If he remained a gentleman and didn't start playing I'll-pay-you-back with Murdoch, maybe there was a chance to resurrect what most certainly had been the start of a romantic relationship between himself and Theo.

Smiling pleasantly, through great effort, Jordan extracted a small packet of papers from the file. "Here they are. These are just more of the same type of documents you signed before." He removed the heavy paper clip from the packet, turned the papers so they would be right side up for

Theo and slid them across the desk toward her. "Here's a pen." He held one out.

Theo took the pen, flipped through the first few pages and saw that they were indeed notifications to the court, similar to those that she had previously signed. With that cursory examination, she began penning her name wherever indicated.

Until she came to the last page, which was very different from the others. Her gaze lifted. "Please explain what this is."

Jordan cleared his throat. "Certainly. It's a request for the bank to release funds from one of the estate accounts to pay the costs incurred thus far in the probate process. As you can see, there is money due to the title companies involved, county and state filing fees, some fees to the court and some minor expenses such as postage and long-distance phone calls."

"And your bill."

"Yes."

Theo raised an eyebrow. "Twelve thousand dollars?"

"Well, not quite."

"Very near, Jordan." Theo sat back and looked at him. "I've done very little business where a lawyer was involved, so I'm no expert on the cost of hiring one. Apparently probate is an expensive undertaking, which I didn't realize. What do you anticipate your total fee to run?"

Jordan was fidgeting with a pencil. "That's really impossible to say at this point, Theo. It depends on how much time I have to expend on the case. Wait here a minute. I'll get my time sheet and show you the hours I've spent on it so far."

Before Theo could object or agree, Jordan hurried from the room. Frowning, she picked up the Request for Payment paper and read it again. Based on this first billing of his, if it took a year to complete probate, Jordan's fees could add up to a six-digit figure. It hadn't occurred to her to question the cost of probate, although she'd certainly known that an attorney's time and knowledge didn't come cheap. But twelve thousand dollars for a few weeks of paperwork seemed exorbitant to her.

Jordan was at Marion's desk, speaking in an undertone. "Give me that time sheet I told you to hang on to."

"The first or the second?"

"The second, damn it! The one we used for billing," Jordan hissed. The first one, which had been in the file for Theo's signature before they'd talked on the phone, would probably have shocked her out of ten years' growth. It had been for twenty-five thousand dollars. Jordan had hurriedly compiled a new time sheet and billing figure, as he'd been afraid of Theo's mood. He still was, which infuriated him.

"Please don't get mad at me," Marion whispered tearily, taking the time sheet from a desk drawer. Her expression was drawn and worried. "Jordan," she whispered. "She gave me my car keys."

"I heard. We'll talk about it later." Grabbing the paper from Marion's hand, he swung around and hastened back to his office. Theo was up and pacing, which alarmed him further. Something was definitely out of sync, and it hadn't been the last time he'd been with her. It was all Murdoch's doing, he'd bet anything. Maybe he had no choice but to discredit Colt with a few stories of his own.

Relying on all of his acting skills, Jordan smiled pleasantly. "Please come and sit down, Theo. Why are you so jumpy today?"

If she was going to let him have it, this was a perfect opportunity. And she was tense enough to do it, too.

But it just wouldn't be smart to declare open warfare with anyone in Hattie. Wearing a stiff and unapproachable expression, she returned to her chair. To her discomfort, Jordan casually perched on the front edge of his desk, putting himself very close to her.

He held out the paper in his hand. "Please take a look at this."

She accepted the time sheet and saw dates and numbers in neat little boxes. The top of the paper contained the title Evans-Hunter Probate. The numbers, apparently, represented hours and fractions of hours expended in the estate's behalf. What bothered her was that there was no explanation as to what work had been done during those hours. Still, she was in no position to question Jordan's figures and computations and she handed back the paper.

"I'll sign the Request for Payment form now," she said, indicating by inflection that she couldn't do it until he moved out of the way.

"Theo, something's terribly wrong. Please tell me what it is." Jordan's face wore a pleading expression. There was no sign of relenting in her eyes, so he tried another tack. "Tell you what. Let's go to a nice restaurant, order lunch and talk about whatever it is that's bothering you. If it has anything at all to do with me, I'm sure I can alleviate your concerns."

Theo's gaze was steady and rock hard. "There's only one thing I want from you, Jordan, and that's for you to get through probate as quickly as possible. Since it's entirely in your hands, I have to rely on your word that you're moving it along as rapidly as the law allows."

"I am, of course," Jordan said hastily. It was a bald-faced lie. He'd been using every delaying tactic in the book. Maude's estate was so clean—no debts at all, the real property owned free and clear for a good many years—that the whole process wouldn't take more than a couple of months at the outside, handled properly. The thing was, once Theo finished going through Maude's office she was bound to catch on that there was no substantial reason for her staying in Hattie. And if she returned to California, Jordan's plan to woo her into marriage would be in the ash can.

It might already be, he thought with a renewed onslaught of fury. His eyes narrowed into menacing slits.

"Colt Murdoch's behind this, isn't he?" he said, all but snarling the accusation. "The last time we were together I felt affection from you, Theo. Today you're acting as though you not only mistrust me but you don't even like me. What the hell did he tell you about me?''

Theo looked at his angry face for a moment, then calmly got up, walked around his own desk, reached for the Request for Payment paper and scrawled her signature on it.

"That concludes our business for today," she said. "Let me know if and when I'm needed in the future. Goodbye, Jordan." She walked out.

Jordan stared at the vacant doorway in disbelief, but just for a moment. Almost running, he took off after her.

"Theo, wait." He caught up with her at the front door, where he took her arm. "I don't deserve this, Theo. Nor do I understand it."

She glanced down at his hand on her arm, then back to his face. "It seems that a lot is going on that none of us deserve or understand." Her gaze went to Marion, who was cringing in her chair. Another revelation struck Theo: Jordan's sins were not Marion's fault. "Goodbye, Marion," she said quietly.

"Goodbye, Miss Hunter," Marion said in a whispery voice.

"Tell me what Colt said, damn it!" Jordan's clasp on Theo's arm tightened.

"Let go of me!" Theo said with sudden fury. "I'm not telling you anything. Whatever stupid feud there is between you and Colt, I am not a part of it, nor will I ever be." Giving her arm a violent shake, she broke Jordan's grip. Her chin lifted. "From now it, it's strictly business between us, Jordan. Please try to remember that." Pushing against the door, she made a haughty exit.

Her relief at being outside was short-lived. Jordan followed her clear to the street. She started walking, but he kept up with her stride. "You think Murdoch's so great, don't you, and you're wrong, Theo. Dead wrong. Did he tell you that he's a jailbird? Ask him about that. Ask him why he spent six months in prison!"

Chapter Ten

Heading back to Maude's house, Theo walked fast. But her feeling of breathlessness wasn't entirely due to physical exertion. Jordan's snide remarks about Colt and prison kept repeating in her head, causing a tightness in her chest.

It was a little scary how that information had affected her. Personally distancing herself from Jordan hadn't been easy to do—she'd had no desire to hurt Jordan and still didn't—but it was done and she felt no backlash from it. In Colt's case, however, she felt an extremely unnerving backlash. What had that sudden sensation in Jordan's office about Colt being important meant? Obviously her feelings for him were much different than those she'd held for Jordan, with or without her consent.

But she didn't know the man, damn it, she didn't know him at all! Not in a thousand years could she have imagined him as an ex-convict. What had he done to warrant six months in prison? If she had asked, Jordan would gladly have told her. But she'd had to get away from him, as though running from him would eradicate what he'd said.

Theo felt terribly torn up and edgy about this whole thing. Pray God that she hadn't judged Jordan falsely, she thought unhappily, even though the proof of his perfidy had been all but thrown in her face today. Strangely, she harbored no ill will toward Marion. Some women fell in love with the wrong man, and Theo suspected that Marion deserved pity, not censure.

She also felt miserably stupid. Being taken in by both Jordan's and Colt's lines was really too much. What had come over her to bask in their pseudo-flattery and then worry in a simpering female fashion because there were suddenly two very attractive men in her life?

Almost to the corner of the block containing Maude's house, Theo stopped dead in her tracks. Across the yards of other homes she could see Colt walking from her front door toward his vehicle parked at the curb. Quickly she took a backward step, moving closer to an immense copse of lilac bushes.

Her heart was pounding, her mouth dry. Now was the perfect opportunity to set Colt straight once and for all, but the idea was the most unappealing prospect she'd ever faced. She really didn't think she could do it today. The episode with Jordan hadn't been exactly pleasant, and she suspected it would be much worse with Colt.

Cautiously moving a leafy branch aside, she peeked through the opening. Colt was sitting in his Bronco! Was he going to wait for her to get home? Why was he here? Only yesterday she'd told him to call before dropping in, that unannounced visitors were no longer welcome. Her lips pursed in silent reproach of his audacity. Apparently Colt took orders from no one and did exactly as he pleased. Which was probably why he'd spent time in jail!

A car drove by slowly, nearly stopping for the cross street. Theo gave it a glance. Its driver, an older man, was peering at her with a curious expression. Her lips twitched in a weak smile in an attempt to allay his curiosity. But why wouldn't he wonder why a woman was lurking in the lilac bushes?

Well, it was obvious that she couldn't lurk here for long. Someone was apt to call the police and report a woman acting peculiarly on the corner of Central and Bismark Streets.

Okay, so she had to face Colt and get it over with. Drawing a deep breath, Theo rounded the corner and started walking, totally ignoring Colt's vehicle and him in it, acting as though she didn't know he was there.

But Colt saw her at once. He frowned. What was she doing on foot? Glancing at her vacant driveway, he wondered where the red car was that had been there since her return. That car had been vaguely familiar, though he hadn't really given it any thought, assuming that she had rented it.

It came to him suddenly. That car belonged to Marion Roth! He was certain that he'd seen Marion driving it for about a year now. What had Theo done, returned it to Marion this morning? Because of his letting the cat out of the bag yesterday about Jordan and Marion's relationship? He'd rued his loose tongue the rest of the day and on into the night. He hated gossip and tale-telling, and then he'd gone and committed the disgusting sin himself. And what had it accomplished, other than causing trouble?

Colt got out of the Bronco and began walking in Theo's direction. She couldn't pretend not to see him anymore, not when he was coming down the sidewalk toward her.

He looked uncomfortable and God knows she was uncomfortable. Everything seemed to be in an awful mess, and she wished again that she could just go home to California.

They stopped in the middle of the sidewalk. "Hello, Theo." He wasn't smiling.

"I didn't expect to see you here." Neither was she smiling.

"I have to talk to you."

"Here? Now?"

"Preferably in private," he said with a wry nuance to his voice and a glance at the neighborhood. "We could take a ride or talk in your house. I'll leave it up to you."

"Big of you," she said with heavy sarcasm. "I asked you to call before coming by, didn't I?"

"I did call, but there was no answer."

"So you decided to come by anyway and wait until I got home. Didn't it occur to you that I might have gone somewhere for the day?"

"You didn't, though, did you? By the way, where's that red car?"

"That's really none of your business." She brushed past him and began walking again.

Colt turned and fell in step beside her. "You found out whose car it is, didn't you? Or did you know all along?"

She sent him a dirty look. "I don't want to see you today, Colt. Just leave me alone." They had reached her gate, and she went through it with the intention of latching it before he could follow. He was quicker than she'd thought, however, because they were both on the yard side of the gate. "Colt, I'm asking you to leave," she said in a taut voice.

"I will . . . in a few minutes." His expression was as tense as she felt. "But I have to talk to you first. It won't take long. If you don't want to invite me in, take a ride with me."

"I am *not* taking a ride with you." Theo glanced around, wondering how many neighbors were peeking out a window and watching this little tableau. Obviously Colt wasn't going to go away, however many different ways she let him know he wasn't welcome.

The disturbing thing was that some idiotic part of herself was glad to see him. Certainly the weakness in her knees and the pounding of her heart had nothing to do with common sense. Colt was not a man for her to be playing games with, which only frightened her more, because the chemistry between them didn't feel like a game.

But he'd been in prison, and she'd never known anyone who had been sentenced to jail for a crime. What was Colt's? And could she discount Jordan's warning her right from the beginning against Colt, certainly before he, himself, had developed any fondness for her? Theo's mouth twisted as she mentally added, *or pretended to.* Her inheritance was causing her nothing but trouble. No damned wonder Maude had kept her wealth a secret.

"Then invite me in," Colt said almost harshly.

Theo started, as though coming awake. Her thoughts had taken her out of the yard and into a world rife with questions.

"I'm not going away," Colt added when she merely looked addled. "I guess we could talk here."

"Here?" In the front yard, with Lord knows who looking on? "Uh, no. Not here. Come inside." Turning, Theo went up the sidewalk, all too aware of Colt on her heels. Inwardly she winced, sighed and groaned in rapid succession. She didn't want to talk to Colt today. In fact, the things she'd said to him yesterday were probably as hardnosed as she'd ever be able to be with him. Was that frailty of spirit a result of falling for him?

Silently groaning again, Theo unlocked the front door and went in. Colt entered and closed the door, as Theo had gone on into the living room. He leaned against the archway between living room and foyer and admired her in that pretty sundress. Her bare shoulders, throat and arms were giving him some very erotic ideas, which he'd do nothing about as he hadn't come here to make another pass. Quite the opposite, in fact.

Theo laid her purse on a table and, without looking directly at him, asked, "What did you need to talk to me about?"

Colt pushed away from the archway. "An apology."

Theo's gaze darted to him as an eyebrow shot up. "Oh?"

"Yes. That conversation we had yesterday about an apology compromising my principles was pure hogwash.

I've thought of little else since I left here yesterday, and it's obvious you're not ready to hear how I feel about you. Anyway, I'm sorry I jumped the gun. It won't happen again.''

He wasn't promising not to talk about her being the "one" again, Theo realized, he was just putting it on hold. Until she was ready to hear it. What made him think he was any judge of her readiness?

Her hands lifted, her fingertips going to her tension-taut temples. Her interior was a mass of nervous confusion. How quickly things had changed. Yesterday morning she had liked and respected both Jordan and Colt; this morning she had no reason to think of either of them as anything but fortune hunters.

"What's wrong?" Colt asked. "Got a headache?" Had he given her a headache? On second thought, maybe Jordan had done that. There must have been some sort of scene when she returned Marion's car. Jordan certainly wouldn't have let it pass without some questions, and, in fact, it was a little odd that he hadn't insisted on driving Theo home. If things had been friendly between them, that is.

A feeling of elation suddenly zinged through Colt's system. It was great to envision Jordy out of the picture. Maybe Theo had even taken the probate of Maude's estate out of his hands. In Colt's opinion that was the smartest move Theo could ever make, but it wasn't one he'd suggest if she hadn't already come up with it herself. No, he would stay out of Theo's business dealings with Jordan, unless, of course, he ever saw anything that wasn't strictly on the up-and-up. But he could never be anything but elated over the idea of a personal break between Theo and Jordy.

Theo's hands dropped. "I don't have a headache, though not having one could qualify as a minor miracle, considering all that's happened since I came back to Hattie."

Colt frowned. "Is there a message for me somewhere in that statement? Theo, I never meant to cause you any problems, and I'm damned sorry if I did." She looked like a forlorn child trying to put up a brave front, he realized, alarmed that the strong, bright, independent woman he'd met the day of Maude's funeral seemed to be deteriorating into an unhappy, confused being. His lips thinned grimly. It was Jordan's doing, that sap, courting Theo when he was committed to another woman. Naturally it would hurt her, damn him.

Colt also damned himself. Even though Theo should have been told about Jordan and Marion, he shouldn't have been the one to do so. It sure hadn't boosted Theo's opinion of him, had it?

"Aw, hell," he mumbled, looking away from her crestfallen face. They were still standing, Theo at one end of the room, he at the other. But it was a small room loaded with furniture, and they weren't more than eight feet apart.

His *aw, hell* startled Theo. "What?" she said.

"It's easy to see you're not happy." Colt narrowed his gaze on her. "Why don't you talk to me? Tell me what's bothering you. You need to talk to someone."

"For your information I talk to my mother in California almost every day."

"Oh. Well . . . do you tell her everything?"

Theo's chin lifted a bit defiantly. "Nearly everything."

"Then you've told her about us?"

Theo blinked in amazement. "Do you actually believe there's an *us?*"

Colt stared at her for a long moment. Was he that wrong about them? No, he couldn't be. She was just upset, probably over her encounter with Jordan and Marion.

"Yes," he said calmly. "I told you yesterday . . . no, I'm not going to say it again. Not yet."

"Meaning that you'll say it again when you think I'm ready to hear it. Listen, Colt, I don't want to hear it, do you understand? Not today, not tomorrow, not next year. Oh, hell," she moaned, sinking to the sofa and covering her face with her hands. "You and Jordan have got me half-crazy."

"*I've* got you half-crazy? Why? What'd I do?" Jordan, he could understand. But what had *he* done, other than let her know how deeply his feelings went for her? Sure, maybe he'd spoken too soon, but by the same token, telling a woman she was special wasn't so terrible.

Colt moved to the sofa and sat down next to her. "Theo, we're not communicating very well."

"No kidding," she said dully.

He tried to pull her hands from her face and she turned her back on him. "I really wish you'd go," she said hoarsely. Her throat was closing; she was on the verge of tears. And God forbid that she ended up crying on Colt's shoulder. Why couldn't she just say it? *Colt, I never want to see you again. Except for your purchase of that land, and maybe not even then. It would be best if a third party handled the transaction. In other words, get the hell out of my life!*

Yes, that was what she should be saying, or something to that effect. Why couldn't she? What made him any different than Jordan? They were both after her inheritance, weren't they? Pretending to fall for her so they would be first in line to get their greedy paws on what Maude had left her?

She felt his hands on her shoulders and a flame instantaneously ignited in the pit of her stomach.

"Theo?" he said softly.

"Don't." She tried to shrug off his grasp, despising the weakness she felt within herself just because he was touching her.

"I hate seeing you like this," he said.

"Then go away and you won't have to see me at all." He hadn't let go of her, and the warmth of his big hands on her bare skin was radiating throughout her entire body. It wasn't fair that he had this sort of power over her, not when he was a man she should steer completely clear of.

"Look at me, honey." Colt tried to turn her around.

She wriggled and refused to do so because she was afraid to look at him, afraid to look into those blue eyes and that handsome face. Oh, yes, this was much worse than it had been with Jordan. For one thing, other than telling him to leave—which she'd done several times—she couldn't be hard with him. For another, she really didn't want him to go.

No, that wasn't true, either. Part of her wanted him gone and another part wanted... Theo gulped. How could she be so traitorous to herself by thinking of sex with this man? His uppermost thought wasn't about making love, she'd bet. His goal was the fortune she'd inherited. And besides, he had a criminal record. Oh, God, what was wrong with her?

She had to let him know that she knew his manipulative game. "You only want one thing from me," she mumbled thickly.

Startled for a second, Colt then chuckled. "Guess you've got my number, honey."

Was he actually admitting his treachery? Startled herself, she turned to look at him, which was a dire mistake. Colt took her altered position as an invitation, and he wasted no time in acting upon it. Pushing her back against the sofa cushions, he pressed his mouth to hers.

Theo's gasp went unheeded. Certainly Colt didn't notice it, not when he was immediately lost in the wonder of kissing her. He hadn't apologized for kissing her yesterday, merely for talking about serious feelings too soon. Granted, he'd arrived here vowing not to make another pass, but he was only human, wasn't he?

So was Theo only human. Her hands lifted to twine through his hair, and her mouth opened for his tongue. Right or wrong, she couldn't stop herself from responding. He left her lips to feather kisses over her face, and she closed her eyes to savor the sensation. Colt slipped a strap of her dress down, then kissed the smooth skin of her throat and naked shoulder. Working his way back up to her mouth, he kissed her with more hunger.

She could barely breathe, but it didn't seem to matter. She opened her eyes to see him looking at her.

"You're so beautiful, Theo," he whispered huskily. "I've never met anyone like you before."

Her tongue flicked, dampening her lips. "I've never met anyone like you, either." It was the truth, the whole truth and nothing but the truth. His good looks far surpassed any man's she'd ever known; he was after her inheritance and willing, apparently, to do anything to get an inside track on it; last but certainly not least, he had a police record for God knows what crime. She was insane to get mixed up with him, and yet here she was, all but lying under him on Maude's sofa and wishing she could stay there forever. Obviously Marion Roth wasn't the only stupid, weak-willed female in this part of the world.

"I told myself I wasn't going to do this today," he whispered raggedly, dipping his head to nuzzle her throat. "I don't think you really grasp what you do to me."

If all he was talking about was physical arousal, she grasped it very well. How could she not when the proof of his desire was pressing into her side?

Vaguely she knew that she didn't have to allow what was happening. She could push him away, calmly or violently, she could tell him in plain English to get the hell away from her, or she could lie there like a stick until he got the message all on his own.

But she wanted him right where he was, kissing her, caressing her. Even his heavy breathing was exciting, and his scent? Oh my Lord, his scent. He smelled so good, of soap and coffee and after-shave. No one kissed like him; no one smelled like him; no one *felt* like him.

This had nothing to do with intelligence or good sense, she knew in the back of her mind. Lying with Colt on a too-small sofa was sheer idiocy, but she couldn't stop him or herself. Her entire body felt soft and strengthless, while his felt vibrantly alive and utterly masculine.

He claimed another kiss, a slow-burning mating of their mouths that destroyed her ability to think at all. She felt his hand sliding up under her skirt, gliding over her thighs, up and down several times. A moan built in her throat until he finally reached her panties, then it escaped, a guttural sound of total acquiescence.

Colt's desire exploded. "Theo...Theo." Kissing her hard, almost roughly, his hand went into her panties. She was hot and wet, and touching her, stroking her until she couldn't lie still was arousing him unmercifully. Somehow he managed to slide down her panties. She helped by lifting her hips and then wriggling against him while he maneuvered them down her legs.

He didn't take the time to undress, merely unbuttoned and unzipped his jeans and shoved them and his briefs down just far enough. Then he moved on top of her, kissing her all the while.

She tore her mouth from his to gasp, "Use...use something."

Damn, he hadn't even thought about protection. Digging out his wallet, he pulled out a foil packet and tore it open. His hands were shaking, he realized, but he'd never wanted a woman more and, in actuality, was shaking all over. She was so beautiful, with her eyes glazed with passion and her skin dewy, her lips sensually swollen from their kisses. Her hair was a tangle of curls, spread out beneath her head, and her expression was beckoning, beseeching. His heart was beating so hard it echoed in his own ears.

Quickly he did what was necessary and lowered himself into position between her thighs. Her lips were parted seductively, and he brought his head down to nip gently at them.

But only for a moment. Her arms locked around his neck, and she moved her lower body to align it with his. He sucked in a rough breath and, looking into her eyes, slowly slid into her.

Her eyelids drifted shut as she whispered, "Oh." She breathed deeply and there was an expression of pleasure on her face. It was what every man hoped to see while making love to the woman he loved.

Yes, loved, Colt decided. He would tell her, of course. It was on the tip of his tongue to say it now, but the words got lost in the passion of another feverish kiss. One led to a second, a third. He had to touch her bare breasts, and somehow he managed to unbutton the bodice of her sundress.

It was amazing what two people could do on one small sofa, he thought. While his hips moved in an even, steady rhythm, they kissed and touched each other all over. The pressure was mounting, however, and her legs lifted and clamped around him.

"Oh, baby," he whispered raggedly. "It's good, so damned good. Tell me it's good for you, too."

She didn't want to talk. Talking could lead to thinking, and thinking might shatter her mood. Even so, in the back of her mind she knew she was going to regret this. It was just that she'd never gotten so hot for a man before, and the idea of stopping now, vague as it was, was terrifying.

But maybe he wouldn't talk again if she conceded to saying two little words. "It's good," she whispered so faintly Colt barely heard her.

That was fine. He was climbing the final summit and concentrating on Theo's physical responses, making sure she was going with him.

His concern was gentlemanly but unnecessary. The only thing that would have prevented her ascent to the top of the mountain was if he should suddenly desert her before she reached it.

"Colt...Colt..." she moaned, moving in unison with him, clinging to him, digging her fingers into his back.

It was a cry from the depths of her soul. He heard and recognized its significance, and he moved faster and went deeper. He felt her fingernails on his back right through his shirt. Her lips sought his, and he gave them to her. Her tongue plunged into his mouth, and then, abruptly, she broke away and turned her head to whimper and moan.

"Don't stop...don't stop."

"Never, baby, never," he said gruffly.

Her body shuddered as the delicious spasms began. It was what he'd been waiting for, and he released every restraint on his own completion.

"Oh...oh...yes...yes...*yes!*" Her voice was hoarse and sounded choked.

He cried out. "Theo...Theo."

Then it was over. Breathing hard and unevenly, they lay still. Theo felt her heartbeat slowing down. Without passion he was heavy. Without passion...oh, no, now she'd done it. Tears filled her eyes.

Colt raised his head and smiled at her. "Is it okay if I say it now?"

Say what now? she thought within the maelstrom of emotions buffeting her brain. Oh, no, not that line about her being the one.

"I...I wish you wouldn't," she said, her voice cracking. "In fact, I wish we hadn't..." His smile vanished, replaced by a scowl, and she said no more.

"You wish we hadn't what?" he demanded.

They were still locked together, and she felt like a fool. She sighed. "I think you know what I was going to say. Please move so I can get up."

"You're joking, right? About wishing we hadn't made love?"

She turned her face away. "Do you see me laughing?"

Hurt and perplexed, he awkwardly moved away from her, got to his feet, hunched up his jeans and headed for the bathroom.

Theo sat up and put her face in her hands with a groan of despair. Where was all that uncontrollable passion now?

Damn, how could anyone behave so stupidly?

Chapter Eleven

Sick to his stomach, Jordan chewed antacids and paced his office like a crazy man. Mentally he had called Colt every vile name he could think of, but there was enough clarity within his murderous rage to know that name-calling was childish and futile, even if he should shout his fury directly into Murdoch's despicable face. He wasn't physically afraid of Colt, never had been, never would be, but there was no getting around the fact that the fear gripping him now was because of that bastard. What had he told Theo? Obviously Marion's name had come up or Theo wouldn't have returned her car.

But had he said anything about Jordan's financial situation? Other than conjecture, did Colt know anything about his financial situation? Sure, there was gossip around town about Jordan's life-style, but with the exception of Marion, he was certain no one in Hattie really knew the hard facts of his debt load. He didn't even bank here, deliberately keeping his financial affairs private by banking in Helena.

He had attended a good law school on the money his mother had received from a life insurance policy after his father's death. Edna Hamilton had requested only one thing of her son in exchange for his costly education: that he return to Hattie to practice his craft. Since it was his own wish to go that very route, he had agreed without debate, thus making Edna a very happy lady in her final years.

Of course, neither of them had known those were her final years. Jordan had just passed the Montana bar with the intention of setting up a small office in rented space above the drugstore, when Edna had a fatal heart attack. Though his grief was genuine, it had definitely been tempered by the receipt of a check for $112,343.58, the amount of his mother's paid-up life insurance policy plus the interest earned thereon.

His plans had changed immediately. Besides the insurance money, his mother's home, furnishings and car had value. He sold everything, watched his bank account swell and hired an architect out of Helena to draw up plans for his own building—this building, the one in which he was treading the expensive carpet and worrying about how he was going to continue meeting its astronomically high mortgage payments. He owned nothing free and clear. He had payments on the BMW, and payments on the house he had purchased in the classiest subdivision in Hattie. His cash had been all but gone for nearly a year now, used for the architect's exorbitant fee, for down payments on the building, the house and the car, for a wardrobe befitting an up-and-coming young attorney, and for furniture and the general costs of living and operating a one-man law office.

The bottom line was that he was on the very brink of bankruptcy. His vision of drawing clients from around the state, earning a name for himself and eventually getting into politics was in the ash can. The clients hadn't materialized, and he'd learned the hard way that it took years to build a profitable law practice. He didn't have years.

Sweat broke out on his forehead and under his arms. Without Murdoch's interference, his plan to marry Theo would have worked, damn it, it would have worked!

Was there any way to salvage the relationship? Any way to make Theo like him again? She had, he knew. She had liked him a lot, even if she did possess the sexual nature of a cold fish. And considering the way she had asked about his billing listed on the Request for Payment form today, he suspected, very strongly, that she was going to question every bill he presented to her. Had Murdoch told her to do that, too?

Jordan cursed under his breath again. Rubbing the back of his neck, which felt as tight as a drum, he caught movement at the door in his peripheral vision. He turned to see Marion standing there.

"What?" he said brusquely.

"Please . . . don't be unhappy," she stammered in a teary little voice. "I . . . I can't bear it, Jordan."

He narrowed his eyes on her. His present plight might be blamed on Colt, but Marion, too, had something to do with it. A great deal to do with it, in fact. If he was to regain any chance at all with Theo, he had to get rid of Marion. Or at least make it appear that Marion meant nothing to him.

Yes, of course. That was his only chance of resurrecting Theo's attention and respect.

"I have a new plan," he said to the distraught woman in the doorway. "You're not going to be able to work here anymore."

Marion reeled, then hung on to the doorframe for support, as though her own legs weren't enough to hold her upright. "Are you firing me?" Her voice was weak with shock.

"Call it anything you want," he said impatiently. "But you and I cannot appear to be connected in any way."

"After today you're still thinking of marrying Theo Hunter?" Marion said incredulously. "Jordan, why can't you see . . . ?"

"Just stop right there," he shouted. Drawing a breath, he spoke more normally, though his agitation was still apparent. "Marion, either you're with me or you're not. If you love me . . ."

Marion cut in. "I think you know how I feel. What's at stake here is how you feel about me."

"Feelings aren't important right now. Can't you get that through your thick head?"

"Stop shouting at me! And why would you say something so . . . so demeaning? My head is no thicker than yours, Jordan Hamilton! You keep on hurting me, over and over again, and for no good reason. I've tried so hard . . ." Turning to the wall, she began crying.

Jordan gave her a disgusted look. "Great, that's just great. When things don't go your way, you turn on the waterworks. Well, listen to me, Marion, and listen well. I am not going to sit by and do nothing while everything I have dribbles down the drain. If you cared for me in the least you'd grasp where I'm coming from without arguments or tears. Don't you get it? If things go on as they are, I won't even have a damned roof over my head!"

Sniffling, Marion turned around. "You could move in with me. Jordan, anything I have is yours. You must know that. We could be married. You could start over."

"In this town?" he sneered. "You're so incredibly dense I can't believe it. I'd be the laughingstock of Hattie. Is that what you want?"

"Jordan, you're wrong. Why would anyone laugh? Other people in Hattie have worked their way through financial problems and I didn't hear anyone laughing." Jordan was glaring at her, as though all of his woes were her fault. "You're blaming me, aren't you?" she whispered hoarsely.

He looked at her for a long time before answering. "This is my plan. You can go along with it or not, but you're not going to stop me. I want you to take all of your things with you when you leave at five. I'm going to actively look for a new secretary, broadcasting far and wide that you and I no longer have a relationship, personal or otherwise. Theo will hear about it from some source, either from another party or directly from me." His lip curled cynically. "Then I'm going to do everything I can to convince her that marrying me would be the wisest move she could ever make. Do you have all that? Do you get it?"

"I...get it." With a heartbroken expression, Marion turned to the door. "Goodbye, Jordan."

He merely sent her another disgusted look, which she didn't see as she had left the office. Now she would pout and act as though he'd committed some unpardonable sin, he thought angrily. Moving to his desk, he sat down and anxiously ran all ten fingers through his hair.

What he had to do now was figure out how to get back into Theo's good graces.

There had to be a way, there just had to be.

Colt stood in the living room doorway to see Theo pretty much put back together. The only remnant of their episode on the sofa that was really visible was the sexy and appealing disarrangement of her hair.

She was up and circling the room, unaware of him watching her. The frown between her eyes—conveying worry and uncertainty—disturbed him.

He stepped into the room, leaned against the wall and folded his arms across his chest, wondering how long it would take her to notice him. Obviously she was deep in thought, and from that crease in her forehead, ruing what had happened. Her regret hurt. To his knowledge there was no reason for her to regret anything, no reason for her to feel any guilt, which also seemed present in her expression.

Unless she and Jordan were closer than he'd thought. Maybe his "knowledge" was influenced by his own ego.

Colt's stomach dropped. Had she made love with Jordan, too?

No, he thought with a fierce clenching of his jaw. She wasn't that kind of woman. She didn't sleep around willy-nilly, he'd bet on it.

"What's wrong?" he asked quietly.

Startled, Theo spun around to face him. "You have to ask?"

Her anger felt like a blow to Colt. "Are you mad at me?"

Her lip curled. "I think that's a safe assumption." After a second she added, "Maybe disgusted with myself is more accurate."

"I don't understand you." How could he? Not more than ten minutes ago she had been writhing under him, kissing him wildly, passionately, and now she was angry. Why was she angry? Why was she regretful?

"I think you do," she said with an accusing look in her eyes and an angry tilt to her head. "I think you know exactly where I'm coming from."

She had no more than gotten that opinion out of her mouth than the telephone rang. There were three phones in the house—in the kitchen, in the bedroom Maude had used and in the office. Theo's first impulse was to let the damned things ring themselves to death. She was in no mood to talk to anyone, except for maybe a few more scathing remarks to Colt before she kicked him out of her life once and for all.

"Aren't you going to answer it?" Colt asked gruffly after the third ring.

It could be Helen calling from the boutique, Theo thought, or her mother. She had to answer it. Shooting Colt a dirty look, she passed him by and went to the kitchen extension.

Grabbing up the receiver, she said rather curtly, "Hello!"

"Theo, we have to talk."

It was Jordan, sounding desperate. If one more person—especially a man—told her they had to talk today, she would scream. As for Jordan's desperation, she couldn't muster up any sympathy over it.

"We do *not* have to talk, Jordan. Not unless it's about the estate. Is it?" she said bluntly.

"Honey... Theo... you're breaking my heart."

"Oh, get a grip, Jordan. Do you think I'm a complete moron?" Theo winced. After what she'd just done with Colt on Maude's sofa, how did she have the gall to even mention the word *moron* in a derogatory fashion?

"Theo, I think your change of attitude was because of Marion. I want to explain. She and I had a thing going a while back, but it's been over for a long time. She's been sullen and inefficient in the office ever since, and—"

"Jordan, stop. Your private life simply doesn't interest me."

"But it has to!" He cleared his throat. "Theo, I fired her."

"You what?"

"I let her go. Today is her last day as my secretary."

Theo yanked out a chair from the table and sank onto it, weakened by the knowledge that Jordan had fired Marion because of *her!* It had to be so. Why else would he have called her and announced the information as though she would render it good news.

She looked up to see Colt standing near the refrigerator. He'd followed her to the kitchen to listen to her conversation, probably when he'd heard that Jordan was the caller. It was damned nervy of him, and she told him so by sending him a scathingly venomous look. He responded by leaning a shoulder against the refrigerator and symbolically digging in his heels.

Men! She was sick of them.

"Listen, Jordan. If you fired Marion because of me, you made a terrible mistake," she said coldly into the telephone. The expression she showed Colt was every bit as cold as her voice. She saw his chin come up and his eyes narrow slightly, but he stood his ground.

"Theo, she wasn't fired because of you or anyone else," Jordan said smoothly, only because he'd been prepared for something like that from Theo. "I let her go for inefficiency and a bad attitude. My mistake wasn't made today, Theo, it was made when I became involved with an employee. I learned my lesson, believe me. When the romance peters out, a professional relationship just isn't possible. At least it wasn't for Marion.

"At any rate, I have the feeling that you heard about my previous relationship with Marion. Naturally you would think I was a jerk, courting you when I was involved with another woman. Theo, it just isn't true. It hasn't been true for a long time. You have to believe me."

Looking at Colt and thinking of their almost savage lovemaking on the sofa, Theo realized that it really didn't matter to her if Jordan was telling her the truth or lying through his teeth. As upset as she was with Colt—and herself for behaving so imprudently with him—he moved her. Jordan didn't. She had started out liking each man equally, one as much as the other, but Colt had outdistanced Jordan in such a way that she could never go back to thinking of them as equals.

"I believe you," she said into the phone, rather absently, her eyes looking into Colt's. There was something so powerful between them that she could want him while knowing she shouldn't, while realizing that she didn't really know him, while worrying about his past and a woman named Ruth and while questioning what kind of man he really was. It seemed to be a very sad commentary on her own character, which she had always deemed to be of the highest moral fiber. Obviously she hadn't known herself as well as she'd thought.

The lack of enthusiasm in her reply caused Jordan to frown. And yet it was a first step and encouraging. "Theo, will you please have dinner with me this evening? Just to talk, honey, I swear it. I want you to get to know the real me, just as I yearn to know you better."

"Dinner?" Theo's gaze was still locked with Colt's, and it was becoming difficult to concentrate on anything but the intensity she saw in his eyes. "No, I don't think so. Was there anything else, Jordan?"

She sounded so vague, as though her mind were a million miles away. Sweating, Jordan pressed her for something, anything. "Uh...tomorrow night, Theo?"

There was a lengthy silence before she answered. "No, not tomorrow night, either. Jordan, I'm going to hang up now. Goodbye."

Jordan heard the click of her phone and slammed his own down with a vicious curse. Firing Marion hadn't helped his case an iota. "Marion," he yelled. "Come in here."

All he heard was silence. "Marion?" Getting up from his desk, he hurried down the hall to the reception area. It was vacant. Was she in the ladies' room? Striding to that door, he rapped. "Marion?"

Opening the door, he peered into the small room, then with mounting dread, gave the door an unnecessarily hard yank to close it.

Quickly he returned to the reception area and started opening desk drawers. Marion's personal items were gone, her hand lotion, her box of tissues, her little bag of cosmetics, her paperback books.

But the expensive gold pen he had given her for her birthday last year was lying on top of the desk next to the computer. Beside it was the sapphire-and-diamond ring he'd paid a small fortune for last Christmas.

He picked up the pen and ring and sank into her chair. Her scent was all around him. He felt totally alone, totally deserted, and he sat there for a long time feeling sorry for himself.

Then he got up and stalked down the hall to his office. He'd show them all, by God. He wasn't finished yet.

"Did I hear you say that Jordan fired Marion?" Colt still leaned against the refrigerator, his gaze on Theo.

"Yes." Theo was again unnerved over Jordan's news. Frowning, she bit her lip. "He...he said she was sullen and inefficient since he broke up with her." Maybe it was true, she thought, hoping it was. If Marion had lost her job because of Jordan's infatuation with *her,* she would never forgive herself.

"He's a damned fool," Colt said sharply. "I've never done business with Jordan myself, but I know people who have and I've heard nothing but praise for Marion's efficiency."

Theo's shoulders slumped. "Wonderful," she mumbled. Once again she was in the middle of Colt and Jordan's feud. Frankly she would much rather believe Jordan's explanation of Marion's termination than Colt's caustic comments. But believing anything either man said was becoming a test of her own intellect. It was emotionally trying and physically tiring to constantly doubt everyone around her, even though "everyone" consisted almost solely of two people—two overbearing, overly confident, macho males. How in heaven's name had she gotten herself into such a mess? Certainly not by choice.

She rose, a bit unsteadily. "I have work to do," she said, which was only the truth, though she had to wonder if she'd be able to concentrate on stacks of dry-as-dust papers after today's fiasco.

Colt knew she wanted him to leave, but he couldn't go when she was so obviously resentful of him. So needlessly resentful. He took the few steps that separated refrigerator and table, then put his hands—palms down—on the small, circular tabletop and leaned over it, putting his face very close to Theo's.

"Talk to me," he demanded. "Tell me why our making love put you in this frame of mind."

"What frame of mind?" she asked, automatically hedging for God knows what reason. Why not tell Colt in minute detail why she wasn't doing handsprings over their antics on the sofa?

But the whole thing was extremely complex, she was realizing. He wasn't just some guy with whom she'd stubbed her toe and immediately regretted it. Like it or not, there seemed to be some sort of mysterious connection between them. Certainly she felt him in the pit of her stomach, and aside from physical recognition of the malady, Colt was embedded in her mind, her brain. Nervous suddenly, she clenched her hands into fists at her sides.

"Angry, resentful. You know damned well what I'm talking about," Colt said, his dark and brooding eyes all but boring holes into her. "Do you think I do this sort of thing everyday? Maybe you think I've got a milk run, a string of women I can drop in on and have a roll around their sofa with anytime I get the urge. It's not like that, Theo. This was special to me. *You're* special to me." Dare he mention love? He was thinking it.

His chin lifted slightly. "Is there someone else?"

She could see in his eyes that he was asking about Jordan. What made him think there was no one in California, that Jordan was his only rival?

She was upset enough to throw him a curve. "If there was, why would I tell you about him?"

His eyes narrowed to slits. "Don't play games with me, Theo. If there is another man, just say so."

"And, of course, you'd walk out of my life, right?" Maybe it was that simple. Maybe all she had to do was tell Colt there was someone else, and he'd vanish into the sunset. Her heart began pounding. Why was she procrastinating? Why not tell him that lie and then watch him puff up with territorial pride? Apparently that would be the end of it for him. The end of it for them.

She stiffened as it struck her: she didn't want it to be over between them!

Her breath was caught in her throat as she waited for his answer. She was nearly choking when he finally said, "With anyone else, yes. With you...no, I wouldn't walk that easy." His lips twitched with a hint of a grin as his mood changed before her very eyes. "That's because I think you're worth fighting for, babe."

It came out of her mouth so quickly she couldn't stop it. "My net worth?"

Colt's expression changed to utter shock. Slowly he took his hands off the table and straightened his back. He spoke coldly. "Don't confuse me with Jordan, Theo. Give your damned inheritance away and see if I stop coming around."

He glanced at his watch. "I've gotta go." He looked at her for a tension-filled moment. "Can I come back this evening?"

The smoky cast in his eyes told her why he wanted to see her again this evening. Her pulse took off, and it was suddenly difficult to breathe normally.

But she couldn't fall into his arms on his timetable or whims. If she said yes to this evening, he'd be back tomorrow. They'd be involved in a full-blown affair in a matter of days, and she couldn't allow it, not when there so many questions about him roiling in her mind.

"No," she said, trying to keep her voice steady. "I need some time."

"Time to do what?"

"To finish my work here, for one thing," she said somewhat sarcastically.

"But that's not all, right? You want time to think about us, don't you? What are you going to ask yourself, Theo? Is he good enough for me? Is he after my inheritance? God, I can't believe that would even enter your mind," he finished disgustedly.

Walking out of the kitchen, he called over his shoulder, "See you when I see you, I guess."

Theo swallowed hard, then ran after him. "Why wouldn't it enter my mind?"

He stopped at the front door and turned to face her. "Is that how you're going to live the rest of your life, worrying that every man who appears to like you is after your money?" Colt shook his head, again conveying disgust.

"Don't put me on that list, Theo. I couldn't care less about any part of your inheritance, except for that one piece of land, for which, if you'd care to remember, I told you to set your own price."

She looked positively frazzled, and his heart softened. "This hasn't been a picnic for you, has it? Isn't that strange. Everyone hopes and prays for wealth, then if by some fluke they get it they don't know what to do with it."

"Colt . . ." She sounded helpless, which right at the moment was a fair assessment of her state of mind.

"Com'ere," he growled, reaching out to slide his hand under her hair to the back of her neck and drawing her forward. For a moment he looked deeply into her beautiful green eyes. "You worry too much," he whispered.

She knew he was going to kiss her, and she did nothing to prevent it. Rather, she stood there and permitted his lips to play with hers. Whatever else he was, he was a gorgeous bundle of sizzling sexuality with the power to melt her bones with a single touch. Though it was discomfiting knowledge, he was capable of destroying her common sense and raising her pleasure gauge to a degree she'd never before experienced.

She was falling for him, hard and fast, and she didn't know how to halt the plunge or even slow it down. Her fingers curled into the front of his shirt as he stopped playing and settled his mouth on hers for a real kiss. It stole her breath and made her mind spin. His arms wrapped around her and brought her up against him, until they were tightly joined from their chests to their thighs. Her insides became murky and moist; she could make love with him again.

When he broke the kiss, raised his head and looked at her, his eyes, hot and smoky, revealed similar thoughts.

"Can I come back this evening?" he asked again, speaking huskily, hopefully.

Theo licked her lips. A glimmer of reason was still alive in her brain, thank goodness. "Not . . . not tonight," she managed to say in a hoarse and unnatural voice.

"Do you believe you're special to me?" he asked.

She drew a breath. "Yes, I believe you." It wasn't that she was special to him that was suspect, but his reason for feeling that way. A woman with a fortune might be special to a lot of men.

"Then why don't you want to see me tonight?" He lifted a hand and brushed some curls from her cheek. "I sure want to see you."

From somewhere within herself she found the strength to push away from him. With some space between them, she was able to think with more clarity.

"I told you I need some time," she said, ruing the breathlessness she heard in her voice.

Colt looked at her for a long moment. "Why don't you forget your work for the rest of the day and come out to the ranch with me? I'd love to show you the place."

She turned her head to avoid meeting his eyes, which were much too persuasive. "No, I can't."

"You can do anything you want to do, Theo," he said quietly.

Her gaze jerked back to him. "All right, fine. I don't *want* to go with you."

"And you don't *want* to see me tonight. How about tomorrow night?"

Her spine stiffened. "Colt, I am not going to have an affair with you."

A startled expression appeared on his face, then he laughed. "I think it's a little late for that announcement, don't you?"

Theo's face colored. "It happened once. It's not going to happen again."

"Oh, I see. Well, I'm afraid I can't agree with you. You kissed me like a hungry woman only a few minutes ago. It will happen again, babe, count on it." He opened the door. "I'll be back. Count on that, too." Leaving, he left the door hanging open.

Watching him sauntering down the sidewalk, Theo felt a lump in her throat the size of an ostrich egg. "Damn you," she whispered raggedly, then slammed the door shut.

She had to get out of Montana before she became totally demented. Between Jordan's questionable tactics and Colt's irrepressible magnetism, she couldn't possibly remain sane for very long.

Chapter Twelve

While Theo showered, her thoughts jumped from Colt to Jordan to what might be happening in California—at the boutique and with her mother—to her inheritance and Maude, and even to Marion Roth, for whom she felt intense, heartrending pity. Maybe she had no right to pity Marion, but she couldn't eradicate the emotion. They were women with possibly one very flawed similarity: a weakness for the wrong man.

Furiously scrubbing her hair under the shower spray, Theo's mouth tensed. She couldn't be falling for Colt, she just couldn't! A man she barely knew? Her hands stopped moving in the shampoo suds in her curls. *Why* did she just barely know Colt? Because he rarely talked about himself, or because she had permitted very few personal conversations between them? Could it be that she hadn't wanted to hear the reason he'd spent time in jail?

No, she *did* want to know. It was just that she hadn't been able to bring herself to ask him about it. But suppose, just suppose, that her feelings for him were important, and suppose he wasn't after her inheritance but truly cared for her. Wouldn't hiding her head in the sand be an awful error in judgment?

"Preposterous," Theo mumbled. All she was doing was looking for an acceptable excuse for behaving like a woman with no morals at all. Colt had probably been chuckling up his sleeve from the moment he'd left her door. Not only was she going to be loaded with dough, she was a pushover. Groaning out loud, Theo leaned her forehead against the tile of the shower stall. How stupid could one woman be?

After rinsing away the soap and shampoo, Theo turned off the shower and stepped out of the stall onto a bath mat. She gave her blurred reflection in the steamy mirror a murderous look. It was very easy to dislike herself when the mere thought of Colt's body made her tingle all over, from the crown of her dripping curls to the tips of her polished toenails. Admittedly it had been stupid to lose herself in Colt's arms today, but she had better be honest enough to face the fact that it could happen again.

Whining, even in private, that she didn't know him well enough to accurately judge his motives and integrity was wasted effort. And vowing to be strong the next time he came around was pure bravado. What she had to do was *get* to know him, so that she had a solid base of information about him. Then and only then would she be able to make sound decisions where he was concerned.

Toweling off, Theo frowned. Who could she talk to about Colt? Certainly not Jordan. Nan Butler? Of course, she could go directly to Colt and question him, but dare she trust anything he might tell her?

Nan was her best bet, Theo decided on her way to her bedroom to get dressed. After underthings, she pulled on a pair of shorts and a T-shirt. Nan had said that she knew *of* both Jordan and Colt, which sounded to Theo as though the older woman was pretty well aware of their histories. She was apt to get an earful about both men. That was what she needed to hear, an earful, the whole ball of wax. Yes, Nan was the person to talk to.

Applying a little makeup, Theo left the house with her hair merely towel-dried. Now that she'd actually come up with a plan, she wanted to get to it. Hurrying down her sidewalk and through the gate, she went next door and rapped on Nan's front door. That was when she noticed the drawn drapes in Nan's windows.

Theo's spirit fell. Nan didn't come to the door, and from the appearance of the house Theo feared she had gone somewhere for more than the afternoon.

But maybe she was wrong. She really knew nothing of Nan's habits, and it was possible that Nan darkened her house just for a trip to the grocery store.

Thoughtfully Theo returned to her own little house and went in. She would keep an eye out for Nan, but in the meantime . . . ?

She heaved a heavy sigh. Tackling the paperwork held absolutely no appeal. Besides, her mind was too cluttered for that kind of work. Going to the kitchen phone, she sat at the table and dialed her mother's number.

Lisa answered on the fourth ring. "Hello?"

"Hi, Mom."

"Something's wrong. I can hear it in your voice."

"Well . . . yes and no. It's nothing you should be alarmed about, so don't worry. What I mean is that I'm safe and sound and plan to stay that way."

There was relief in Lisa's reply. "Thank goodness. For a second there . . . well, tell me what *is* wrong."

The last time Theo had called, everything had been fine in Hattie. She had mentioned her faith in Jordan's legal abilities and how lucky she felt that he was the attorney handling the estate, and then joked—as only she and her mother could do—about both Jordan and Colt appearing to be personally interested in her. Things had changed so drastically in such a short period of time that Theo didn't know where to begin.

The truth was that she was suddenly doubting if she should begin at all. Lisa certainly couldn't do anything to alleviate her distress over Jordan firing Marion, or her suspicion that Jordan wasn't as honest as she had so wholeheartedly believed. As for Colt, how could she tell her mother about today's blunder on Maude's sofa?

It had finally happened, Theo thought unhappily. She had finally done something that she couldn't discuss with her mother. She shouldn't have called, not when she was this addled.

"I...I guess I'm just lonesome," she said lamely.

"Oh, honey, if that's all that's bothering you, why don't you take a break and come home for a few days?"

It occurred to Theo that she could do exactly that, if she wanted. In fact, she could box up every piece of paper and file folder in the house and ship them to California, where she could go through them as easily as she could here. She could also tell Jordan that their business would be conducted over the phone or through the mail from now on, and there wouldn't be a damn thing he could do about it. The estate was hers, he worked for her, after all, and if probate took a little longer because she wasn't here, who cared?

Then she thought of Colt and her heart sank. Making a total break with Jordan was one thing, but she wasn't finished with Colt. Rather, she had just *started* with Colt, and putting over a thousand miles between them was apt to cause her a great deal of misery. She had to find out about his past and what kind of man he really was. She wouldn't rest until those goals were accomplished. Running away definitely wasn't the answer.

"No, I'd better stay here, Mom. There are some things that need doing, and I'm the only one who can do them." Things like sneaking behind Colt's back and pulling information out of Nan or anyone else she could find who would talk about him. Theo winced.

"I suppose that's true," Lisa said sympathetically. "But it won't last forever, Theo. When you get really lonesome, try to remember that. I wish I could come to Montana and help you out, be there for you, but . . . well, there's no point in wishing for the impossible, is there?''

"How are you feeling, Mom?"

"Pretty good, actually. You're not to worry about me on top of all you have to do there. I take it that you're staying in touch with Helen at the boutique?''

"Oh, yes. I call her every morning. She seems to have everything under control.''

"I stopped in yesterday afternoon, and the shop looked great. Helen's doing a good job.''

"Yes, I think she is.''

They chatted about this and that for another ten minutes, then said goodbye. Theo put the phone down with a guilty grimace. That had been the first time in her entire life that she had deliberately kept something from her mother.

But explaining her jumbled feelings for Colt just wasn't possible. How could it be, when she didn't wholly grasp them herself?

As brutal as the day had been, Theo finally forced herself into Maude's office and sat at the desk. Opening the first drawer on her right, she sighed: it was crammed to the top with loose papers and file folders. Taking everything from the drawer, she began sorting, putting papers in one stack, folders in another.

The ringing of the front doorbell startled her, and she got up and peered out the window. If either Colt or Jordan had been standing on the stoop, she would have let them stand there until hell froze over or they passed out from exhaustion, whichever came first.

But she saw a young man holding a florist's box, and parked at the curb was a van bearing a sign, Hattie Floral Shop. Theo frowned. Now just who was sending her flowers? Not Jordan, she hoped, and not Colt, either.

The bell pealed again. Dispassionately and without the slightest enthusiasm, Theo walked through the house and

opened the door. The young man smiled broadly. "Theodora Hunter?"

"Yes," she said tonelessly.

"I have a delivery for you." He held out the box, which
Theo accepted.

"Thank you." The young man went down the sidewalk
whistling, and Theo closed the door. It was a large box, ev-
idencing a large bouquet. Taking it to the kitchen, she set it
on the table, removed the ribbon and lifted the lid. Long-
stemmed red roses, at least two dozen, filled the box.

Theo picked up the tiny envelope and extracted a card.

Theo,
Please accept these beautiful roses as a token of my respect and esteem.

                                                    Jordan

"Damn," she mumbled, sinking into a chair. The roses
were beautiful and must have cost a small fortune. But she
didn't want Jordan sending her flowers, especially expensive flowers. It was disheartening to realize that he hadn't
given up on her. What would she have to do to convince him
that theirs was strictly a business relationship now, put it in
writing?

She was still sitting there staring at the roses arranged so
perfectly among lovely greenery in the box when the phone
rang. Instinctively she knew who was calling, and she let it
ring six times before finally reaching out for the receiver.

"Hello," she said dully.

"You *are* home. The phone rang so many times, I was
about to hang up. This is Jordan. Have the flowers I sent
arrived yet?"

"They're here."

"Well . . . do you like them?"

"Everyone likes roses, Jordan, but I wish you hadn't sent
them."

"Look at them as a peace offering, Theo."

"However I look at them, I still wish you hadn't sent them. Jordan, let me be honest. I'm not very happy with you right now, and expensive flowers are not going to alter my feelings."

"Tell me why you're not happy with me, Theo, please. I think I at least deserve an explanation, don't you?"

"I think I made myself quite clear in your office this morning."

"You mean because you were jealous of Marion? Theo, I told you that was a thing of the past."

"My God, I wasn't jealous of Marion! I'll tell you something, Jordan. I feel sorry for Marion, and your firing her to impress me is the cruelest, most ridiculous thing I've ever heard of. And since you have no compunctions about pressuring me about my attitude, I'll tell you something else. If you have one ounce of good sense, you'll put her back to work! Goodbye, and please don't call me again unless you have something that needs saying about the estate. And don't send me any more flowers!"

Theo slammed the phone down and in the next heartbeat realized that her hands were trembling. Her whole body was shaking, in fact. She couldn't deny that she had initially encouraged Jordan's interest, and she wished to God that she hadn't done so. But how much plainer could she let him know that he was no longer anything to her but the attorney handling the probate of Maude's estate? She would never believe that he was suffering from love for her, no matter what he did. What was wrong with him? Couldn't he accept defeat? Was her inheritance really that important to him that he would lie and cheat and then continue to harass her?

Running her fingers through her hair, she got up and went to stare broodingly out of the window over the sink. Why would a man with so many costly possessions and a successful law practice make a fool of himself over a client? Could it be that his law practice *wasn't* successful? Was it possible that Jordan needed money and she, with her impressive net worth, looked like the solution to his problems?

It was a discomfiting theory, but since she couldn't believe his line about his having immediately recognized the two of them as being soul mates, it was the only one that made sense.

The person getting hurt in all of Jordan's shenanigans was Marion Roth. Theo's lips thinned. She certainly hoped that Marion didn't blame her for this mess. Turning slightly, Theo eyed the telephone. Maybe she should talk to Marion.

Then again, maybe Marion wouldn't want to talk to her. God, what a ludicrous situation.

The traumatic day still wasn't over. Theo was just finishing the light dinner she had prepared for herself when the phone rang. Again she stiffened. Again she went through the exercise of not wanting to answer then deciding she had to because it could be Lisa or Helen calling.

Warily she picked up the phone. "Hello?"

"Hi, beautiful."

Colt's voice went through her like a hot knife cutting butter. Her reaction startled her. Knowing she was intensely attracted to Colt was one thing; physical proof was quite another.

"Uh, hi."

"I was wondering if you'd changed your mind about my coming over this evening." His tone was smooth as silk, a bedroom voice if she'd ever heard one, and she didn't have to think about it to know what was on his mind.

Well, it was on her mind, too. Behind everything else she had thought, said or done since Colt had left the house lay the hot, steamy memory of what they'd done on the sofa.

Before she could pull her thoughts together enough to answer, he asked softly, "Are you still wearing that sexy sundress?"

She swallowed nervously. "No, and I haven't changed my mind about your coming over, either."

"What *are* you wearing?"

"Nothing that would give you any funny ideas," she retorted, albeit weakly.

He laughed lazily in her ear. "Sweetheart, all I have to do is think of you and I get all sorts of ideas. I wouldn't exactly call them funny, though. Everyone sees things differently, however. Do you feel that what we did today was funny?"

"I'm not talking about ha-ha funny, and you know it."

"Then you mean peculiar? Strange? I really don't think those words fit, either. Let's try for another term, okay? How about exciting? Fantastic?" His voice dropped to a lower pitch, all signs of levity gone. "Theo, invite me over. Tell me you want to see me. I sure want to see you."

Her heart was beating in double time. He was right. Exciting and fantastic were much better terms than strange and peculiar for what they'd done. But there was more to a relationship than great sex, much more.

Besides, she didn't trust him. Maybe he was a little more subtle than Jordan—displaying total boredom over her inheritance—but that could be because he was smarter than Jordan. A little wilier, craftier.

No, until she scratched his outrageously handsome surface and understood who was really lurking under his tanned and glorious skin, it was hands-off, no matter how much she herself wanted another session such as had occurred today between them.

"Don't come over," she said coolly. "I'm going to bed early."

"Ah, what a picture that paints in my mind. What do you wear to bed, light of my life? Something lacy, I'll bet. Short and lacy. Or maybe nothing. Maybe you sleep in the buff like I do."

"Colt, stop it!" Damn him, his sexy remarks were giving her hot flashes. He slept nude. Great, just great. Now she had another discomfiting image to endure. She'd probably roll and toss all night because of today.

"Colt, I'm hanging up now," she said stiffly. "Goodbye." She started to put down the phone.

"Wait!"

Theo returned the phone to her ear. "What?"

"Theo, I have to be out of the area for a couple of days. I'm leaving early in the morning. There's a piece of land I want to take a look at over by Miles City. Why don't you come with me?"

"Don't be absurd. In the first place I've got too much to do here to be going anywhere for a couple of days, and in the second, what makes you think I'd want to spend that much time with you?"

"You'd love every minute of it, I guarantee it," he purred.

"I most certainly would not!"

"The nights, especially."

"Oh, go to hell!" This time Theo slammed the phone down, hard. Overly agitated, she picked it up and slammed it down again. Then, groaning, she put her face in her hands. She was losing it, obviously. Getting so angry that she battered the telephone wasn't like her. But how dare Colt rub her nose in her misstep today? *The nights, especially.*

"Conceited jerk," she muttered.

Theo kept looking out her windows at Nan's house. The front porch light and one at the back of her house had come on with darkness, but Maude's place had the same sort of apparatuses, light-sensitive timers that automatically turned on the outside lights when the sun went down. Nan still hadn't come home.

As Theo had suspected, when she finally went to bed she rolled and tossed instead of falling asleep.

This couldn't go on. She either had to get Colt out of her system or learn to trust him. Maybe his trip to Miles City was the opportune time to do her snooping.

She could…she could do what? Frowning in the dark of her bedroom, she struggled with ideas on how best to learn about Colt, both his past and the present. Going to the law and asking questions about him seemed a bit much. She discarded that idea at once.

But there had to be people who would happily gossip their hearts out about everyone in Hattie, Colt included. All she had to do was find them.

Yeah, she thought cynically. All she had to do was find them. Tall order, Theo, very tall order.

Chapter Thirteen

The next morning, still in her robe and slippers, Theo ran out into her front yard to check what she believed to be Nan's living room windows. The drapes were still drawn; Nan *must* have gone somewhere.

But what if...? Theo's heart nearly stopped. Nan wasn't inside and too ill to come to the door, was she? Worse scenarios than that raced through Theo's mind. Frantic suddenly, she looked around the neighborhood. Nan had lived here for years; everyone on the block had to know her.

Spotting a middle-aged man coming out of his house across the street, Theo left her yard and darted toward him. "Sir? Hello? Could I speak to you for a moment?"

The man was heading for his car in his driveway. He stopped with a curious expression. Theo arrived a bit out of breath. "I'm sorry to bother you and I apologize for the way I'm dressed, but do you know Nan Butler?"

The man nodded. "Certainly. Why?"

"Well, I'm living in Maude's house...."

"Yes, I know you are. You're her granddaughter, I believe."

"No...no, I'm not. But that's neither here nor there. I'm worried about Nan. She appears to be gone, but then it occurred to me that she might be home and..." Theo's fears got stuck in her throat. She took another tack. "What I'm getting at is, would you have any idea if she really did go somewhere? Or if you don't, do you know of someone in the neighborhood who might know where she is?"

The man offered his hand. "Bill Parsons."

Theo smiled thinly but shook his hand. "Theo Hunter. About Nan..."

"She went to visit her sister in Helena. Does that about three, four times a year. She'll be back in a few days. Never stays very long."

Theo heaved a relieved sigh. "Thank you. I don't know why I got so alarmed. I mean, I hardly know Nan, but things happen, and..."

"Don't apologize, Theo. In this neighborhood we look out for one another. I think it's highly commendable that you even noticed her absence." Bill Parsons smiled. "You're going to fit in very nicely. Is there a Mr. Hunter?"

"Uh...no." And she wasn't going to fit in very nicely for long, either, but she couldn't explain herself to Mr. Parsons, especially while dressed in her nightgown and bathrobe. "Thank you," she said again, easing toward the street. "It was very nice meeting you."

"Nice meeting you, Theo. Stop in and say hello to the missus sometime. We should all get acquainted."

"Thanks, I'll try to do that."

Theo dashed back across the street and into her house. Okay, she thought. Nan really was gone. Mr. Parsons figured she wouldn't be back for a few more days, so there would be no conversation with her elderly neighbor today and probably not tomorrow.

In the meantime, because Colt, too, was out of the area, Theo had come up with several other ideas. She ate breakfast, then for today's outing dressed in one of her really striking summer slack suits. It was white with navy blue piping around the lapels, and her accessories were navy-and-white mid-heeled pumps and handbag. When her hair and makeup were perfect, she sat down at the kitchen table to call a taxi.

Then she remembered what Marion had said about Bob Turlow renting out his used cars. Yes, that would be much better than a taxi, Theo decided, looking up Turlow's Used Cars in the phone book. Some of the things she had in mind really required her own transportation.

It took a while, but she finally secured the kind of vehicle she wanted, using one of her credit cards for payment. Mr. Turlow had been most cooperative, and had promised to deliver the vehicle within a half hour.

Theo poured herself a cup of coffee, heated it in the microwave and sat down to wait.

Locating the Murdoch Land and Cattle Company was a snap, though Theo was surprised when she arrived in her rented, immaculate four-wheel-drive vehicle and saw an attractive A-frame building. The entire front of the structure was glass, except for a minimum of cross beams for window supports. The rest of the structure was weathered cedar shakes, and the many pine trees around it added to its rustic appearance. It had a large front porch with wooden half barrels spilling brightly colored petunias and marigolds, and Theo also noted two umbrella tables, each with four chairs.

The parking area contained one car, a light blue sedan. Theo parked next to it, turned off the ignition, then drew a breath that wasn't altogether steady. Colt wasn't here, so why was she nervous? Was she afraid that she might meet a woman named Ruth in that office building?

But wasn't that one of the reasons she was here? There definitely was a woman inside. Theo could see her through the front windows, not in detail but clearly enough that she wasn't confused about the woman's gender. The woman seemed to be watching her, as well, probably wondering why she had parked and not come in.

Taking the keys from the ignition, Theo dropped them into her purse and got out. It was a lovely morning with clean, clear air, and climbing the four stairs to the building's porch, Theo noticed water droplets sparkling on the flowers in the split barrels. Obviously someone had recently watered the plants, and just as obvious, someone was keeping this place in very good order. The porch was swept clean and the outside furniture was dust-free and ready for usage.

Pushing open the door, Theo walked in. The woman smiled invitingly and stood up from her desk. "Good morning," she said brightly.

"Good morning," Theo replied. "I was admiring your flowers on the way in." She was eyeing the woman, who was extremely attractive with her honey blond hair and dark eyes, but at least forty-five years old. Could she be Ruth?

"They really perk up the porch, don't you think? I love flowers. My yard is full of them. Gardening is a passion of mine. Please, come and sit down."

"Is it all right if I look around first?"

"Oh, yes, of course. Look around all you want." The woman came around the desk. "I'm Terry Driscoll." She held out her hand.

Theo took it. "I'm—" she cleared her throat "— Elaine Hunter." Elaine was her middle name, so it wasn't a lie. But it was entirely possible that Colt had mentioned Theodora Hunter as being the new owner of that eight-hundred-acre tract he wanted to buy, and she preferred to talk to Terry Driscoll as a total stranger. Hopefully Terry wouldn't pick up on the name *Hunter*.

Relieved that she wasn't Ruth, Theo heartily shook her hand.

"Are you interested in a particular type of land?" Terry asked as Theo wandered over to a freestanding billboard displaying photos of land.

"Not really," Theo answered, turning to survey the office in general. Besides Terry's desk, there was another—Colt's, undoubtedly. And there was a long table with six upholstered chairs neatly placed around it. There were green plants, a good half-dozen file cabinets, and the usual office equipment—typewriter, copy machine, calculator—with the notable exception of a computer. No computer. Odd in this day and age, Theo thought.

"Actually, I'm just nosing around at the present," she told Terry.

"You're new to Hattie," Terry said.

"Very new."

"It's a great little town, Elaine. The people are friendly and we're not that far from Helena, which takes up the slack in the shopping department. We're proud of our progressive school district, and we have some very good doctors and a small hospital. Do you have children?"

Theo smiled. "No. I'm not married."

Terry smiled back. "Well, neither am I, but I was and I have two teenage sons." She rolled her eyes humorously. "You haven't lived until you've dealt with teenage sons." Her smile remained firmly in place. "How about a cup of coffee?"

"Yes, thanks."

Terry went to a counter at the back of the room. "Milk or sugar?" she called.

"Milk, please."

Terry returned with two ceramic mugs of steaming coffee, one of which she passed to Theo. "Be careful. It's hot. Come on, let's sit down." Instead of leading Theo to her desk, Terry brought her to the long table.

The chair Theo sat in was comfortable, and she placed her mug on the table when Terry set hers down. Since there were no rings or scars on the tabletop, Theo decided it must have a protective finish.

"I love your suit, Elaine." She smiled. "I'm sure you didn't buy it in Hattie. Where are you from?"

Theo hesitated, but then spoke honestly. "California."

Terry nodded knowingly. "Many of our buyers are from California. I've never been there, but from what they've told me, I have the feeling the only things I've missed by not visiting the state are smog and traffic."

Thoughtfully Theo took a sip from her mug. Lord knows California had smog and traffic problems, but it had so much more than that, positive things, good things—the ocean, mountains and desert to name three. And every cultural advantage one could think of—theater, art, music, it was all there. However, she wasn't here to discuss California, either its good or bad points.

"Do you own this company?" she asked, merely to start the ball rolling in the direction she wanted it to go.

"Me? Good heavens, no." Terry laughed, and she had a very nice laugh, Theo decided. Warm and friendly. She liked this woman, which she hadn't anticipated happening, and deceiving her to gather information about Colt suddenly made her feel uneasy. "Colt Murdoch is the owner, Elaine," Terry said. "He's out of town today, but I'm sure I can help you with any questions you might have about the area or any land we have for sale."

Theo sighed inwardly. She was here, and she had already committed her crime by leading Terry to believe she had merely wandered in. She may as well stay and learn what she could about Colt.

"Then you work for Mr. Murdoch," Theo murmured. "Are you his only employee?"

"In here, yes. He has employees at the ranch, of course."

"He owns a ranch, also?"

Terry nodded before sipping her coffee. "It's been in his family for several generations."

Theo smiled indulgently, woman to woman. "Does *he* have teenage sons?"

Terry laughed. "He might as well have, but no, he has no children of his own."

The quixotic remark made Theo sit up straighter. "But he's married," she said quietly, fishing for more, needing to hear more.

"Oh, no," Terry said with a shake of her head. "He's never been married, though only the good Lord knows why not. He's the best-looking guy in Montana, I swear. If I were fifteen years younger..." She chuckled. "Actually, he's a great boss. I really love my job. I've had to work since I got out of high school and this is the best job I've ever had. How about you? Do you have a job in Hattie?"

"Uh...no."

"If you're looking for one, maybe I can help you out. Ask around, you know? I know almost everyone in town and would be more than glad to—"

Theo cut in. "Terry, that's very nice of you, but I'm not looking for work."

"Oh. Well, if you change your mind..."

"I won't. I'm not staying in Hattie for long, Terry."

"But you're interested in buying some land?"

She was perplexing Terry, Theo realized. Here was her first real lie, and it didn't come out easily. "Strictly for investment purposes." She had absolutely no intention of investing in anything in or around Hattie. Good grief, she already had a list of real estate to get rid of. Why would she burden herself with more?

But the lie worked. Terry's expression of perplexity vanished. "Many of our customers buy for investment. And land *is* a good investment, Elaine. Land values are doubling, tripling, appreciating at a rapid rate. Ten years ago you could have bought any number of parcels around Hattie for a hundred dollars an acre, and today some of them are worth five thousand an acre."

"Five thousand?" Theo's left eyebrow shot up. Surely the eight-hundred-acre piece that Colt was going to buy from her wasn't worth that much. Why, that added up to four million dollars! No, she couldn't believe he had that kind of money, nor could she believe the land—as beautiful as it was—was worth that kind of money.

"Of course, those are very special tracts," Terry added. "Now, we have some very nice pieces for four and five hundred an acre. And higher, if you're interested in more expensive property. May I show you some photos of them?"

Theo had to turn the conversation back to Colt. "Terry, I'm sure you're aware of the reputation of some land developers. I don't mean to imply that Mr. Murdoch isn't honest, but..."

Terry looked aghast. "Colt Murdoch is the most honest person I've ever known, Elaine. Believe me, you need have no qualms about doing business with him. If you do, you really should check with the Better Business Bureau and the Bureau of Consumer Affairs. They have offices in Helena. Call them. I promise that you'll hear only positive information regarding Colt's business ethics."

Before Theo could respond, the front door opened and a couple walked in, a man and a woman dressed in jeans and boots.

Terry got up and smiled at the newcomers. "Hello. Would you mind waiting for a few minutes? I'll be with you shortly."

This looked like the perfect time to make an exit, Theo thought. Gathering her purse, she got to her feet. "Terry, I really must be going. Thank you so much for your time."

"They won't mind waiting, Elaine," Terry said in an undertone. "Please don't rush off."

"I'm sorry, but I have an appointment." Her second lie.

"Oh, I see. Well, let me give you some information on various pieces of land to take with you. You can look it over and get back to me if you have any questions."

"Thank you."

Terry dashed about, gathering photos and papers, which she put in a file folder and handed to Theo. "Even if our land doesn't interest you, Elaine, stop in again. I enjoyed talking to you," Terry said.

"Thank you, I will. Goodbye."

Back in her vehicle, Theo released the tight control she'd maintained on her emotions in a long sigh. What had she learned? Terry's opinion of Colt's honesty was bound to be biased. But what had that strange remark about Colt and teenage boys been about? *He might as well have sons, but no, he has no children of his own.* Did his friend Ruth have sons?

Theo drove away with an ache in her stomach and a frown. This detective business wasn't her forte and she didn't like it in the least.

But she'd gone this far, and something within her was forcing her to continue her quest. If she could learn all of the truths there were to know about Colt, she would also know how to deal with him when he returned from Miles City. He would contact her, she'd bet on it. It was definitely in her best interests to be prepared.

After all, she was afraid she was falling in love with him, and falling for a man she neither knew very well nor trusted was dangerous business.

Sighing again, Theo wished that Nan hadn't picked this particular time to visit her sister. For some reason Theo felt that the elderly woman could tell her everything she yearned to know about Colt.

It would be much simpler to have a nice long chat over a cup of tea than run around the country playing detective, that was certain.

Jordan was sitting at his desk. The silence of the building was driving him up the wall. Without Marion's warm and pleasing presence the place felt as dead as a tomb. In four hours the telephone had rung exactly once. A woman seeking information about a divorce was thrilled to find herself talking to a lawyer rather than a secretary, and she had immediately begun a barrage of questions with barely a breath between them. Finally Jordan had broken in coldly, saying, "I'll be happy to answer all of your questions, ma'am, but you'll have to make an appointment." Marion had been his buffer between people looking for free advice and him, and he sorely missed her efficient tactfulness.

He sighed despondently. He missed her. In every way possible. Nothing was working out. Theo had resented his sending her flowers almost as much as she'd resented his firing Marion. The hard, painful truth was beginning to sink in: he had no chance with Theo.

And now he probably didn't even have Marion. He'd called her house three times this morning and gotten her answering machine. He'd hung up each time without leaving a message. How could he talk to a damned machine? He needed to talk to her. Face-to-face would be best, but he doubted that she would let him in if he knocked on her door.

Life was the pits right now. Everyone and everything was against him, even Marion.

It wasn't fair. He didn't deserve what was happening to him.

Or did he? Fear rose in his throat, tasting like bitter bile. There had to be a way out, some sort of solution to his dilemma.

Trembling, he popped an antacid into his mouth. Then he reached for the phone and dialed Marion's number again.

"Hello. I'm not available at the moment, but please call back or leave a message. I'll return your call if you leave your name and number. Thank you."

Cursing violently, he slammed down the phone.

It was almost four hundred miles to Miles City from Hattie, a long drive. Colt had started the trip before dawn and reached his destination around one that afternoon. Locating the Realtor with the land for sale, he obtained maps and directions, telling the man that he preferred looking at the property alone.

At first sight of the land he knew immediately that it wasn't for him. Ordinarily he paid very little attention to advertisements listing property for sale that wasn't near Hattie, but the price of this particular land was so low, he'd thought he should take a look at it. It was easy to decide against it. Barren and rocky, it held absolutely no eye appeal. He'd known beforehand that it was too far away from his base of operation, but had it been good land, he would have adjusted his sales routines to the distance and made money from it.

Feeling the need for a little exercise after sitting behind the wheel all day, he got out of the Bronco and walked onto the property. No, it wasn't for him, he decided again. But it was a beautiful sunny day and a short hike before driving back to Miles City would feel good. He had nothing better to do for the balance of the day anyway. His plan was to spend the night in a motel and return to Hattie in the morning.

It was isolated land, with nothing—not even wandering beeves—or no one in sight. Tramping around for about a half hour, he stretched his back and then sat down on a large gray boulder. He'd thought of Theo for most of the day, and again she invaded his mind.

The thing that kept eating at him was her remark about her net worth, her innuendo that he was more interested in her inheritance than he was in her. How could she think that about him? Didn't she sense how he felt about her? The kind of man he was?

But then, he hadn't always been the man he was today, had he? Maybe she'd heard old tales. For dead certain, good old Jordy would be glad to fill her in, anytime she gave him an opening.

Squinting his eyes at the horizon, Colt wondered just how much Jordan had told Theo about him. Not that the truth was all that bad, but it was bad enough and Jordy might have made it sound a hell of a lot worse than it was. Remembering how Jordan had delighted in stirring up trouble in his youth, Colt wouldn't put it past him, especially if he thought it would help his own case with Theo.

Colt heaved a sigh. No matter how far a man went in this world, he brought his past with him. Young people didn't realize that. A lot of them thought they could do anything they pleased, act tough and throw their weight around, give their folks one problem after another, ditch school and hang out with punks, finally end up in trouble with the law, and none of it would matter.

Well, it did matter. He was living proof that it mattered. He'd gone a little wild in his teens. His mother was dead and his old man was well on his way to drinking himself into the same cemetery. The ranch was neglected and Colt didn't give any more of a damn about it than his father did. He went from bad to worse, skipping school, mouthing off, staying out all night if he felt like it, until the night when the police picked him up driving a stolen car. He hadn't known it was stolen. Hell, he'd just met the kid in the back seat who'd told him to go ahead and do the driving. They and three other boys had been drinking beer and driving up and down Hattie's main streets yelling obscenities out the windows, laughing uproariously at people's reactions and just begging for trouble.

Well, they'd gotten it. More than they'd wanted. Certainly a hell of a lot more than Colt had wanted.

He'd changed real fast, Colt recalled wryly. Getting arrested that night had been the best thing that could have happened to him. Not that he'd felt that way at the time, but where would he have ended up without a shock? And six months in "juvie," juvenile detention, had been one hell of a shock.

But none of that had anything to do with his feelings for Theo. And God knows he didn't want her inheritance. The problem was, how did a man convince a woman that he wanted her and to hell with her money?

He really loved her, Colt thought with a sinking sensation in his gut. Why her? Why not one of the many other women he'd dated over the years? Odd how fate, or something, took a man's feelings out of his own hands. He sure hadn't set out to fall in love with Theo, but it had happened all the same.

Like he'd told her, she was the one, the woman he wanted to spend the rest of his life with.

Lord help him if she never reached the point of feeling the same way.

After renting a motel room for the night, Colt carried in his one small bag, set it down and headed for the phone. He placed a credit card call to his office. Terry answered promptly.

"Good afternoon. Murdoch Land and Cattle Company."

"Hi, Terry, it's me. How's everything going?"

"Oh, hi, Colt. Well, so far it's been a pretty good day. The Polsons came back for that twenty acres you showed them last week, and I wrote up the sale. Two other couples hung around for a while, looking at photos and such. I think they're both pretty interested and will be back. And, oh yes, a single woman was in this morning, looking for investment property."

"Sounds like you've been busy."

"That's the name of the game, boss," Terry quipped.

"Sure is. The single lady you mentioned . . . do you think she's a serious buyer?"

"Well . . . it's hard to say. She's really pretty, and her clothes were gorgeous. I think she's got the money to make investments, but you know, she seemed more interested in talking about you than land."

Colt's eyes narrowed. "Is that a fact? Hmm. What color hair did she have?"

"Auburn. Long and curly. Really beautiful hair. Why?"

"And green eyes, by any chance?"

"Yes! How'd you know?"

"What name did she give you?"

"Elaine Hunter."

A broad smile broke out on Colt's face and elation suddenly zinged through his system.

"Colt, do you know her?" Terry asked.

"Yep, sure do. Thanks, Terry. See you tomorrow."

He hung up grinning.

Chapter Fourteen

When Theo got home from her second outing of the day, the sun was low on the horizon, beginning its descent behind the mountains to the west of Hattie. After her visit to Colt's office, Theo had rushed home, changed into jeans and walking shoes, then gone shopping in search of a good pair of binoculars. She'd found some at the hardware store and bought the best the proprietor had in stock.

Only a little worried that she might have trouble locating her eight hundred acres, she'd driven her rented four-wheeler out of town, heading, she'd believed, in the right direction. Ultimately she had found the tract, then she'd locked the vehicle into four-wheel drive and taken it onto the property, pointing it at the hills separating her land from Colt's ranch. When the terrain became too steep and rough even for the four-wheeler, she'd gotten out with the binoculars and hiked the rest of the way.

At the crest of the hills, it had surprised her to see that the Murdoch ranch lay directly below her point of view. Great, she'd thought, and had settled herself down with the binoculars to get a really good look at the place.

She'd seen plenty, though what it all meant eluded her. There were cowhands working at various jobs, but they were all boys, or rather, very young men. Teenagers, by the look of them. And she'd seen a woman and a very young boy—about six or seven years of age—as well. Something had told her she was looking at Ruth, and it wasn't a pleasant sensation, because the woman was slender and attractive.

She had also checked out the ranch itself—the large, old-fashioned two-story house, the barn, several buildings she couldn't identify, corrals, fences and animals.

But the people were the most intriguing. Did Colt hire boys to do the work on his ranch because they came cheaper than seasoned cowhands? That idea didn't sit very well with Theo, forming some uneasy questions in her mind about Colt's business ethics—regardless of Terry's high praise.

At any rate, she had returned home feeling puzzled, unnerved and even more questioning about Colt than she'd been before today. Adding to her disappointment was Nan's dark house: Nan still hadn't come back from Helena.

There was only one other person she could think of who might have information about Colt and be willing to pass it on: Marion Roth. Of course, there was Jordan, but Theo didn't trust anything he might tell her about Colt, not when he so obviously viewed Colt as an enemy.

But how would Marion receive a call from her? Theo had nothing to feel guilty over. Jordan had deliberately misled her about his being a totally unencumbered man, but did Marion know that? Theo doubted it. And it was entirely possible that Marion blamed Theo for losing her job, besides resenting her for coming between her and Jordan.

Marion should be informed of the truth on several matters, Theo thought grimly. And it was possible she knew something of Colt's history. Theo weighed the idea while taking a shower, necessary because she had gotten very hot and sweaty on that hilltop spying on the Murdoch Ranch and its occupants through her expensive binoculars.

God, she was doing things she never would have thought herself capable of before meeting and falling for Colt, she realized unhappily. Was that what falling in love did to a woman? Turn her into someone else? Why was she crossing moral boundaries that she wouldn't even have gotten near prior to the past few days?

Theo knew the answer to that question: somewhere inside her resided a hope that Colt really did love her. A hope that her inheritance had nothing to do with his declarations of affection or his desire for her. He had made such fantastic love to her. Should nothing come of their relationship, his lovemaking wasn't something she would get over easily, and certainly it would remain a memory with painfully durable ramifications.

"Okay, where's your courage now?" she muttered to her reflection in the steamy mirror while drying off. Marion wasn't an ogre, after all. She was a woman with a wound, possibly an unhealable wound, but perhaps she would talk to Theo. It could be that a good long talk would help both of them with their men.

Before she could change her mind, Theo threw on a robe and went to the office. Sitting at the desk and snapping on the lamp, she perused the Hattie telephone directory for Marion Roth's listing. It was easily located, and again, before her courage deserted her, Theo dialed the number.

She frowned through an answering machine message, then spoke at the beep. "Marion, this is Theo Hunter. I would very much like to see you. I think we should talk. Please call me back. My number is—"

"Theo? I'm here. I . . . I've been monitoring my calls."

Marion's voice suddenly in her ear startled Theo, but she quickly recovered. "I do the same thing sometimes, Marion. Listen, the reason I called . . . how do you feel about a meeting between us?"

"I . . . I'm not sure. Do you really feel that we should talk?"

"Yes, I do." Theo was encouraged by Marion's quiet voice. "About several things, to be honest. It's up to you, of course, but I'd like to invite you to come here this evening, or I could go to your place, whichever you'd prefer."

"Well . . . either place would be fine. But do you have transportation? I live on the other side of town from you."

"I rented a car, so transportation's no problem."

"Then come here, if you don't mind."

Theo could hear the tremulous quality that had entered Marion's voice. She was beginning to question Theo's reasons for this call, Theo realized, wondering what topics needed discussion.

"Is your address the one listed in the telephone book?" Theo asked.

"Yes. You shouldn't have any trouble finding my house."

"How about eight?"

"Eight would be fine. I . . . I'll be watching for you."

"Thank you, Marion. See you at eight."

Putting the phone down, Theo sat back feeling satisfied and thankful. Marion hadn't sounded at all angry with her, which was a major step toward a forthright conversation.

Rising, she went to her bedroom to get dressed. She had time to prepare and eat something before going to Marion's, but that was all. She would skip dinner altogether if she wasn't so hungry. But she'd already skipped lunch, and she really did have to have some dinner.

Colt went to a restaurant at six. Back in his motel room an hour and a half later, he kicked off his boots, switched on the TV set and stretched out on the bed. After absent-mindedly flipping through the available channels with the remote control, he turned off the set and laid the remote on the bedstand. Locking his hands behind his head, he stared at the ceiling.

Since talking to Terry, he'd thought of nothing else but Theo going to his office. She'd deliberately gone there when he was out of town, which indicated what? That she wanted to see what he owned without his knowledge? Did that mean that she'd also paid a visit to the ranch?

Reaching out to the phone, he dialed nine for an outside line and called the ranch. Ruth answered. The voices, loud music and laughter in the background evidenced a normal evening in the big old ranch house.

"Hello, Ruth. How's it going?"

"Oh, hi, Colt. Same old same old. Are you still in Miles City?"

"Still here. I'll be back tomorrow. By any chance, did you have a caller today?"

"A caller? I had several, if you're talking about the phone."

"No, a visitor. A woman."

"Nope. Didn't see any sign of a woman." Ruth chuckled. "One of your girlfriends catching up with you, old pal?"

Colt laughed easily. "That's what I'm trying to find out, you Nosy Nellie."

"Well, you can rest easy, sir. She hasn't tracked you to the ranch yet," Ruth said pertly. "Should I post lookouts in the morning, just in case she's armed?"

Again Colt laughed. "Not necessary. How's Petey?"

"My rambunctious six-year-old son has just been put to bed, exhausted as usual."

"Well, say hi to the other boys for me. I'll sign off now. See you sometime tomorrow."

"G'night, Colt. Sleep well."

"You, too. Good night."

Hanging up, Colt lay back on the pillows. So...Theo had gone to his office but not to the ranch. What should he think about that, or should he think anything at all about it? Maybe it meant nothing. Maybe she really was looking for some investment property.

"Naw," he mumbled, immediately deeming that idea as preposterous. She'd gone to his office to snoop, the little imp. He smiled, pleased that she would bother.

In fact, her snooping pleased him so much he felt an enormous urge to talk to her. Looking up her number in his little black book, he placed the call.

Theo was on the run, clearing the table and dropping the few dishes she'd used into the sink. When the phone rang, she tossed it an impatient look, but as usual felt duty-bound to answer it.

Grabbing it, she tucked it under her chin and continued to clear away the dishes and leftover food from the table. "Hello?"

"Hi, beautiful."

"Colt?" She would swear that her heart did a somersault in her chest. "Uh...aren't you supposed to be in Miles City?"

"That's where I am, sweetheart. I'll be home tomorrow—probably early afternoon. Can I stop by and say hello before I go to my office and check in with my secretary? I like to keep track of any customers that come in during my absences." He had to clear his throat to keep from laughing, because he'd bet anything Theo was mentally squirming about now.

She was. "Um, I...I'm going to be busy," she said nervously. Putting a carton of milk and a bottle of catsup into the refrigerator, she closed the door then leaned against it. If he kept track of every customer who walked through the door of his office, Terry would tell him about her visit, she thought weakly.

But she'd known, or at least suspected, that Colt would find out what she'd done. To hell with it, she thought, pushing away from the fridge to take the cutlery she'd used for dinner from the table to the sink.

"I'm in a motel room," Colt said, grinning devilishly as he spoke. "Real nice room, cozy as can be and with a great bed. King-size. Much too large for one lonely man."

"I'm sure you don't have to be lonely if you don't want to be," Theo retorted. Imagining him in a "real nice" motel room with a king-size bed caused her pulse to flutter. He'd asked her to go with him. She could be in that room with him right now.

"Yeah, but I'm real picky about who I invite into my life, Theo."

"Are you?"

"Do you doubt it?" His voice had become soft and silky.

"I don't know what to believe or doubt about you, and I think you know that." Theo glanced at the wall clock and decided she had about ten minutes to spare. Flirting with Colt on the phone was exciting ... and safe. She could say anything she chose and he was too far away to act upon it. The thought made her smile.

"I know only one thing right now, sweetheart. I wish you were here with me."

Theo's heart went *kaboom!* "For what reason?" she asked coyly.

He laughed, deep in his throat. "Take a wild guess."

"Obviously you're thinking about that big bed."

"Bingo," he breathed in her ear. "Now, tell me you're not too busy to see me when I get back tomorrow."

"Oh, but I am."

"You were busy today, too, right?" She'd been busy, all right, checking him out. He sure did like that picture.

"Very busy. You were, too, weren't you? You're probably worn-out from tramping over that land you went there to see." The teasing, flirtatious tone of her own voice surprised Theo. Flirting with Colt just came naturally, apparently, especially when he was too far away to do anything about it.

"I'm not a bit worn-out," he said with a sexy chuckle. "I'd prove it, too, if you were within reach."

"But I'm not within reach."

"You will be tomorrow."

Smiling, Theo drew a breath. "But I'll be busy working."

"You little devil. You know you're driving me crazy, don't you?"

"Of course not. We're having a simple conversation. Why would that drive you crazy?"

"Simple conversation, my eye. What were you doing when I called?"

"Clearing the table. Does that excite you?"

"Anything you do excites me."

"Well, the next time I see you, I'll clear the table and give you some kicks."

He chuckled. "Yeah, right. Listen, if you're going to be too busy to see me when I get back, how about dinner together tomorrow night? The restaurant might even let you clear the table. Just think how worked up and excited I'd get, how I'd suffer. That should be incentive enough for you to say yes."

Theo had to laugh. "Do you think I would enjoy watching you suffer?"

"Yeah, I think you would." His voice dropped to a lower, more intimate pitch. "I'm suffering over you, Theo. I never thought falling in love made people suffer. I wonder if it's that way with everyone."

Theo's heart was suddenly in her throat. "I...wouldn't know."

"You've never been in love?"

Not until now. Oh God, she really was in love with him. And she had so many unanswered questions about him. Disturbing questions. Disturbing doubts.

"Change the subject, Colt," she said in a barely audible whisper.

"Makes you uncomfortable to talk about it, doesn't it?"

"When I'm so uncertain, yes." Her gaze fell on the clock again. "Colt, I have to hang up. I...have an appointment."

"At this time of night?" Colt's stomach dropped. "Do you have a date, Theo?" Not with Jordan, he prayed. But not with any other man, either.

There was nothing wrong with her going to see Marion, Theo thought, no reason to keep it a secret.

"I'm going to Marion Roth's house. I told her I'd be there at eight."

Colt was silent for a moment. "I see."

"You don't approve."

"I don't have any feelings about it, one way or the other. It just surprised me. I didn't know you two were becoming friends."

"Well, I hope that will be the outcome," Theo said. "Anyway, I have to hang up. I don't want to keep her waiting."

"Right. Theo, about dinner tomorrow night...?"

Theo heaved a sigh. They weren't talking silly and flirting now. There was something deadly serious in his voice and certainly she felt it in her own system.

"Colt, I don't know," she said slowly, uneasily.

"You told me to call before coming by, and that's what I'm doing."

"You're asking for a date," she said, a little sharply. "If I believed all you wanted was dinner together..."

"But you know I want more."

"Don't you?"

"Let me tell you what I want, Theo. I want to make love to you, every day and every night. I want us to discuss a future together. I want to show you my ranch, and introduce you to the people on it." His lips formed a little half grin. "I want to show you around my land company, introduce you to Terry, my secretary." His grin disappeared. "I want you in every part of my life. In short, baby, I want you, your thoughts, your time, your love."

Theo's knees gave out, and she fell onto the nearest chair. "You want only a few trivial things, I see," she mumbled, attempting levity and failing entirely.

"God, I wish you were here." Colt sounded almost angry, and certainly impatient. He wished something else, that he'd driven home this afternoon instead of staying the night. Flirting on the phone was fun for a while, but he should be saying these things to Theo in person. He wanted her in his arms so badly right now, he ached.

"I . . . I have to go," Theo croaked in a weak little voice.

"Yeah, I know you do. I'll see you tomorrow. Good night."

The click of his phone in her ear startled Theo. He was going to see her tomorrow, whether she objected or not.

Trembling, she put down the phone and got up. If she was going to arrive at Marion's on time, she had to leave now, shaking in her shoes or not.

As Marion had promised, Theo easily found her house. She pulled into the vacant driveway, thinking that Marion's car must be in the garage. It was a very nice brick house with white trim, and the double garage was attached. There was a light on at the front door and a lamp in a window. The backyard was fenced, and there were so many large shrubs and decorative bushes around the house, Theo couldn't see anything else.

Getting out, she took a breath—admitting some nervousness—and walked to the front door. There was a doorbell, which she rang. After a moment, the door opened.

Marion smiled at her. "Hello."

"Hello, Marion."

"Come in." Marion stepped back and Theo went in.

Marion brought her to the living room. "Please sit down." She waved her hand. "Anywhere."

"Thank you." Theo sank onto the sofa, glancing around the nicely decorated room. "Your home is very attractive."

"Thank you. It was my mother's house. I grew up in Billings. After my father died—about five years ago—Mother moved us here and bought this place. She passed away two years ago."

"I'm sorry," Theo murmured. Marion was wearing white jeans, a pink blouse and white canvas shoes. She looked very pretty...and very young.

She was still standing. "I'm going to have a glass of wine. Would you care to join me?"

"Why...yes. Thank you." Being offered wine surprised Theo, but maybe it shouldn't have, she thought. Maybe wine was best for this meeting, more relaxing than tea or coffee. And God knows she could do with less tension. Colt's call had really thrown her for a loop, and now this, although Marion seemed calm and collected, thank goodness.

Marion left for a few minutes, then returned with two stemmed glasses. It was white wine, Theo saw, and when she took the glass Marion held out, she could feel that it had been nicely chilled. "Thank you."

"You're welcome." Marion sat in a wing chair that directly faced the sofa. She lifted her glass. "Well, here's to...to what, Theo?"

"Friendship?" Theo waited, all but holding her breath. Marion could cut her to pieces, if she chose.

But Marion merely nodded. "To friendship."

They sipped from their glasses, with Theo feeling enormously relieved. Colt had said Marion was a nice woman, and it appeared that he was right.

"I feel as though I should still call you Miss Hunter," Marion said quietly.

Theo smiled. "Please don't. Feel that way, I mean. This is very good wine," she added after another sip.

Marion looked down at her glass, appearing to be studying its contents. "Jordan bought it." Her eyes rose to meet Theo's. "He always buys the best of everything."

It was as though Jordan himself had just entered the room. Theo sat up straighter. "You know he's one of the reasons I came to talk to you, don't you?"

"I suspected."

"Marion, I'm so terribly sorry if I hurt you in any way. I didn't know there was anything between you and Jordan."

"He led you to believe that," Marion said softly. "It was necessary to his plan."

Theo frowned. "His plan?"

"His plan to marry you for your inheritance." Marion got up, as though she'd suddenly become too agitated to sit still. "I've struggled with this ever since your call. Should I tell you the truth or should I protect Jordan with lies? I love him, you know. I'll probably always love him. But..." She brushed away a tear and laughed shakily. "I told myself I wasn't going to get emotional, but I've been nothing but emotional since he fired me."

Theo felt utterly wretched. "I was so worried you might think I had something to do with that. I didn't, Marion, I swear it."

"I know you didn't. He...he's been calling. Almost hourly. Mostly without leaving a message, but I know it's him. I haven't talked to him. I can't. Not yet. Maybe...someday, but not yet."

"He's probably terribly sorry for what he did."

"Knowing Jordan I'm sure he is, but I've discovered that a woman reaches a stopping point. I really can't deal with any more pain from him." She sighed. "No matter how much I love him."

"I understand," Theo murmured.

"Do you? Have you had a similar experience?"

"Every woman probably has a story to tell about a man, Marion. Maybe not similar to yours, but no less painful." Theo smiled tremulously. "Actually, I'm...I..." She stopped for a swallow of wine, wondering how to proceed, how to turn the conversation to Colt.

Marion was looking at her curiously. "Do you have someone in California?"

Theo shook her head. "No, but..." She hesitated a moment. "Marion, do you know Colt Murdoch?"

"Colt? I know him well enough to say hello, but that's about it. Are you aware how much Jordan dislikes him?"

"Yes, and I have to ask. Do you know why he's so dead set against Colt?"

"No, I really don't. Not precisely, anyway. I think it goes back to their childhood, as silly as that sounds. I mean, we all remember kids we didn't like when we were kids ourselves, but don't most people outgrow such foolishness?"

"Apparently Jordan hasn't."

Marion returned to her chair. "Theo, are you asking about Colt for a reason?" Her voice became gentle. "Is he your story?" She looked thoughtful then. "It just occurred to me. If Jordan thought you were seeing Colt...? *Have* you been seeing him?"

Silently Theo nodded. "Marion, I met both Jordan and Colt on the same day, the day of Maude's funeral. They're charming, handsome men and I liked them both. I'm afraid my fondness for Jordan diminished greatly when I learned about you. Especially since he hadn't told me about you himself. You said he had a plan to marry me for my inheritance. Do you think that he actually believed I was that gullible?"

Marion sighed. "Yes, I think he did. The male ego can sometimes be astounding."

"More often than not," Theo said with a frown. Colt could be wearing the same hat as Jordan. Had she learned anything about him today to convince her otherwise?

She gave a shaky little laugh. "I have the feeling that you and I are in the same leaky boat, Marion."

"You're in love with Colt," Marion said with some sadness. "And you're wondering if he isn't doing the same thing Jordan was, wooing you for your inheritance."

Theo finished the wine in her glass before answering. "I keep wondering if I'm even close to the truth of Colt's true nature. Jordan told me that Colt spent six months in prison. Do you know anything about that?"

Marion's pretty face registered shock. "In prison! Colt? I find that very hard to believe. Of course, you have to remember that there are things that have happened in his life before I even knew who he was." Her expression softened. "Have you asked him about it?"

"No, and I'm not sure I can. But I think that's why I keep doubting what he says about his feelings for me. Wouldn't you think he would tell me about it without my opening the subject?"

"He's told you he loves you?"

"Yes, but so did Jor—" Theo stopped. "I'm sorry, Marion. I want you to know one thing. Jordan and I were never intimate." It was a delicate subject and Theo prayed that Marion believed her.

"I know. He told me about the night he kissed you." Marion moistened her lips, appearing uncomfortable. "You see, he came from you that night to me."

"He didn't!" Theo exclaimed incredulously.

"I'm afraid he did. Then he convinced me that his plan was sensible, and that your marriage would last for no more than a year. I would be waiting in the wings, so to speak. Once he divorced you, he would be a wealthy man and marry me." She sighed despondently. "I'm ashamed to admit it, but I actually went along with it for a while. Unhappily, unwillingly, but I did agree." Her gaze dropped, then lifted. "So you see, it's I who owe you the apology."

Theo raised her glass and saw that it was empty. "Do you have any more of that wine?" she asked. So Jordan had drawn Marion into his nefarious scheme. The cad.

"I'll get the bottle."

"Please do. I think we have a lot more to discuss about Mr. Murdoch and Mr. Hamilton," she said dryly.

Chapter Fifteen

Jordan drove by Marion's house around eleven that night, hoping for...something. He honestly didn't know what was his hope, or maybe he was just afraid to put it into words. Since Marion wouldn't even talk to him on the phone, she wasn't apt to greet him at her front door with a smile. But he'd never been unhappier, and Marion was the person he longed to see, yearned to talk to.

Everything about her home looked normal to him, except for the strange vehicle parked at the curb. Slowing down to barely a crawl, Jordan gave the dark blue four-wheeler a curious once-over. It looked familiar, but he couldn't quite connect it to anyone. The muscles in his stomach suddenly tensed with dread. If she already had another man...?

He gunned the engine and sped down the block. He had made a mess of his life and didn't know how to correct it. Miserable and heartsick, he drove on home.

* * *

It was after midnight when Theo unlocked the front door of her house and went in. The evening had gone so remarkably well that she couldn't help smiling while getting ready for bed. If nothing else had been accomplished tonight, she had made a friend. After thoroughly dissecting Jordan and Colt, her and Marion's conversation had drifted to themselves, their respective families and events in their lives that had nothing to do with the men they loved. Not only had they talked easily and comfortably, they had laughed together. Giggled, actually. Over the silliest things. It had been a fun, relaxing evening.

But...she had learned very little about Colt. Marion knew nothing of his history, not even gossip, which was probably due to Jordan's attitude toward Colt. Apparently he'd had so little contact with Colt, there'd been no reason to discuss him with Marion. Maude's death and Theo's appearance in Hattie had seemingly refueled an old, old feud between the two men. What was strange was how each man viewed it. Colt took it with a grain of salt, even finding humor in Jordan's animosity, while Jordan disliked Colt to the point of bitterness.

Lying in bed, Theo thought about Colt returning tomorrow. Instantly she felt warmer, languid. She knew he was going to come by, he'd said it plain enough. Sensible or not, his determination was exciting. She frowned. Becoming putty in any man's hands was a horrifying thought, and yet women in love behaved peculiarly, sometimes in direct opposition to their own beliefs and ethics. Marion was a perfect example. Theo would swear that the young woman didn't have a deceitful or dishonest bone in her body, and yet the man she was deeply in love with had convinced her— for a time—that his marrying another woman for her money made sense. If Jordan hadn't panicked and gone too far by firing Marion, she *still* might be involved in his scheme.

But Theo had herself to worry about now. Feeling sexy just from thinking about Colt was a danger signal, if ever there was one. What was she going to do tomorrow when he showed up? How was she going to react if he touched her? Tried to make love to her again?

She swallowed the nervous lump in her throat. If only today's snooping had produced better results. She'd learned nothing negative, she reminded herself. Except for what she'd seen from that hilltop and considered rather unethical, his hiring underage boys to keep his ranch going. But that was really only an infraction of her own personal standards. Terry had had only good things to say about her boss, of course, but then, how many employees would say anything else to a stranger?

Turning over, Theo punched her pillow into a more comfortable configuration. If only she'd been able to talk to Nan. Why, in God's name, hadn't she done so when she'd had the chance?

Yawning, Theo closed her sleepy eyes. It had been awhile since she'd stayed up this late. She hoped that she would be able to sleep a little later in the morning than she usually did to make up for it.

Colt's visit tomorrow could be a real trial. It would definitely be beneficial for her to be clearheaded and alert.

Theo awoke to the lulling sound of rain on the roof. Glancing at the clock, she shuddered. It was only 6:10 a.m. and she was still tired. Snuggling deeper into her blankets, she tried to go back to sleep. But once awake, her brain went into worry mode and her eyes simply wouldn't stay shut.

Finally, grumpily, she threw back the covers and got up. Trudging to the kitchen, she put on a pot of coffee, then trudged to the bathroom for a wake-me-up shower. It worked. Feeling much better, she dressed for the day—choosing off-white slacks and an aqua cotton sweater—fixed her hair and makeup and returned to the kitchen for some breakfast.

The rain sounded pleasant to the ear, but the gray pall outside made it a gloomy day. She would work in Maude's office, she decided, all day unless interrupted.

Maybe Colt wouldn't come by. Her heart fluttered wildly at the thought, almost frighteningly so, and her reaction irritated her.

Theo Hunter, you don't know what *you want! Get a grip, would you?*

Muttering to herself, Theo tidied the kitchen and went to the office to begin working.

Colt's trip back to Hattie followed the same time frame as his drive to Miles City the day before. He left early and arrived in Hattie around one in the afternoon. Pumped up and energetic, even though it was drizzling rain, he drove to the office to check in with Terry.

She had a stack of calls he had to return, and he sat at his desk to do it. He was just finishing up about an hour later when he noticed a red car stopping out front. Recognizing it as Marion Roth's car, the one that had been parked in Theo's driveway for several days before she realized whose it was and had returned it, he got to his feet.

Terry had seen it, too. "Someone's coming," she commented from her desk. Maybe because of the rain it had been a quiet day. She sounded glad to finally see a potential customer.

"It's Marion Roth," Colt told her.

"Oh, you know her."

"Yes. You might, too. She works for Jordan Hamilton." Or she used to, Colt thought wryly, thinking what a horse's behind Jordy truly was. He could have had only one possible motive for firing Marion: to prove to Theo that Marion was unimportant. Well, it hadn't worked. Colt felt proud of Theo's intelligence and ability to see through people's little games.

"Oh, yes, I've seen her before," Terry said. "I've never actually met her, though."

They both watched Marion get out of her car and hurry to the building. She walked in, looking nervous.

Terry smiled in her naturally friendly way. "Hello. Nasty day out there, isn't it?"

"Yes, it is." Marion's eyes were on Colt. "Hello, Colt."

"Marion," he said quietly. "Come in and sit down."

"Uh . . . could I talk to you?" Her glance darted to Terry and back.

Colt understood. She wanted to talk to him in private. "How about going to Herb's for a cup of coffee?"

Marion nodded. "That would be fine, thank you."

Colt grabbed his hat. "See you later, Terry." He escorted Marion from the building and to his Bronco. With the windshield wipers on low, Colt drove to a small café just down the road. The only thing Marion said during the short drive was about the weather. Colt followed her lead, though he was almighty curious about why she wanted to talk to him. They barely knew each other, so this must have something to do with Jordan, he decided a bit uneasily. The last thing he wanted to do was get involved in Marion and Jordan's problems.

They went into the café and took a corner booth. There were only a few occupied tables and booths in the place, so they would have all the privacy Marion seemed to want for this conversation.

Two cups of coffee were delivered to their table, along with a thermal pot so the waitress would not have to keep running over to refill their cups.

Colt took a swallow, while Marion added milk and sugar to her cup. He laid his arms on the table and looked at her, remarking casually, "This must be important."

"It is," Marion said, then stopped to bite her lip. Taking a breath, she spoke again. "I . . . I've never done anything like this before, but I owe it to Theo."

"Theo?" A deep crease appeared between Colt's eyes. "This is about Theo?"

"She came to see me last night. We . . . we talked about a lot of things."

"About me?" His frown went deeper.

"Yes." Marion sipped from her cup, then, nervously, her eyes lifted to meet Colt's across the table. "Are you in love with her?"

As though struck, Colt fell back against the booth. "Marion, at the risk of sounding rude, is that any of your business?"

"No, it isn't, but I still have to know. Are you in love with her?"

Colt shook his head in utter amazement. "Did she send you to talk to me?"

"Lord, no," Marion said with a shudder. "And to tell you the truth, I pray she never finds out about it. After last night I consider her a friend. I realize I'm risking that friendship with this meeting, but if there's anything I can do to help her, I'll do it. She doesn't deserve the treatment she's received in Hattie, Colt. She's warm, friendly and very nice. I really like her. But she's also a very unhappy woman, and that's because of you."

"She told you that? She actually said she's unhappy because of me?" The good mood Colt had arrived in Hattie with was deteriorating rapidly.

"She also said that she's in love with you," Marion said softly.

"In other words, she's unhappy because she's in love with me?" He couldn't even be thrilled over hearing that Theo was in love with him, not when she was unhappy because of it.

"She thinks you're..." Marion hesitated, swallowing hard. Sticking her nose into other people's business didn't come easy for her. But this was so crucial, and she felt so guilty over abetting Jordan's disgusting scheme. "She thinks you're after her inheritance, just as Jordan was. Maybe he still is. I can't believe he would stop trying."

Colt caught the sparkle of tears in her eyes. Marion was emotional about all of this, and why wouldn't she be? He was pretty damned emotional about it himself.

He muttered a curse under his breath, then gulped the rest of the coffee in his cup. After refilling his cup from the pot, he leaned forward.

"Listen, I don't give a sh . . . tinker's damn about Theo's inheritance! I told her that. Why won't she believe me?"

"Is there any reason she should?"

"I'm not a liar, Marion."

"How does she know you're not? After what Jordan pulled, she'll probably never believe another man for as long as she lives."

"Jordan," Colt snarled. "He caused trouble all the time he was growing up and he's still doing it. I'd like to pop him one right on his arrogant nose."

Marion smiled wanly. "So would I."

Colt stared at her. "You're still in love with him."

A sigh lifted Marion's shoulders. "It's unfortunate, but we don't seem to have the power to chose whom we fall in love with."

Recalling himself wondering why he'd fallen for Theo rather than one of the other women he'd dated and known through the years, Colt could only agree.

"Yeah, fate or something seems to do that for us, all right. Well, you came to me. What do you suggest I do?"

"Do? The answer is simple, though actually doing it probably won't be." Marion leaned forward. "Colt, you have to convince Theo of your love. If you really do love her, that is. You still haven't admitted or denied it."

"I do," he said grimly. "I love her more than I ever thought possible. Damn it, I thought falling in love was supposed to make a person happy. None of us are happy, are we?"

"No," Marion said in a quiet little voice.

"I'll bet even old Jordy is miserable. Which is only what he deserves," Colt added bitterly. He studied Marion's forlorn face. "Would you ever take him back?"

"Not without a lot of changes."

"He'll never change, Marion."

She tried to smile. "Never say never, Colt."

There was a pause. They drank coffee and sat there without speaking, each involved in their own thoughts.

Then Colt spoke. "It's all about trust, Marion. I don't see any way to make Theo trust me. She's lumped me with Jordan and that's that."

"Are you giving up then?"

He didn't answer, merely sat there looking grim and defeated.

"Talk to her, Colt. Don't give up. She wants you to prove yourself to her. Do you know what she did yesterday? She went to your office and talked to Terry. She was fishing for information about you, Colt. Then she drove out to that land you want to buy from the estate, hiked up the hill to the property line and spied on the ranch with binoculars."

"You're kidding." She'd spied on the ranch? What in hell for? He'd invited her there and she'd refused to go, several times. What had she expected to see from those hills?

But, mulling it over, he decided that Marion was right: Theo did want him to prove himself. She was afraid to trust him, maybe because of Jordan's bag of tricks, maybe because he himself had done something wrong. He'd moved in on her pretty fast, after all, even though he'd known he should stay away from her until their business deal was consummated.

And that damned inheritance was bound to influence her thinking, too. Wouldn't it influence anyone? Make them wary about advances from the opposite sex? Especially when things were happening so fast?

His eyes narrowed on Marion. "You said you came to me with this because you owed Theo. What makes you think you owe her something?"

Marion was worrying a paper napkin. "Because . . ." She swallowed, appearing anxious and upset. "Because I went along with Jordan's plan to marry her for her inheritance. I let him talk me into it, even though every cell in my body hated the idea. I . . . feel responsible for her unhappiness.

Even for her mistrust of you. I thought that if I told you how she really feels, you'd be able to do something about it. If she didn't love you, it wouldn't matter. But she does. She . . . does." Marion blotted her eyes with the shredded napkin. "I'm sorry, but I've done a lot of crying lately."

"Don't apologize. It took a lot of courage to come to me, Marion, and I'll never forget it." That wasn't to say that he knew what to do with Marion's information. But at least Theo's feelings and qualms weren't just suspicions in his own mind now. It should be so simple. He loved her, she loved him. But circumstances had made a complex relationship out of one that should have gone smoothly from the onset.

Colt drove Marion back to her car. He went into the office to tell Terry he'd be gone for the rest of the day, then returned to the Bronco to wonder what his next move should be. How could he prove himself to Theo? And prove what? That he was trustworthy? That he wouldn't care if she never had a dime of her own?

Driving away, he felt almost crushed from the burden of having to prove intangible things about himself. There was no way to prove something that one couldn't hold in his hand or see with his own eyes, he decided grimly. All he could do was keep on telling Theo how he felt about her. If she never believed him or learned to trust him, he was in for a sorrowful future.

But if she really loved him, so was she. Maybe that was his one ace in the hole.

He pointed the Bronco toward Theo's neighborhood.

Seeing Colt drive up to her curb through the office window, Theo's pulse began racing. Striving for calmness, she took several big breaths, though the way her heart and stomach were fluttering didn't evidence much success. *You're actually feeling giddy, just because he's getting out of his car and coming to your front door!*

It was the God's truth. Because that man out there w. coming to see her, she felt breathless, light-headed and emotional. It was no way to maintain the upper hand, she thought weakly, no way at all.

The doorbell chimed. Pushing her chair back from the desk, Theo forced herself to her feet. Walking through the house at a normal pace, she opened the door. The first thing she noticed was how utterly gorgeous he was with rain glistening in his black hair.

She cleared her throat. "Hello."

Colt replied soberly. "Hello, yourself."

After his flirtatious phone call last night, his almost somber expression surprised Theo. But what had she expected? That he'd grab her and throw her down onto the sofa, or something to that effect?

"Come in," she said, standing back so he could.

"Thanks." Colt stepped over the threshold and then preceded her into the living room. Without an invitation to sit, he sank down on a chair.

Theo perched on a sofa cushion, her hands in her lap. "Uh, you seem different. Is anything wrong?"

"I think something could be wrong, yes."

"Oh. Well . . ." She was at a loss. Something amiss in his life didn't necessarily involve her. In fact, it probably didn't. He must have a lot on his mind at any given moment of any day, what with running both a ranch and a land sales company.

Colt leaned forward, laying his forearms on his thighs. His eyes bored into her. "You're what's wrong."

"Me? What'd I do?" Oh, hell, Terry had told him about Elaine Hunter visiting his office during his absence, he'd put two and two together, and he didn't like the answer.

"I've been doing a lot of thinking," Colt said, almost brusquely. "About you, about me, about us, and I have to ask you something. Do you want me to stop coming around?"

His question nearly floored Theo. Her gaze darted from him, took a turn around the room and returned to his face.

"Is that all it would take, a simple yes from me?" She couldn't believe it, not after the way she'd sniped at him several times and all but thrown him out once or twice.

"Yes," he said. "That's all it would take."

"Why are you putting me on the spot like this?" Her chin tilted up rather defiantly, though she didn't feel defiant, she felt slapped in the face. He hadn't come to this conclusion from doing a lot of thinking about them. Something had happened, and she wanted to know what it was.

"Is that how you feel, that I'm putting you on the spot?"

"How else would I feel?"

"Okay, fine. I guess that's what I'm doing then. You see, Theo, I'm in love with you, and you're not contributing one damned thing to our relationship."

"Not contributing! That's absurd," she scoffed. "In the first place, what makes you so certain there is a relationship?"

"There is as far as I'm concerned." Colt pointed a finger at her. "It's all up to you, isn't it? I wonder if that's fair."

"Well, I certainly have the right to choose who I do or do not like. Everyone does," she said rather sharply.

"Nope, that's where you're wrong. We don't choose who we fall in love with. It just doesn't work that way. Either there's a special chemistry between two people, or there isn't. I feel we have it. Do you?"

They sat there staring at each other. Theo finally took a breath. "Well, I'd certainly like to know what got you on this tangent."

"You're not going to give me a straight answer, are you?" Colt's eyes narrowed to slits. "You're a master at evasion, Theo. Why can't you tell me in plain English how you feel about me?"

Folding her arms across her chest, she looked away from his eyes, which contained an intensity that she found extremely discomfiting. "Maybe I don't know," she mu. bled.

"Like hell you don't," he said softly.

Her head jerked around. "I am not a liar!"

"Neither am I. Nor am I a fortune hunter, a cheat, a swindler or a womanizer. How do you feel about those apples?"

"I…I…you're confusing me!" Getting to her feet, Theo then wondered why. She couldn't just go off to another room and leave him behind. For one thing, if he took the notion, he'd follow her. It was just that she didn't know what she should be doing about now. Maybe she should tell him yes, that she didn't want him coming around anymore. But it wasn't true. In fact, it was so far from the truth that the mere thought of it made her stomach roll sickishly.

"*You're* confusing me," Colt retorted accusingly. "That's what you've done best since the day we met." He grinned slightly. "Except for that one time." Deliberately he looked at the sofa.

Theo flushed hotly. Not from embarrassment, but from her own feverish memories.

"If I'm such a confusing person, why do you even want to come around?" she asked acidly.

His reply was instantaneous. "Because I hope someday to convince you of my feelings for you. I don't want you to doubt me, Theo, not about anything. I know you're worried that I'm only interested in your inheritance. Well, I'm not. I told you that before. The problem there is that I don't know how to earn your trust. Maybe you know. Tell me what I can do to make you trust me."

She looked so forlorn standing there that he got up and went over to her. She didn't recoil or try to elude what she had to know was coming. Tenderly Colt put his arms around her and drew her head against his chest. He pressed a kiss into her hair and inhaled its clean scent.

"Tell me what I should do, Theo," he whispered. "If you leave it up to me, you know what I'll do. I think of you all

...e time. I want you. I love you. I want us to be together in
...very way possible. You have to open up with me and tell me
what to do. Don't be afraid. I will never knowingly hurt
you.''

She wanted to believe his every word so badly she ached.
Being in his arms was like heaven on earth. But theirs was
no ordinary relationship and they both knew it.

Well, *she* knew it, anyway. She sighed heavily, despondently.

His arms tightened around her. ''Hey, take it easy,'' he
said gently. ''You know, the world isn't going to come to an
end whichever way you decide. It might be a pretty sad place
for a while if you tell me to get the hell out of your life, but
I'll survive and so will you.''

Would she? Tears filled her eyes. Her arms crept up to
hug his waist.

''I . . . I want to love you,'' she whispered.

''What? I didn't hear you. What did you say?'' Colt took
her chin and tipped it up to see her face. Her swimming eyes
touched his soul. ''What did you say, honey?''

Her lashes dropped, concealing her eyes. ''Something I
shouldn't have said. Please forget it.''

He sucked in an unsteady breath. She'd said something
important, too low for him to hear, and now she was reneg-
ing on it. Probably sorry as hell that she'd actually revealed
her true feelings to him.

His patience was running out. He'd begged, pleaded and
groveled enough. If Marion had told him the truth, and
there was no reason to think she hadn't, then Theo loved
him. At the same time she didn't trust him not to betray her
as Jordan had done. Being lumped with Jordan Hamilton
was an insult, and Colt wondered if she knew how big an
insult it really was.

Okay, fine. He'd tried it her way. Now he'd try it his way.
Without warning, he clasped the back of her head and
pressed his lips to hers. It was a rough, aggressive, chal-

lenging kiss. His tongue plunged into her mouth, and he moved closer to her so that their bodies touched at every erotic point. What made his pulse go wild was that she wasn't struggling to break away. Her tongue toyed with his, and when he rubbed his lower body against hers, she only snuggled closer.

He kissed until he needed air, then he took a breath and kissed her again. His hands moved up and down her back, cupping her hips, urging her closer still. He was achingly hard, and she had to know it. His head was spinning; so must hers be. The wanting between them was almost tangible. He thought again of the things that weren't, like trust and love. But sexual desire, though not really visible—unless one were to take a good look at the straining seams of his jeans—*felt* tangible.

There was a roaring in his ears. She would make love with him right now if he continued the kissing and the touching. Did he have the strength of will to deny his own painfully intense desire to prove a point? The thing was, he'd already proven that day on the sofa that he could make her want him sexually. But he wanted more from her, so much more.

He took her by the arms, raised his head and stepped back. Her glazed eyes registered surprise. "Wha...what's wrong?" she whispered raggedly.

"I'll tell you what's wrong, light of my life. We're not going to make love." She blinked at him. "When you're sure of your feelings for me, *then* we'll make love," he said.

Her face lost color when what he was doing really sank in. Humiliated and furious with herself, she wrested free of his arms.

"I can give you an answer to your question now," she said through clenched teeth. "Don't come around anymore."

He grinned. "Too late, sweetheart. You see, I would have believed you a few minutes ago. Now I don't." He walked to the foyer doorway, stopped and turned to give her another slightly wicked grin. "I'll be in touch. Count on it."

"You—" he went through the outside door, closing it behind him "—bastard!" she shrieked.

Then she collapsed on a chair and bawled her eyes out.

Chapter Sixteen

Theo answered the phone begrudgingly. She didn't want to talk to anyone, with the possible exception of her mother. To be honest, she was so down in the dumps that she really didn't even want to talk to Lisa. Still, she couldn't ignore the phone, their only connection while she was in Montana.

"Hello," she said after three rings.

"Hello, Theo."

It was Jordan. Theo wilted even more. Her head was pounding from a nerve-grating headache that had taken root during her crying spell after Colt's departure. Her usual painkillers had barely taken the edge off, and she knew it was a tension headache because her entire body felt rigid.

"How are you?" Jordan asked.

Theo had never heard the subdued, almost timid tone in Jordan's voice that she was hearing now. Not that he was a blustery sort of man, but he'd always struck her as completely confident. He didn't sound confident this evening.

In fact, he sounded a lot like she felt, as though the bottom had dropped out of his world.

"I'm all right," she answered, though she could hear the aloofness in her voice. Not too many days ago she would have spoken with warmth and asked him how *he* was. Thinking of that merely added weight to what felt like a lump of lead in her midsection.

"Theo..." He stopped to clear his throat. "I have some papers that require your signature. May I bring them by?"

"You mean now? Tonight?"

"Yes. I've been working on them all day and only finished up a short time ago."

"Can't they wait until tomorrow?" She was in her robe and didn't feel at all well. Dealing with Jordan this evening, in any capacity, seemed beyond her capabilities.

"I have to deliver them to the court in Helena at ten tomorrow morning, which means I'll have to leave Hattie very early. It's only seven now, not late, Theo, and it will take just a few minutes of your time."

He was right, of course. Seven wasn't late. It was just that she'd hoped to avoid seeing anyone ever since Colt left, and as the afternoon had evolved into evening she had stopped worrying that someone might come along. Jordan being that someone was especially annoying. This whole damned mess was his fault, caused by his greed.

And yet he was the attorney in charge of Maude's estate. Unless she fired him and took everything to another lawyer, she was going to have to see Jordan on a fairly regular basis. Maybe she should fire him, she thought. It was no more than he deserved. Still, it was a very big step to take, and maybe she didn't have the desire to start over with a different attorney.

"All right," she said, speaking in a dull, flat monotone. "Come right now, if you must. I'm planning an early bedtime."

"Thank you, Theo. I'll be there in ten minutes."

Putting down the phone, Theo decided that she didn't want to meet with Jordan in her nightclothes. Going to her bedroom, she threw on a pair of slacks and a long-sleeved T-shirt. She didn't bother checking her hair or her makeup, though she probably looked a fright. But it simply didn't matter what Jordan might think of her appearance.

The doorbell rang, announcing Jordan's arrival. Heaving a vexed sigh, Theo walked to the door and opened it. Jordan was standing on her stoop, but he wasn't looking at her; he was staring at her rental vehicle in the driveway as though in a trance.

"Jordan?" she said.

He brought his gaze to her, and she saw a rather dazed expression on his face. "It was you at Marion's last night?"

Her first good look at Jordan startled Theo. His skin was pasty and gray, his eyes bloodshot. She had never seen him any other way but immaculate, and his suit was rumpled, his shirt collar was open and he wasn't wearing a tie. He was carrying his briefcase, and he didn't seem very steady on his feet.

"Jordan, are you all right?" she asked with a concerned frown. He looked ill, to be honest. Considering his abominable behavior, she probably shouldn't care. But total indifference to anyone's misery just wasn't in her.

"No...yes," Jordan stammered. "It...it doesn't matter. Were you at Marion's last night?" His eyes veered back to the driveway.

Theo caught on. He must have driven past Marion's house last night and seen her four-wheeler. He'd probably wondered who was visiting Marion, who was inside her house. He was suffering, Theo realized, just as she was. As Marion was. Her heart softened with a ponderous sadness for all of them.

"I was there. Come in." Stepping back, she held the door open in invitation. She led him to the sofa in the living room. "Sit down, Jordan."

He seemed disoriented. "Yes . . . yes, thanks." Seated, he opened his briefcase. Theo noticed how his hands were shaking.

She sank into a chair. "What's wrong, Jordan?" she asked gently. Whatever he'd done, however much trouble and heartache he'd caused her and Marion, she hated seeing him in this condition. So would Marion hate it, Theo knew. Marion loved this foolish man and it would break her heart to see him like this.

Jordan tried to smile and only looked sad. "Too many things to mention, Theo." He took a sheaf of papers from his briefcase, then lifted his eyes to Theo. "I didn't know you and Marion had become friends."

"I like her very much, Jordan."

He swallowed hard, as though a huge lump had developed in his throat. "Everyone does." Dropping the papers to a sofa cushion, he covered his face with his hands and groaned. "God, I've been such a fool. She won't take my calls, or come to the door. I've tried to see her so many times."

Theo felt herself choking up. "She . . . she feels terribly hurt, Jordan."

"I know she does, and she should. But . . ."

Theo could tell he was crying. She felt like joining him. They could both sit in Maude's living room and weep for hours, but what good would it do?

She got to her feet. "Let me get you something, Jordan. Would you like some coffee?"

He dragged a handkerchief out of his pocket, wiped his eyes and blew his nose. "I'm sorry. No coffee, but thanks. I've already drunk so much coffee today, my stomach's rebelling."

She remembered Maude's blackberry brandy. "I know what you need. It'll calm your nerves and might even help your stomach." Going over to the little cabinet in the corner, she got out one of the bottles of brandy. Hurrying to the kitchen for glasses, she returned to the living room. Opening the bottle, she splashed a little brandy in each of the glasses and brought one to Jordan. "Here, take it."

With her own glass, she resumed her seat. Jordan took a tentative sip of the liquor. "Taste's good. What is it?"

"Blackberry brandy. It was Maude's. Jordan, you're terribly unhappy, aren't you?"

"Miserable," he admitted in a shaky voice. "I know it's my own doing. Theo, I don't know what got into me. I owe you an apology and you have it. Marion..." Tears filled his eyes again.

"What got into you, Jordan," Theo said distinctly and without faltering, "is the fact that you're broke and on the verge of bankruptcy."

He looked shocked. "Marion told you that? It's true, but I never thought she'd talk about it." His nervousness seemed to increase.

"We talked about a lot of things last night, Jordan. We got along famously. I told her my problems, she told me hers."

Jordan hung his head. "I'm her biggest problem, right?"

"Bingo."

"Probably yours, too."

"You're one of my problems, yes, but not my biggest. Let me rephrase that. You *were* a problem to me. But you're not anymore. I understand you now, Jordan." Theo studied the dejected man on her sofa. "You love Marion, don't you? You've loved her for a long time, and yet you plotted to marry me for the estate Maude left me and even managed to convince Marion that it was a sensible plan." She shook her head. "I don't know if she'll ever be able to truly forgive you, but..."

Theo hesitated. Dare she break a confidence and tell Jordan how much Marion really did love him? But he looked so lost, so broken, as though he had nothing at all to even go on living for. He needed to hear something that would give him hope, she realized, making her decision.

"She still loves you, Jordan," Theo said quietly.

Jordan's head jerked up. "Did she say that?"

"Very plainly."

"Then why won't she talk to me?"

"I think she needs a little time, Jordan. Try to be patient."

"I...I'm putting my building up for sale, Theo." He looked shamefaced. "And my fancy house and car. I don't need any of it."

"Sounds to me like a very wise decision. You'll still be practicing law in Hattie, though, won't you?"

"Yes. I can't leave Hattie. This is where Marion is." His eyes blurred with tears again. "Theo, I'm so sorry for what I did to you. I feel like the worst fool there ever was."

"Drink your brandy, Jordan," Theo murmured. "And try to remember one thing. Probably every person alive has done something they wish they hadn't. It'll work out. You'll see."

It was amazing to Theo that she could bolster Jordan's badly damaged ego so well when her own was in shambles. She signed the papers he'd brought and he left her house walking a little taller, a little straighter.

She stood on her front stoop and watched his car disappear down the street, wondering if he would attempt to see Marion yet tonight. Her heart skipped a beat; it was entirely possible that Marion wouldn't thank her for telling Jordan anything she'd said last night. Theo could only hope that she'd done the right thing.

With a heavy, overloaded sensation, she turned to go back inside. She stopped then, peering intently at Nan's house. There was a light burning inside! It appeared as a faint glow, as it wasn't completely dark outside yet. But that light had not been on during the past few nights.

Theo's hand rose to her throat. Nan had come home. This was her chance to talk to her.

Or was it? Maybe Nan had just walked in the door and wouldn't welcome an unexpected guest.

But it was also possible that Nan had been home for hours and Theo had been too wrapped up in frustration and self-pity to notice. Certainly she hadn't come outside this afternoon to check Nan's house.

Pulling the door of her own house closed, Theo bounded down the steps and sidewalk and all but ran to Nan's front door. She heard first music coming from inside, then voices: the TV set, obviously. Nervously she pushed the doorbell button.

The door opened. "Why, Theo. How nice. Come in." Nan was smiling, looking sprightly and happy to see her.

"It's not too late for a call, is it?"

"Heavens no. Come in."

Theo entered and Nan led the way to her living room, where she switched off the television set. "Sit down. This is a very pleasant surprise. Did you know I'd been gone? Just got home this afternoon. I was visiting my sister in Helena." Nan chuckled. "We get lonesome for each other, but after a few days we start bickering. Her memory is bad, but she thinks she remembers long-ago incidents and that I'm the one with the bad memory. At any rate, a few days together is about all we can take." Nan laughed again. "Until the next time. Sit down, Theo. Make yourself comfortable. What can I get you? A cup of tea?"

"Please don't go to any trouble, Nan."

"Brewing a pot of tea is no trouble at all. You just sit down and relax. I'll only be a few minutes." Nan hurried from the room.

Theo looked around, then sat down. Nan's living room was cozy with chintz-covered, upholstered furniture constructed on a small scale, and quite a few beautiful potted plants. It was spotlessly clean, which even from the little she knew of Nan didn't surprise Theo. Maude and Nan may have been the best of friends, but Maude had obviously liked clutter and Nan didn't.

That thought led to another for Theo: Maude's personal belongings. She wanted to go through them and should have asked Jordan tonight to have them returned to the house. What prompted Theo's desire to look through Maude's things was the fact that she was almost finished in the office and hadn't run across any of the letters she had written to her through the years. They had to be with her clothes and things, as she felt certain Maude hadn't thrown them away. Not when her office was proof that she'd never discarded anything. Now that the office was pretty much organized, Theo felt that she could begin discarding items. Certainly no one needed to keep ten-year-old bank statements, ancient advertisements and outdated miscellaneous papers that made no sense at all.

Nan returned with a tray, which she placed on the coffee table. There was a ceramic teapot, matching cups and saucers, and small containers of sugar cubes, lemon and milk.

"What do you like in your tea?" the bright-eyed little lady asked Theo.

"I like it plain, Nan, thank you." While Nan poured the tea, Theo glanced around the room again. "Your home is lovely, Nan."

"Thank you for saying so. I'm very comfortable here." Nan passed a cup and saucer to Theo. Taking her own, she sat on the small sofa. "My, this is nice. I've been hoping for an opportunity to chat with you."

Theo took a sip of her tea. "You said that you and Maude had been friends for many years. Have you always lived in Hattie?"

"No, dear. I moved here in 1959. John, my husband, worked for the state highway department, a supervisor, and he was transferred to this area from Missoula. We bought this house and I've lived in it ever since. Finished raising my children right here. John died in 1985."

"I'm sorry," Theo murmured.

"Yes, well, one must look at death as a part of life, I believe. He was a good man and I'm sure he's in a good place. I know you're not married, Theo, but you must have family."

"Only my mother, Nan. Dad passed away years ago, and I'm an only child. Mother and I are very close. She has some serious medical problems, so I call her every day."

"That's very considerate." Nan's eyes twinkled suddenly. "But tell me how a pretty, intelligent woman like yourself eluded marriage. I'm sure the young men must be lined up at your door."

Theo laughed. "Afraid not." Theo talked about the boutique, starting with her initial idea to become a shopkeeper and ending with how successful the boutique had become. "I have a woman managing it in my absence," she said.

"In that case, I'm sure you're anxious to return to your own home."

Theo paused. "I . . . was. Now . . . I just don't know," she said slowly, thoughtfully. It was a revelation of sorts. One that was a little sad, somewhat disturbing and at the same time rather exciting. She *wasn't* anxious to leave Hattie anymore. She wasn't anxious about the shop or about Helen's management. There was really only one person she cared about in California and that was her mother.

Was that startling change of heart due to her feelings for Colt?

Setting her cup and saucer on the coffee table, she drew a breath. "Nan, you said that you knew of Colt Murdoch and Jordan Hamilton."

"Yes, I remember saying that. Why, Theo?"

"Well . . . I have some questions. I've tried to find out the answers for myself, but I really haven't gotten anywhere."

"Which young man are you interested in?" Nan asked with a wise little smile.

Theo took another deep breath. "Colt."

"Ah, yes. Well, he's certainly a handsome devil, isn't he?"

"Gorgeous," Theo murmured with a telltale stain of pink in each cheek. "Anyway, if you wouldn't mind talking about him, I'd really appreciate anything you could tell me."

"Oh, I don't mind." Nan smiled. "I don't mind in the least." She got up to refill their cups.

Theo returned home around eleven and felt as though she were walking on air. She was saturated with tea and information, hordes of information. What was so euphoric was that none of that information was bad or even slightly negative. According to Nan, Colt was a man to be respected and admired. Why hadn't he himself told her what Nan had? If anyone had a right to tout his accomplishments, even brag a little, it was Colt.

Damn Jordan for planting doubts and suspicions in her mind, Theo thought irately. It was fine if he didn't like Colt, though it was his problem, not hers or anyone else's. Of course he'd planted those poisonous seeds to keep her away from Colt, thus paving a clear path for himself. He'd probably caught on the day they'd all met at Maude's funeral that Colt and she were attracted to each other.

Theo stopped in midstride to think about that. Was it really true? Had she and Colt felt something special for each other at their very first meeting?

Knowing she was too keyed up to sleep, Theo poured herself a small glass of brandy and curled up on the recliner chair. Sipping slowly, she let everything Nan had told her drift through her mind. It was a remarkable story; never had she heard anything more remarkable, to be honest. Colt wanted to buy that piece of land from the estate? No way. After what she'd learned about him tonight, she would give it to him!

And the rest of the estate? What was she going to do with it? She still hadn't made any decisions regarding so much money, but all along she'd felt that it should be used for something more than the pursuit of pleasure. An unusual excitement began churning within Theo. "My Lord," she whispered as an idea took shape. Would Colt agree with it?

Oh, if only it wasn't so late! She wanted to talk to him now, tonight!

But she'd have to wait until morning, she realized with a disappointed sigh. There were two other calls she had to make tomorrow, as well. One to Jordan to tell him that she wanted Maude's things returned to the house, and the other one to Marion. As difficult as it could turn out to be, she had to confess to Marion that she'd told Jordan portions of their very private conversation. If Marion became angry...? Theo chewed on her upper lip, praying that wouldn't happen. It would be wonderful if Marion thanked her, in fact, as farfetched as that notion was. Theo took another sip of brandy. However Marion took her confession, she would have to deal with it.

Thinking of Colt again, Theo got warm all over. She smiled, then laughed in anticipation. Tomorrow was going to be a very interesting day.

She could hardly wait.

Awake at 5:00 a.m., Theo jumped out of bed and went directly to the kitchen phone. After looking up Jordan's home number, she placed the call. He answered on the second ring.

"Jordan Hamilton here."

"Good morning, Jordan. This is Theo."

"At five in the morning? Theo, is something wrong?"

"No, not at all. I just wanted to catch you before you left for Helena."

"Well, you just barely made it. I was on my way out the door when the phone rang." He sounded more like his old self, Theo realized, so maybe hearing that Marion still loved him had done some good. "What did you need to talk to me about?" he asked.

"About Maude's personal things. You said they're stored in your garage."

"They are."

"I want them returned to the house, Jordan. When you get back from Helena, would you please see to it?"

"Yes, of course. I'll take care of it at the first possible moment."

"Thank you. I'd appreciate it. Goodbye, Jordan."

"Bye, Theo. Oh ... by the way, thanks for what you did last night. I slept better than I have in a long time."

"You're very welcome. Marion's a special person, Jordan." *Don't hurt her again. If you love her, don't hurt her again.*

"I know she is. Thanks again. Talk to you later."

Theo put down the phone, then prepared the coffee-maker so it would brew while she showered. One call down, two to go.

Showered and dressed, Theo dialed Marion's number. The message machine came on and she waited for the beep. "Marion, this is Theo. If you're home, please pick up. I need to talk to you."

Marion didn't come on the line. "Please call me back when you can. It's quite important. Bye." Theo hung up. Maybe Marion was a sound sleeper and still in bed. Or maybe she too had risen early and was already gone somewhere.

The time had come, she thought with a sudden spate of nervousness. Drawing a deep breath, she reached for the phone book to look up Colt's ranch's number. Jotting it down on the pad by the phone, she closed the book.

But instead of immediately placing the call, she sat there. After a few minutes she got up for a cup of coffee and brought it back to the table and the telephone.

This call could change her entire life. In fact, she hoped it did exactly that. So ... why was she so hesitant about making it? She believed in Colt now, didn't she? Trusted him? Admired everything he was doing? Loved him?

Yes, yes, yes and yes.

"You nitwit," she muttered to herself. "What are you afraid of now?" Irritated with herself, she grabbed the phone and dialed Colt's number.

A youthful male voice answered. "Murdoch Ranch."

Theo cleared her throat. "Colt Murdoch, please."

"Sure. Hold on."

Theo heard the phone being dropped on something hard, a tabletop perhaps, then the voice of the young man who'd taken the call. "Colt? You're wanted on the phone." It was a shout, as though Colt were some distance away. There were other voices, she realized while listening intently to the sounds of a large and boisterous household.

The phone was picked up. "Hello?"

"Uh... Colt?"

"Theo?" There was surprise in his voice.

She gave a nervous little laugh. "Yes. Caught you off guard, I'll bet."

"You win the bet. I never would have guessed it was you calling in a hundred years." His voice became lower, more intimate. "Everything okay?"

"Everything's... wonderful. Um, Colt, would it be possible for you to come by this morning?"

Thrilled to death over this call, he chuckled softly in Theo's ear. "Anytime you say, sweetheart, anytime at all. Give me an hour or so to get things lined up out here and I'll be on my way."

"Thank you. See you then."

With her heart beating a mile a minute, Theo hung up the phone. Her very next thought had to do with clothes. What she was wearing, slacks and a plain shirt, wouldn't do at all. Not for this meeting.

Rushing to her bedroom, she began going through her wardrobe.

Chapter Seventeen

Theo was ready and waiting at eight. By the time Colt parked his Bronco at her curb at ten, she was a bundle of nerves. Checking her makeup and hair in a decorative mirror on the living room wall, she went to the door and opened it before Colt could knock or ring the bell.

He took one look at her and whistled. "Babe, you look fantastic!"

She'd done her best to look that way and was glad he appreciated her efforts. Her dress was white with large, splotchy black flowers in no apparent design. It was cut low at the neck and had tiny cap sleeves. The bodice fit like a dream, enhancing every curve she possessed, then the skirt flared becomingly from her narrow waist. Her hair and makeup were perfect; they should be, she'd checked herself in one mirror or another every ten minutes for two hours.

"Come in, Colt." Surprisingly, her nervous tension had vanished. Most of it, anyway. He was here, and he looked so handsome, so crisp and clean in his white western-cut shirt and jeans. Her welcoming smile was radiant.

"Happy to. Thanks." Colt was grinning from ear to ear. Obviously some mysterious event had altered Theo's attitude toward him; he'd sensed it the second he saw her standing there looking so pretty in that black-and-white dress. Her smile cinched it for him. Whatever had occurred, he was grateful as hell. In fact, he felt so confident with the especially warm and friendly expression on her face that once the door was closed he pulled her into his arms and kissed her on the lips.

What was really exciting was her sweet-as-honey response—leaning into him, putting her arms around his waist, kissing him back with lips and tongue and passion.

Raising his head, he looked into her eyes and sucked in a deep breath. "Dare I ask what brought this on?"

"Yes," she whispered huskily. "Dare anything you want."

His eyes sparkled wickedly. "That's a mighty wide door you just opened, sweetheart."

"Yes, isn't it?" she said softly. "I can almost see the wheels turning in your head, Mr. Murdoch. You're wondering what's going on. Why did she change? Does she really mean that I dare do *anything?*"

"You're reading my mind, baby," he whispered before settling his mouth on hers again. This was incredible. *She* had called *him. She* had dressed seductively for *him. She* was kissing *him,* and had blatantly suggested he do anything he wanted.

Well, he wanted plenty. Breathing hard and taking kiss after kiss, he ran his hands up and down her back. Then he remembered that the neckline of her dress was cut enticingly low, and he dipped his head to adoringly nuzzle the tops of her breasts.

Her fingers wove through his hair. He heard a laugh bubbling deep in her throat, a purely female laugh that suddenly had his blood pressure soaring. She was going to make love with him, had instigated it, in fact, and there was a lilting happiness about her this morning that he'd never seen before.

He had to know what had happened to make her so loving. Straightening, he held her face in his hands and probed the depths of her eyes. But before he could say a word, she laid her finger on his lips.

"Let's talk later," she whispered, her eyes smoky with sensual mystery. Slowly her finger slid down his chin, followed the contour of his throat and stopped at the first button on his shirt. She flicked it open, stating clearly with that one gesture where she intended this to go.

Suddenly Colt didn't care what had transpired to alter her attitude so drastically. Having her, loving her, was the one and only thing in his mind. Groaning hoarsely, he yanked her up against himself, seeking her lips with his. Her response evidenced a hunger as overwhelming as his own.

"Not the sofa this time," Theo whispered between a steady stream of wild, passionate kisses. She felt her skirt being drawn up, then his hands on her bare skin. He groaned again: she wasn't wearing panties.

Slipping from his arms, she took his hand and said two words. "My room."

Numbly, his mind spinning, he let her lead him to her bedroom. The bed was already turned down! He looked from it to her and received a smile that turned his knees to mush. All at once he was a man in a hurry. He tore at his shirt buttons and dropped the garment on the floor.

Theo turned her back to him. "Unzip my dress," she said in a tremulous voice.

He slid the zipper down, then pressed kisses to her back and shoulders. Moving her hair aside, his mouth lingered at her nape, raising goose bumps on her feverish skin.

"Am I still the one, Colt?" she asked breathily.

"The one and only, baby. Don't ever doubt it." Taking a small step back from her, he slid the dress down her arms and to the floor. She walked out of it, then turned to face him and bent over to pick it up.

He was staring, his eyes moving up and down her body. "You are so beautiful."

Her chin lifted slightly. "Do you really think so?"

"I don't think, I know." His hands rose to his belt buckle and he started undressing.

Theo brought her dress to a chair then lay down on the bed, on her stomach with her arms curved around a pillow and her eyes on Colt.

"You're beautiful, too," she said as his clothing fell away.

He chuckled softly. "I guess beauty is in the eye of the beholder."

"Are you saying you don't feel that you're a handsome man? You have to know, Colt. You see yourself in a mirror every day, to shave if nothing else. You must know how utterly gorgeous you are."

This time he laughed out loud. "Flattery will get you everywhere, sweetheart." He walked to the other side of the bed and stretched out next to her. She started to turn over. "No, not yet," he whispered, running his hand down the exciting curve of her spine to her hips. "Your skin is perfection, as smooth as satin." His fingertips danced lightly over her behind and down the back of her thighs.

The bed shifted slightly as he moved closer to her. Her lips parted for air. Against the bare skin of her hips she felt his arousal, hot and hard and throbbing with life. His hand came around her and cupped a breast. At the same time he feathered kisses down her backbone. She shivered at the sensations he was causing.

"Oh, Colt," she said in a barely audible whisper.

But he heard her and knew what she was feeling. It was the first time since they'd met that he believed he knew, without doubts or reservations, what she was feeling and thinking. Some of it, anyway. There was a reason why she'd called him this morning, a reason why she was on this bed with him, naked and womanly and responding to his every caress. But why guess at it? he thought. She'd said they would talk later, and later was fine with him.

He turned her over, placing her on her back, and looked deeply into her eyes. The words *I love you* were in his soul and on the tip of his tongue

But . . . they would talk later.

He moved on top of her, keeping most of his weight on his elbows. But when he started kissing her again and her body began rubbing against his, everything fled his mind except her and what they were doing. What she'd invited him to do.

Burning with desire, he thrust into her. In the next second he pulled away abruptly, muttered, "Protection," and felt around the floor for his jeans.

"Hurry," Theo moaned. Without the heat of his body warming hers, she felt chilled. Separation was intolerable. She was hanging by her fingernails and needed him desperately.

He returned to her in seconds. She wrapped her arms and legs around him, holding him as closely as possible. "Oh, Colt . . . Colt. My love . . . my love."

"You got that right, sweetheart," he growled raggedly. He was her love. He always would be. It was astounding that she had apparently suddenly accepted that fact when she'd been so flagrantly uncertain only yesterday.

Theo was in a dreamy state. *This* was making love. What they'd done on the sofa before had been tempestuous sex, hot and exciting but nothing like what was happening now. He was so tender with her, and she felt his emotions mingling with her own. It was as though they had become one person, one body, one spirit, one brain. Never could two people be any closer than she and Colt were at this moment, she thought as emotional tears filled her eyes.

She couldn't help it. The words came spilling out. "I love you . . . I love you."

He stopped to look at her face, his own containing an adoring expression. "I know you do. And you know I love you."

"Yes…yes." She brought his head down. "Kiss me. Love me."

"Forever, Theo. Forever and always."

They said no more. Lost in the wonder of their lovemaking, they neither thought nor spoke, except for small murmurings of pleasure. They reached the heights together, cried out together and then became very still, together.

After a wonderful interval of silent, total satisfaction, Theo opened her eyes and pressed a kiss just below his ear. He lifted his head and smiled. She smiled in return.

"I need to get up for a minute. Don't go away," he said.

"I won't."

When he was gone, she stretched languorously and smiled again. Everything was going to work out, she knew it now. He really did love her, and there was no question in her mind about her love for him.

Her smile stayed fixed. They would talk now. There was so much to talk about, all of the elements of his life and hers that somehow had to be blended into a single path to happiness for both of them.

Colt came back wearing a towel. Theo was lying under the sheet. She lifted a corner of it in invitation, and he dropped the towel and crawled in beside her, immediately nestling her into his arms. He kissed her lips, then her forehead and sighed contentedly.

"I doubt there's a happier man alive this morning," he told her.

"Or woman," she said softly. "Colt, tell me about your ranch," she added after a moment.

"I'd rather talk about what it was that changed your mind about me," he said with a tender kiss to the tip of her nose. He tilted her chin to look into her eyes. "What was it, honey?"

"I'm not sure where to begin."

He laughed a little. "It couldn't be that complex, Theo. Yesterday you didn't trust me and today you do. Whatever happened took place pretty fast."

"Well . . . it is complex. Sort of. Colt, do you know Nan Butler?"

Colt frowned slightly. "The lady next door?"

"Yes."

"I know who she is, but that's about it. Why?"

"She knows everything there is to know about you," Theo said serenely. "And she was delighted to fill me in."

"Oh, really?" He sounded doubtful. "How would she know so much about me?"

Theo laughed. "She knows everything about everyone in and around Hattie. She's quite a gal. I spent hours with her last night."

"Last night. I see. Okay, what'd she say?"

Theo took a breath. "Why didn't you tell me that you've been helping troubled boys by bringing them to your ranch? She said you've been doing it for years, that you've saved a lot of them from spending time in jail, and that many of them finished high school, went on to higher education and made something of themselves. Colt, you should be so proud. How could you not have told me?"

"That's" what made you start trusting me? Hell, if I'd known that was all it took, I'd have told you about it the first day we met."

"I wish you had. I wish *someone* would have. Of course, it could have been the company I was keeping. Jordan certainly had nothing good to say about you. Why on earth does he dislike you so much?"

"Theo, if I knew the answer to that, I'd be a much smarter man than I am. We didn't get along when we were kids and it's been that way ever since. Jordan's a funny guy. Between you, me and the gatepost I think he's totally without morals or standards. Take his relationship with Marion, for instance. . .."

"I spent an evening with her," Theo said.

Uh-oh, Colt thought. He'd better not bring Marion into this conversation. What she'd told him about Theo's visit to her home had been in confidence, and if he let something slip, he'd never forgive himself.

"Regardless of what a jerk Jordan is," Theo said thoughtfully, "I feel sorry for him. He's about finished financially, and he's putting his building up for sale. His house and car, as well."

"Oh? Did Nan Butler tell you all of that, too?"

"Jordan himself did. He brought some papers by for my signature yesterday. He looked terrible, as though he hadn't slept in days. He's repenting what he did to Marion, Colt, suffering over it."

"Yeah, well, he brought it on himself."

"Yes, he did, but I hate seeing anyone so unhappy." She snuggled closer to him and smiled. "Especially when I'm floating ten feet off the ground."

Colt laughed and kissed her. "Is that what you're doing, just because you heard about my work with troubled youngsters?"

"It's very important work, Colt." She was suddenly nervous. "Um, since I talked to Nan, I've been thinking about something."

"Obviously," Colt said with a laugh, assuming she meant him. He hugged her. "Guess gossip isn't all bad."

Wriggling out of his arms, Theo sat up. Tucking the sheet under her arms, she looked at Colt with a serious expression. "Nan said it was common knowledge that you put most of your profits from both the ranch and your land sales company into the ranch. She said the state cooperates with you on the disposition of the boys, but that you receive no money from anyone, the government or otherwise, to help support your program. She also said that you took in a woman, a widow and her young son, Ruth and Petey Conway, when she became ill and couldn't work for several months."

Colt was watching her closely. "Ruth has paid me back a hundred times over, Theo. She runs the house, cooks, cleans and plays a big part in keeping a bunch of high-spirited and not always pleasant boys in line.''

"I...I was worried about Ruth," Theo said quietly. "Jealous. The day you took me to that eight-hundred acres you want from the estate, you said that Ruth had made our lunch. I... assumed she was your girlfriend.''

"Good God," Colt muttered. "We sure haven't been communicating, have we?''

"No, we haven't.''

"Ruth's a friend. That's all she's ever been.''

"Oh, Colt, you're such a good man," Theo all but whispered. "I let Jordan's behavior influence my judgment of you. How unfair. Why did you put up with it?''

He smiled, raising his hand to touch her face. "Because you're the one.''

"I didn't believe that, either. Not when Jordan had just upset me with ridiculous statements about he and I being soul mates." Theo heaved a sigh. "It's all been so... disturbing. Maude leaving me a fortune, meeting you and Jordan...''

"Wondering if both of us were after your inheritance," Colt added quietly.

"Jordan was.''

"Maybe I am, too.''

"No, you're not. Any man who would work hard and invest his money into the future of young boys in trouble isn't greedy, Colt. You want to know something? I'm not greedy, either. I want to do something real, something important with Maude's money.''

Colt nodded, feeling pride in her goals. "Good girl." But where was she going to do this real and important thing, in Montana or in California? "Listen, honey, about us." A crease had developed in his forehead. "Are you going back to California? Theo, I don't want to lose you. I've never been in love before, and I don't know what I'd do without you.''

"I don't know what I'd do without you, either," she said softly. "Let's not ever find out, okay?"

A gladness entered Colt's eyes. "Then you're not going back to California?"

"Off and on, yes. I have to do something about my business, and my mother isn't well. I'd love it if she would move here, but she probably won't want to leave her doctors. I'm going to discuss it with her."

"Maybe we should be talking about marriage," Colt said, watching her to see how that idea affected her. It was what he wanted, love, marriage and children with the only woman he'd ever loved. But Theo might feel differently. He believed she loved him, but not everyone thought marriage was the best conclusion to falling in love.

Her smile was slightly teasing, though her eyes contained the glow of utter happiness. "Are you proposing?"

His heart skipped a beat. "Would you say yes if I were?"

"Yes, I think I would." She saw him reaching for her. "Wait."

He sank back to his pillow, confused suddenly. "Wait for what, sweetheart?"

She took a breath. "We're not through talking yet. Colt...I..." How would he perceive her idea? It was really so crucial to their future, but after the way she had all but accused him of courting her for her inheritance this had to be handled tactfully.

He was frowning, wondering uneasily what she was having such difficulty in saying. "What is it, Theo? What's wrong?"

"Nothing's wrong," she said quickly. "It's just that...oh, darn, I didn't think this was going to be so hard to talk about. I mean, I knew it was going to be hard, but just...not this hard."

He couldn't imagine what was on her mind. She had confessed love for him, he'd done the same with her. They were single-minded on the subject of marriage, apparently, so what else was there?

His heart sank. Her inheritance. Yes, that had to be it. She still wasn't sure that he wanted no part of it.

"A prenuptial agreement should ease your mind," he said quietly.

Her eyes widened. "What?" Understanding hit her then. "Colt, no! That's not it at all. I ... I want to get involved in what you're doing."

His frown returned. "Involved? Theo, I don't understand."

She sighed. "I know. Let me ask you this, Colt. If you had a great deal of money at your disposal, what would you do with it?"

"Expand the ranch," he said slowly, thoughtfully, beginning to grasp what she was getting at. "I'd build dorms so I would never have to turn down any boy in trouble, hire specialists in the field of teenage psychology and build up the cattle operation for added income and also to give the boys more to do. Keeping them busy is important. The first thing I do when a new boy comes to the ranch is give him a horse that he can call his own while he's there, and explain to him that the animal is his responsibility. Most of these kids have never been given anything, let alone responsibility. They come from broken homes, from the streets, from people who've never given a damn about them. Not in every case. We've had a few who've had both parents worrying themselves sick because the son who was sweet and adorable as a child turned into a complete monster during adolescence."

"You've never worked with girls?"

Colt shook his head. "We just don't have the facilities."

"But you would take on troubled girls if you had the means to expand?"

He thought for a moment, then nodded. "I don't see why not." Despite an effort to remain calm, excitement was building in his system. "Theo, are you thinking what I think you're thinking?"

She gave a slow nod of her head. "You were a boy in trouble, weren't you?"

"Yes. I was arrested and spent six months in juvenile detention."

"Not prison."

"No, not prison. But juvie is no picnic." He studied her. "Where'd you get that prison idea?"

"I'm sure you can guess."

"Jordan. That jerk," he said disgustedly. "Theo, I came out of juvie vowing to better my life. My father was a drunk, every building on the ranch was practically falling down, there was only a handful of scrubby cattle on the place and I still had to finish high school."

"But you overcame it all, didn't you?" she said, the admiration making her voice sound even more caring, loving. "You bettered your own life and then started helping other boys in your previous situation. Colt, I'm so proud of you. I've never known anyone who gave so much of themselves." She paused, then said quietly, "I'd like to put Maude's estate into a special fund, to be used solely for the expansion and operation of the ranch. I'm sure we could arrange a tax-free status with the IRS."

Colt was floored. "*All* of it?"

"Almost all of it. With my mother's health so shaky, I would like to make sure she never has to worry about money. What do you think?"

"I . . . I don't know what to think. Theo, are you sure?"

"I'm sure, but you have to be, too. It would be a lifetime project, Colt, a lifetime commitment."

"I'm already committed to the boys and the ranch, Theo. That's never going to change." His gaze narrowed on her. "But your entire life would change. Are you prepared for that?"

"I'd be with you," she said softly. "Working with you." There was a second's pause. "Committed to you."

This time when he reached for her, she didn't hesitate to move into his arms. "I love you so much," she whispered.

"I don't know how it happened. Or why. But I want to spend the rest of my life with you."

His lips tenderly brushed hers. "I love you in the same incredible way." But he had to ask one more time. It was so amazing, something he'd never dared to hope for, enough money to do some real good for the forgotten and troubled kids he kept hearing about from various law enforcement agencies with which he stayed in touch. Looking down into Theo's eyes, he said, "You're absolutely positive about giving up your inheritance?"

She smiled. "Yes, I'm absolutely positive. From the moment Jordan told me about my inheriting Maude's estate, I felt that it should be put to good use. Oh, I thought of trips and wild shopping sprees, anyone would. But always, in the back of my mind was a bigger idea. I just didn't know what it was. Until last night."

Colt kissed her then, with all of the love he possessed for her. Then he said huskily, "Will you marry me?"

For an ecstatic moment she closed her eyes. When she opened them she was smiling. "Yes. I would be very proud to be your wife."

He hugged her, pressing a kiss to the top of her head. "You'll never be sorry, I promise."

"Neither will you," she whispered, vowing to make it so.

Epilogue

Maude's personal possessions were returned to the house the next morning. After the two men who had brought the dozen or so cardboard cartons left, Theo stood in her living room among the stacks of boxes and wondered where to begin; there was so much more than she'd expected.

It had to be done, of course. More, she wanted it done. Determinedly she slit the tape on one of the boxes. "Shoes," she murmured, digging around in the box. "And handbags." Retaping the box, she wrote on it with a felt marking pen. *Shoes & purses.* Moving that carton to Maude's empty bedroom for the time being, she returned to the living room and opened another.

One by one she worked her way through the boxes. They contained clothing of all kinds, knitting and other handiwork supplies, books, magazines, newspapers, and partially completed pieces—afghans, sweaters, bits of lace—that had been in process at Maude's death. At least nothing had been thrown away, Theo thought gratefully. On each box she marked its contents so she wouldn't have to open it again. About a third of the way through the task, she opened a carton that set her pulse to racing. Lifting out a rectangular wood box, she set it on the floor and sat down beside it to examine its contents.

The second she raised the lid, she knew she'd found her letters. Maude had saved them, every single one by the look of it. Thumbing through them, Theo went way back and read those that she'd written as a child. Some were funny, some were poignant. Her history, from the time she was nine years old, was recorded in these old letters. It touched her deeply that Maude had kept them, although she had done the same with Maude's letters. There had been a special bond between them, a special friendship, Theo thought, not for the first time. Every youngster should be so fortunate as to have an older person for a pen pal.

With all of the old mail spread across her lap, Theo saw something else in the wood box: a small black book and a white envelope tied together with a piece of pink yarn. Curiously she took them from the box and slid the yarn away. The little book was a savings account book from the local bank. Theo blinked at its first page in utter astonishment. The savings account was in her name!

"For heaven's sake," she mumbled as she flipped through the pages. Every dollar she'd sent Maude through the years had been deposited into this account. With interest accrued, the balance was over ten thousand dollars.

Theo was almost too stunned to remember the envelope bonded by yarn to the savings book, but then she picked it up and tore it open. As she suspected, it was a letter to her from Maude.

My dear Theo,
I know this will all be a shock for you, but I trust that you'll recover and handle it wisely. You were so sweet through the years, sending me money the way you did. Do you recall that the first sum you sent me was three

dollars and you were eleven years old? Somehow you had gotten the impression that I was short of money. I never meant to give you that impression, but something I wrote in one of my letters apparently led you in that direction. I could have cleared up the matter at once, of course, but your thoughtfulness and consideration for my welfare was so extraordinary that I selfishly took great delight in opening your letters and finding a five- or a ten-dollar bill tucked into it. When you were older and working, it was more, sometimes a hundred dollars. As you can see from the savings passbook, I never touched a penny of that money. But, oh my dear, how I rejoiced in your generous spirit. I lost my own daughter many years before we began corresponding—perhaps you've heard the story by now— and in a unique and wonderful way, you filled the empty spot in my heart.

Theo, you are to feel free to use your inheritance in any way you wish. Although I preferred to live simply, you have my blessing to squander it on frivolous things for yourself and your dear mother, if that's what you desire. I'm sure by now you've thought the word "eccentric" many times, and probably I was an eccentric. What you must understand is that I lived my life exactly as I wanted. You mustn't mourn nor grieve at my passing. Despite the loss of my husband before his time, and certainly my only child, I lived a full and rewarding life. You added a great deal to it these past twenty years, and there is no one to whom I would rather leave my earthly possessions. Enjoy them.

Your friend always,
Maude Evans

Wiping away a tear, Theo thought of Colt and her mother. She wanted to share this lovely message from Maude with each of them. Colt had stayed all of yesterday and half the night with her. They had talked and talked, becoming excited about the expansion of the ranch, and then, spontaneously, would forget everything but their being madly in love and fall into each other's arms.

How many times had they made love? Four? Six? Theo laughed softly. Never had she been happier. Never had she felt so complete, so whole. She had talked to Lisa early this morning, right after Colt had gone. Lisa was ecstatic for her daughter, but moving to Montana simply wasn't possible for her. "But I'll come for the wedding and visit often." They understood each other very well. Theo would visit Lisa in California often, too, and whenever practical she would ask Colt to go with her.

With a contented, serene sigh, Theo returned the letter to its envelope and got up to put it and the bankbook in her bedroom. She also carried the wood box with her letters to Maude and placed it on her dresser. Colt had said he would return this afternoon and take her to the ranch. She would be having dinner with the "gang," as he put it, and he'd warned her humorously to be prepared for noise and confusion. At the present time the boys lived in the ranch house with him, Ruth and Petey. Theo was looking forward to meeting everyone, and certainly the prospect of a little noise and confusion wasn't at all daunting.

She was on her way back to the living room when the front doorbell chimed. Winding through the remaining boxes scattered about, she went to the foyer and opened the door.

"Marion! How nice. Come in." Theo stepped back and held the door for her visitor to enter.

"Hello, Theo. I hope I'm not interrupting…" Marion saw the cartons. "Oh, goodness, you're right in the middle of something. I should have called first."

Theo had shut the door and was standing in the living room doorway with her guest. "You're not interrupting a thing. I'm very glad you came by. What can I get you? A cup of coffee? Or tea?"

"Nothing, Theo, thanks. I got your message to call you from my answering machine and decided to come over instead of talking on the phone." She smiled shyly. "I have something to tell you."

Theo went into the living room and jostled the remaining cartons into one pile. It took but a minute and then she smiled at Marion. "Please sit down. These boxes contain Maude's personal things. I thought it was time I went through them."

Marion sank to the sofa. "You've had a lot to do because of the estate, haven't you?"

Theo sat on the other end of the sofa. "Yes, but I'm not complaining."

Marion smiled teasingly. "With such a large inheritance, I suppose not."

Theo laughed. "Well, yes and no. I mean, inheriting a fortune does make complaining about a little work rather ridiculous. But the monetary value of the estate isn't nearly as important as Maude thinking so much of me. Do you understand what I'm trying to say?"

Marion nodded. "Yes, I think I do. True friendship is priceless."

"That's it exactly." Theo's expression became poignant for a moment as she thought of Maude, but then she smiled. "You said you had something to tell me."

Marion cleared her throat. "Yes. It's about... Jordan. Jordan and me. The reason I wasn't home yesterday when you called was because I was with Jordan."

"You went to Helena with him?"

"The night before last, he came by the house around nine. I... finally relented and let him come in. At first I couldn't be nice to him. It was as though I had let him come in so I could give him hell, which I did in no uncertain terms. He sat there and took it, without saying one word. He listened to my ranting and raving for a good half hour, until I wound down, actually. He'd never seen me truly angry before, and I don't know if I shocked him to speechless or what. But when I couldn't think of one more nasty thing to say to him, he said, 'I love you, Marion.'

"I started crying then." Marion bit her lip, then drew a long breath. "We both cried."

"And you made up," Theo said gently. "I'm glad, Marion, for both of you. Jordan must have left here and gone directly to your house. He brought over some papers that needed my signature."

"Yes, he told me."

Theo thought a moment, then decided that friendship shouldn't be tested with secrets. "Marion, there's something you should know. When Jordan was here, I . . . I told him some of the things you said the evening I came to your house." Theo's face conveyed her discomfort. "He was so miserably unhappy, worrying so much about you, and I told him to not give up, that you had said you would always love him."

Marion blinked at her. "This is incredible. Theo, I did the same thing with Colt."

"You did?"

"Yes. After my abominable behavior—cooperating with Jordan's plans and all—I felt I owed you something. I wondered what I could do to make it up to you, and after thinking about it, knowing you loved Colt but were afraid to trust him, I went to his office to speak to him. We went to Herb's for coffee, and I told him some of the things you'd said. Primarily that you were in love with him. Afterward, I was terrified that you'd find out and hate me for it.

"Theo, I value your friendship so much. Please don't be angry with me," Marion said in a tiny voice. "I mean, what you told Jordan apparently worked wonders for him and me, but . . ." Marion's voice trailed off as she looked helpless and regretful.

Calmly Theo took her friend's hand. "This may come as a surprise, but Colt and I are getting married."

"What?" Marion's eyes got as big as saucers.

"And maybe I have you to thank for that. I'm sure it didn't hurt our case any for him to *know* the truth of my feelings."

They looked at each other for a long moment, smiled and then started laughing. It felt good to laugh together over something each had worried about.

"Well," Theo said after they had calmed down. "I guess things have turned out well for both of us. I'm really happy about you and Jordan."

"We're getting married, too. Next weekend. Oh, Theo, we have so many plans. Jordan is going to sell everything and move into my house. He's going to start over in rented quarters. I'll continue to work for him, and I just know that once he's out from under the horrible financial burden he's been living with, he'll make a go of it."

Theo smiled warmly and patted her friend's hand. "I know it, too. With you behind him, he can't miss. Colt and I have plans, as well." She gave Marion a brief outline of those plans.

Marion listened, her eyes shining with admiration. "You're a very special woman, Theo."

"Everyone is in their own way, Marion." Theo smiled. "It just takes awhile sometimes to find the right path. Do you know what I wish now? That Colt and Jordan could become friends."

Marion sighed. "I wonder if that's possible."

"Not right now, it isn't. But maybe in time?" Theo smiled. "I'll bet that you and I together can figure something out. Want to give it a try?"

A slow smile built on Marion's face, until even her eyes beamed impishly. "Yes."

They laughed again, both happy, both in love, both looking to the future.

Marion spoke then. "Even if it doesn't work for our men, I hope that you and I will still always be friends."

Theo nodded. "We will be, Marion. As we already agreed, true friendship is priceless."

Her thoughts took her further. True *love* was priceless, a precious gift.

She sighed contentedly. Everything was wonderful.

*   *   *   *   *

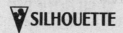

♥ SILHOUETTE

⟩ SPECIAL EDITION ⟨

COMING NEXT MONTH

**Our first six CELEBRATION 1,000 titles!
Join us as we celebrate our first 1,000 books and the
everlasting magic of romance!**

MAGGIE'S DAD Diana Palmer

Powell Long had always been hot-tempered and irresistible, and the
years had done nothing to change that. Just as they hadn't changed
the desire he'd always had for his first love—Antonia. Now she was
back, but why?

MORGAN'S SON Lindsay McKenna

Morgan's Mercenaries

Only Sabra Jacobs could rescue little Jason Trayhern, who'd been
kidnapped. But Sabra was nervous about such a mission with a new
partner. The hard-bitten ex-marine was running from something.

CHILD OF MINE Jennifer Mikels

What was best for Billy? He was only a baby and he needed Carly,
his adoptive aunt and guardian. But Alex Kane was his father. Could
they join forces—as husband and wife?

THE DADDY QUEST Celeste Hamilton

Holly MacPherson's young son had decided he wanted a daddy and
that police officer Brooks Casey would be ideal. But Holly wasn't
looking for a husband, certainly not a cop husband—no matter how
gorgeous.

LOGAN'S BRIDE Christine Flynn

The Whitaker Brides

Samantha Gray made Logan Whitaker notice her. Her children broke
down his defences and her feminine appeal made his pulse pound.
How could he resist the loving wife and family he'd always wanted?

BRAVE HEART Brittany Young

Since childhood, Daniel Blackhawk had been waiting to find the
woman who was the other half of his heart. But now he'd met Rory
Milbourne, he couldn't see how they could ever be together...

V SILHOUETTE

Sensation

COMING NEXT MONTH

MARRIED BY A THREAD Kia Cochrane

Where Dusty McKay came from, wedding vows were forever. But his wife wanted out of their marriage, and nothing he said or did was working to change Tori's mind...until Dusty came home with his orphaned niece cradled in his arms.

CAITLIN'S GUARDIAN ANGEL Marie Ferrarella

Heartbreakers

Protecting a murder witness was proving to be the toughest assignment of detective Graham Redhawk's career. The witness was Caitlin Cassidy, the woman who'd long ago decided he wasn't good enough to spend her life with. But he could ignore the attraction he still felt for her...couldn't he?

AN OFFICER AND A GENTLEMAN Rachel Lee

Dare MacLendon knew that Andrea Burke hid her passionate nature beneath her cool, competent demeanour. Dare was only too aware that his attention could destroy Andrea's career, but still he yearned to convince her that she was a colleague, a friend...and the woman of his dreams.

A MAN LIKE SMITH Marilyn Pappano

Southern Knights

Sexy attorney Smith Kendricks needed reporter Jolie Wade's help. She had information he wanted, but Jolie was vigilantly guarding her source. How could Smith convince Jolie to reveal her informer without losing his heart in the bargain?

SILHOUETTE

Desire

COMING NEXT MONTH

ARIZONA HEAT Jennifer Greene

Paxton Moore was happy with his life just the way it was until Kansas McClellan barged into town, asking him for help in her search for her missing brother. Why were the sultry days—and hot nights—suddenly getting too steamy for comfort?

COWBOY HOMECOMING Pamela Ingrahm

When Steve Williams went back to the old family ranch, he was shocked to find a beautiful blonde sitting at his kitchen table claiming the land was hers. All Steve wanted was solitude, not the irresistible Tegan McReed!

ONCE IN A BLUE MOON Kristin James

Michael Traynor was back, sexier than ever. But Isabelle Gray was no longer the lovesick teenager who had once fallen into his bed. Could she keep hidden the ten-year-old secret she'd harboured since he left?

REBEL LOVE Jackie Merritt

Cass Whitfield had been devastated when rebel Gard Sterling hadn't remembered the passion-filled night they'd spent together. Could Gard now convince her that he wasn't the same bad boy who hurt her all those years ago?

ANGELS AND ELVES Joan Elliott Pickart

Man of the Month

The most important thing in confirmed bachelor Forrest MacAllister's busy life was his family. Until he saw sexy Jillian Jones-Jenkins, who had him thinking about things he'd never considered before—like brides and babies and happily ever after...

WHATEVER COMES Lass Small

Reporter Amabel Clayton was furious when people assumed she'd slept with a man to get a story. Particularly when the man was elusive rock star Sean Morant. Talented, sensuous and sexy...he was *definitely* off limits!

♥ SILHOUETTE
Intrigue

COMING NEXT MONTH

WINTER'S EDGE Anne Stuart

Dangerous Men

After a car accident, Molly Winters woke up with amnesia. Apparently the man she'd been with had been killed, but she was being released into the husband she couldn't remember's care. On the night of the accident, had she been fleeing her husband, or racing towards him?

BEHIND THE MASK Joanna Wayne

Lindsey Latham had hoped that she could come back to New Orleans without seeing the man who'd once stolen her heart. But having witnessed a murder, she had no choice but to run into Graham's arms. For passion and for protection…

UNSPOKEN CONFESSIONS Kelsey Roberts

Shadows and Spice

Shelby Hunnicutt's precious baby had been kidnapped and the agent assigned to the case was none other than her ex-lover. It would be disastrous if Dylan Tanner discovered that the child he searched for was his own!

THE SUSPECT GROOM Cassie Miles

Mail Order Brides

Trina Martin had agreed to become a mail-order bride, but then her groom-to-be was murdered during the wedding. With a blizzard raging outside, all the guests—and the murderer— were trapped. Why was the prime suspect so appealing?

Name that Song

How would you like to win a year's supply of sophisticated and deeply emotional romances? Well, you can and they're free! Simply solve the puzzle below and send your completed entry to us by 30th September 1996. The first five correct entries picked after the closing date will each win a years supply of Silhouette Special Edition novels (six books every month—worth over £160).

Please turn over for details of how to enter 🖙

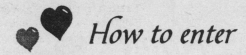 *How to enter*

To solve our puzzle...first circle eight well known girls names hidden in the grid. Then unscramble the remaining letters to reveal the title of a well-known song (five words).

When you have written the song title in the space provided below, don't forget to fill in your name and address, pop this page into an envelope (you don't need a stamp) and post it today! Hurry—competition ends 30th September 1996.

**Silhouette Song Puzzle
FREEPOST
Croydon
Surrey
CR9 3WZ**

Song Title: _____

Are you a Reader Service Subscriber?   Yes ❑   No ❑

Ms/Mrs/Miss/Mr _____

Address _____

_____

————————— Postcode —————————

One application per household.

You may be mailed with other offers from other reputable companies as a result of this application. If you would prefer not to receive such offers, please tick box.   ❑

COMP196
C